PINEAPPLE JAILBIRD

A Pineapple Port Mystery: Book Eight

Amy Vansant

Vansant Creations, LLC / Amy Vansant
Annapolis, MD
http://www.AmyVansant.com
http://www.PineapplePort.com

Copy editing by Carolyn Steele.
Proofreading by Effrosyni Moschoudi, Meg Barnhart & Connie Leap

CHAPTER ONE

Christmas lights blinked on almost every lamppost of Charlotte's street, their cheery twinkling curving into the distance like an airport runway constructed by someone deep into the spiked eggnog. Yawning and stretching for the stars, Charlotte strolled to the base of her driveway to grab the morning paper. Her movement triggered a neighbor's motion-activated Santa into a series of muffled ho-ho-hos. Santa's voice had been failing him as the season waned.

Christmas had been over for a week, but people loved the holidays in Pineapple Port, the fifty-five-plus neighborhood where Charlotte had grown up. The residents dragged out the season until every plastic reindeer on every roof *begged* to be stuffed back into the garage. Many of the locals still had family visiting—sons and daughters and grandkids who didn't want to go back to the freezing Northeast. Or freezing Midwest. Or, heaven forbid, *Canada*.

It made Charlotte shiver just thinking about those places. She had Florida blood. A temperature dip into the fifties was enough to send her scurrying for a snowsuit and gloves. She was a newly minted, fully licensed private investigator, but how people survived winter north of Florida was a mystery she didn't think she'd ever solve.

Luckily, the thermometers hovered at sixty-seven this

December morning—

Charlotte cocked her head.

Hold on. That's not right.

As her fingers grazed the top of her bagged newspaper, the house across the street caught her attention. Mariska lived there with her husband, Bob. Mariska had raised Charlotte after her grandmother died, leaving Charlotte the only permanent resident of Pineapple Port under the age of fifty-five. She'd already been orphaned before moving in with her grandmother, and if Mariska and the other residents hadn't worked the system for her, she would have been thrown into the custody of the state.

Thanks to Mariska, instead of being shuffled from one foster home to another, Charlotte had spent her days wheeling around the neighborhood in a golf cart and shuffling through water aerobics until her fingertips puckered.

Charlotte knew all Mariska's tics and habits, and this morning, something wasn't *right*. She knew what the house across the street was supposed to look like at five a.m. because her dog, Abby, who *used* to fetch the paper, had developed the playful habit of tearing the news to shreds before dragging the remnants back to the door, newspaper streaming behind her like she was a furry parade float.

Charlotte didn't want to fire Abby from her only job, but piecing the paper together so she could read it wasn't easy before her coffee.

The new morning ritual involved Charlotte tootling down the driveway to grab her paper while Abby wandered off to do her business. During this time, Mariska's lights were always on.

Today, Mariska's lights were *off*.

Mariska and Bob took turns waking up too early—he had to go to the bathroom, her legs ached—there was always something.

But the lights weren't on today.

This morning, Mariska didn't wave at her through the

window, holding up her dog, Izzy, and working the mutt's paw, so it looked as if the pointy-eared shedding machine was waving as well. That wasn't *too* strange—Mariska hadn't held up Miss Izzy in a while. The dog had grown into a sturdy *brick* of hair and weighed about as much as a small pickup truck, thanks to Mariska's inability to stop treating her.

But it wasn't just the lack of lights and waving dog paws bothering Charlotte.

She took a step to the left, still peering at Mariska's door.

There it is.

Mariska's door was *ajar.* She hadn't registered the shadow at first, but now she could see the front door of Mariska's double-wide pre-fab home appeared to be hanging at an angle. A trick of the light. The door was simply open.

Charlotte straightened, paper hanging in her hand, until Abby flew by, snatching it from her grasp. The Soft-coated Wheaten gave her prize a good shaking and tore at the plastic sleeve until the paper unfurled like a flag across the driveway. Abby immediately lost interest, spat out the plastic, and returned to sniffing around the yard.

Charlotte sighed and stared at Mariska's daily news, still lying at the end of her driveway. If she or Bob had come outside to fetch it and left the door open, they hadn't finished the job.

Izzy didn't fetch papers. Mariska's dog preferred to stay inside and protect the family from animals on the television set, barking and rushing to slam her nose into the screen whenever a critter appeared in a commercial. She particularly hated a cartoon eagle that mocked her from the screen as she yapped and tried to circle behind the television to find it.

Charlotte took another step toward Mariska's home.

Maybe they went around the back...

She wandered a few feet down the street to peer around the side of Mariska's house.

Nothing. But wait—

Mariska's golf cart wasn't in her driveway.

Charlotte sighed.

Well, there it is.

At least one of them went somewhere on the golf cart. Mystery solved.

Charlotte looked at her watch as she turned back toward her house, only to make a full three-sixty and head straight for Mariska's, her pace quickening.

It was five o'clock in the morning.

Why would they go somewhere on the golf cart at this hour? Was something wrong?

She whistled for the Wheaten to follow, and Abby appeared at her heels, excited to break morning tradition and head to Mariska's house early.

Abby *loved* that woman and her treats.

Charlotte grabbed Mariska's paper on her way past, partially to be helpful but mostly to keep Abby from temptation. She peered through Mariska's glass storm door but couldn't see much. The entranceway opened into a narrow hall. Everything inside sat still and dark.

She opened the storm door and called inside past the open internal door, her voice low and whispery.

"Mariska?"

Izzy barreled around the corner, slipping on the linoleum floor, landing on her hip, and springing back up to continue her approach. She whined, knocking the door open wider as she pressed her nose through, whip-like tail wagging.

Charlotte opened the storm door far enough for Abby to charge into the house, her broad chest bouncing off Izzy's head. Izzy pirouetted and trotted after the Wheaten as the two of them scrambled room-to-room—Abby investigating and Izzy following to make sure her nosy neighbor didn't touch her stuff.

Charlotte entered and peeked into the open-plan kitchen and living room. Bob wasn't sitting in his worn La-Z-Boy chair. She walked through to check the lanai and found the sliding door leading to it closed and locked. Mariska opened the sliding door every morning because Izzy's water bowl was kept in the lanai, an arrangement made necessary by Izzy's inability to drink without throwing water around the room like a sprinkler.

If the door isn't open, Mariska isn't up.

Staring down the hallway that led to the bedrooms, Charlotte weighed the pros and cons of creeping back there. Her presence already felt like an invasion of privacy. Entering Mariska's bedroom would be even worse, but something didn't feel right, and she couldn't leave until she knew everything was okay.

Entering unnaturally still houses in a fifty-five-plus community didn't always end well, but there was no way Mariska *and* Bob both had heart attacks overnight. Charlotte pushed the morbid thought out of her head.

Let's get this over with, so I can get back to my coffee.

Charlotte tiptoed down the hall as the dogs barreled from the spare room and headed back toward the kitchen, nearly taking out her kneecaps in the process.

"Mariska?"

The bedroom door was ajar. The room behind it was darker than the hallway, which bathed in ambient light from the nightlight plugged into the guest bathroom wall.

"Bob?"

Charlotte poked her head into the room and tried to focus on the bed. It looked as if someone was in there.

Good. They're still sleeping.

Maybe they accidentally left the door open last night after walking Izzy.

Huffing a sigh, Charlotte was about to turn and leave when a tickle scurried across the nape of her neck.

Something about the lumps in the bed.

They weren't *lumpy* enough.

Charlotte poked her head back into the bedroom. She

couldn't hear anyone snoring. Her eyes adjusted to the darkness until she could see something in the air above the sleeping bodies.

A hand?

One of the sleepers had their hand in the air, thrust up like a redwood tree as if a teacher had asked a question, and they had the answer.

How can someone sleep with their hand in the air?

"Mariska?"

The arm was skinny.

Very skinny.

That shape of arm didn't belong to Mariska or Bob. But now her eyes were adjusting to the dark, and she could see the fingers at the end of the arm clear as day.

It was definitely a hand.

The time had come to abandon polite caution. Charlotte slapped at the switch on the wall, and the room flooded with light.

She gasped.

Eyes stared back at her.

Unblinking.

The four eyes were *painted* on the faces of the two mannequins occupying Mariska and Bob's bed. Both wore wigs vaguely resembling Bob and Mariska's hair, but nothing else about them rang true. One of them had a permanently straight arm thrust into the air. Something hung looped around that mannequin's frozen thumb, a red ribbon holding an envelope aloft where it dangled against its wrist.

Charlotte moved to the envelope and lifted the ribbon.

Fingerprints.

Sheriff Frank would kill her if she messed up the evidence.

Charlotte ran to the en-suite bathroom and searched under the sink through piles of decorative soaps and cleaning products until she found cleaning gloves. She slipped them on and returned to the bedroom to pull the envelope from the mannequin's grasp.

The envelope proved unlicked, its flap tucked neatly into itself. She slipped it open with her clumsy rubber-sheathed thumb and retrieved a small note from inside.

The white slip of paper held a single sentence scrawled across it.

This is what it feels like to lose someone.

—Jamie

CHAPTER TWO

"My name is Solomon Black. I've been retained to represent you, Ms. Moriarty."

Stephanie scowled at the man across the table from her. She'd been called from her prison cell to meet with her lawyer.

The thing was, she didn't have a lawyer.

The man claiming to be her lawyer looked wealthy and well-put-together in his expensive bespoke suit and gold cufflinks, but the pallor of his face looked as if he'd been throwing up all morning. He appeared wealthy—a fancy lawyer—but not one feeling particularly strong.

She tucked a straggly blonde strand behind her ear. The hard water in the prison showers was *murdering* her hair.

"You don't look so good," she said.

Solomon reached into his pocket and thrust a phone toward her. "I have a phone call for you."

The thin sheen of sweat on his brow glistened under the meeting room's harsh lighting.

Hm.

The expensive suit, the fear on his face, the sweat...the math of Solomon Black's appearance was beginning to add up.

Stephanie looked at the phone.

I know who that is.

She took the phone and placed it against her ear.

"Hello, Mother."

"Did you do it?" said a voice on the other side of the line.

"No. I didn't."

Her mother, Jamie, grunted.

"You sound like you don't believe me."

"I've kept tabs on you. I know you *could* have done it."

"Yes, I *could* have, but I didn't. First of all, it was sloppy. Four people showed up in that warehouse after the shooting. I don't usually kill someone and then sell tickets."

Solomon rolled his eyes and looked away. Stephanie held her hand over the phone and whispered to him.

"Hypothetically speaking."

He nodded. "Of course."

Jamie chuckled. "Tickets. I never thought of that. I could have made a fortune."

Stephanie sniffed. "Anyway, I don't do that sort of thing anymore," she mumbled.

"Since when?"

"Since about two weeks ago, if you must know."

"Oh yes? What happened two weeks ago?"

Stephanie sighed. "I was *inspired*."

"Inspired by whom?"

"I'd rather not say."

"Tell me."

"Declan."

"Declan? The local boy? Since when does he inspire you?"

"Since now. In a way, his new girlfriend did too."

Jamie laughed. "His new girlfriend? That relationship will last about ten minutes after you get out of jail. You two are like peas in a pod."

"No, that's just it, Mom. We're not. You might think you keep tabs on me, but you don't know me, and you don't know Declan. He's...he's not like *us*."

"I know, but he's like a puppy following you around."

"No, he's not. He never was."

"He went to South America with you and your little death squad."

"And he left as soon as things went south. He tried to get me to leave with him. He wasn't following me. He was trying to save me from myself."

Jamie grunted. "How noble. And this new girlfriend. Why her?"

"Why is he dating her?"

"No, why did *she* inspire you?"

"I don't know. She's a drip."

"Sounds inspiring."

"No..." Stephanie paused to think for a moment. "I suppose, in some ways, she reminds me of me, only *good.*"

"What do you mean *good*?"

"She's *good.* It's like she's Superman, and I'm...who's the bad superman?"

"Clark Kent?"

"No, Clark Kent is his mild-mannered persona. I feel like there was a *bad* Superman. Wasn't there?"

"I really couldn't tell you."

Stephanie held the phone down and addressed Solomon.

"Who's the bad Superman?"

Solomon paled another shade. "I don't know. Do I have to know? I could make a call—"

Stephanie shook her head and waved him away. "Nevermind." She raised the phone back to her ear. "You get the idea."

"Yes. *Bad Superman* is pretty self-explanatory. You're saying she's the superhero, and you're the supervillain."

"I guess."

Stephanie shifted in the uncomfortable metal chair. Talking to her mother was always humiliating. She couldn't understand why she didn't cut the woman out of her life completely, the way Jamie had cut her out of *her* life shortly after birth. She guessed it was a little too late to hand her mother over to some Florida trailer trash.

Or maybe too *early*.

Her mother would have to get old someday. Maybe she could put her in a home with *really* low standards...

"Are you there?"

Stephanie snapped from her daydreaming. "Huh? Yes. I'm here. What do you want, anyway? And who's this guy?" Her attention settled on the lawyer, and he seemed to melt beneath her gaze.

Solomon cleared his throat. "I told you, my name is Solomon Black, and I've been retained—"

Stephanie glared at the man, and he shut his mouth.

"He's your lawyer. He's the best. He's from New York."

"You bought me a lawyer?"

"Bought? In a manner of speaking. Let's just say things won't work out well for *him* if he doesn't get you off."

Ah. That explains why he looks like he's about to hurl on me.

"But you didn't even know I was innocent."

Jamie scoffed. "Like *that* matters. I'm a little disappointed you're not, to be honest."

"Does this mean you care about me?"

Jamie's playful tone dissipated. "You know who I am, and you have my DNA. I can't have you in the prison system with nothing to do but think of ways to bargain your way to freedom."

Stephanie frowned. "Stop. You're gushing. It's embarrassing."

"Just tell Solomon everything you can think of to help him find you a way out."

"Well, I didn't kill Jason, so this should be his easiest case ever."

"You *said* you shot at him."

"In self-defense."

"Even so, Steph, it's not looking good. It isn't a coincidence you ended up in that warehouse. Someone set you up."

"But I didn't kill him. He was already in that chair, dead—"

"Tell Solomon everything. And when he gets you out from under these charges, you and I will have a talk about your new life plan. That is if Declan's okay with that."

Jamie spat the word Declan as if it tasted bad in her mouth.

"New life plan? What—"

The air on the other side of the line stopped its subtle hissing, and Stephanie knew the connection had been severed. She handed the phone back to Solomon.

"Your mother wants you to tell me—"

Stephanie held up her palm. "I know."

She wanted to ask her fancy new lawyer what her mother had threatened to do to him if he didn't win her case, but decided it didn't matter. Her psychopath mother would do anything to get what she wanted and this time, what she wanted was to know her daughter wouldn't help the authorities find her.

A chill ran down Stephanie's spine.

She thinks I'm a liability.

It was never a good idea to be a liability in Jamie's world.

It could be prison was the only thing keeping her alive. But trapped here, there was little she could do to hide. Who knew how far her mother's influence reached?

I'll need to stay on my toes.

Jamie's regrets didn't tend to live very long.

CHAPTER THREE

Sheriff Frank ran his hand across his thinning gray hair and stared at the mannequins in Mariska's bed as if they were a trigonometry problem he had to solve. When Charlotte called, he'd run over from his home a few doors down. He stood beside her now, his knobby knees jutting from beneath a well-worn maroon robe, tufts of gray hair sprouting from its deep V.

"So you came in here, Mariska and Bob were gone, and these things were in their place?" he asked.

Charlotte nodded. She'd returned Jamie's note to the envelope and hung it back in the mannequin's hand. She'd used Mariska's cell phone to call Frank, who was like a second father to her after Bob.

Bob.

Bob had a wisecrack for everything. Charlotte wished she could hear his thoughts on the lifeless bodies staring up at her now. Jokes ping-ponged in her head, echoing in Bob's voice.

"That's the most life Mariska's shown in bed in years!"

"Everyone always said we were a couple of dummies..."

The idea that she might never see Mariska and Bob again made Charlotte's throat tighten. She looked away to hide her emotions from Frank.

Be a professional. Everything will be okay.

She pointed to the envelope. "I think the note is for me."

"You read it?"

"Yes."

Frank sighed. "You shouldn't have touched the evidence."

"I know, but I had to find out what was going on, didn't I?" Charlotte held up her own hands, still covered in yellow plastic. "I put on the cleaning gloves, and I was *very* careful."

"Still."

Charlotte stared at the note. "It doesn't matter anyway. Jamie Moriarty did this. You know she didn't leave fingerprints. She's too smart."

From behind Frank, Charlotte heard a tiny whimper as Darla, his wife and Mariska's best friend, entered and pressed her knuckles against her lips. She'd taken the time to throw on red capris and a black t-shirt with *Bike Week '95* stamped on the front in a peeling fat font.

"What is this? Where is Mariska?"

Charlotte frowned. "We don't know."

"Who did this? Why?"

Charlotte plucked at the fingers of her gloves. She liked to think she'd left them on to show Frank how careful she'd been with the note, but in reality, her brain just wasn't working. It felt as though someone had pressed *pause* on all her major organs. Fear had her feeling as frozen as the mannequins.

"Jamie Moriarty. She left me a note to be sure we knew it was her."

"Isn't that the one you thought was the Puzzle Killer?" Darla whispered the nickname of the country's most prolific serial killer and paled.

Charlotte could only nod.

Frank eyed his wife and pushed on to avoid the rising panic they could both see roiling on Darla's face. "How do you know the note's for you?"

"Because Jamie called me while I was at Seamus' grand

opening party over Christmas."

"What? Why didn't you tell me?"

"There wasn't much to tell, and it was Seamus' big night."

Frank grunted at the sound of Seamus' name. "That idiot owning a bar. That's all I need. Don't even get me started."

Charlotte couldn't help but chuckle. Since her boyfriend Declan's uncle Seamus had arrived in town, he'd found more than a few ways to cause trouble. A classic Irish rogue, Seamus always had one scheme or another in play. Half of her thought owning a bar was the perfect vocation for Seamus—he liked to talk, and it gave him something to do besides lolling around Declan's house. On the other hand, she could also imagine all sorts of trouble brewing at his new bar, The Anne Bonny. It didn't help that he'd bought the bar with no warning and with money he swore he didn't have whenever Declan suggested it might be nice if he paid a little rent. Seamus' *temporary* housing in Declan's spare bedroom had gone on for *months.*

Frank stared at the envelope, running the tip of his tongue along the edge of the steel-gray mustache perched above his lip. It was time for a trim.

"So what did Jamie want when she called?" he asked.

"She wants me to get Stephanie out of jail."

Now it was Darla's turn to gasp. "Stephanie? That lunatic Declan used to date?"

Charlotte nodded. "That's the one."

"Why is she in jail?" Darla pointed at the bedroom wall but waved her hand, invoking, one had to infer, somewhere farther away than the bedside table. "She just opened a lawyer thingy...I see her sign down there when I go to get the dog groomed. *Attorney-at-law.*"

"She might have killed an assistant D.A."

"Stephanie? Really? I read about his murder in the paper. Jason something?"

"Mm hm. Jason Walsh."

"But what's all that got to do with Mariska and Bob?"

"I found his body. And her, near it."

Darla gasped again. "They didn't say that in the paper."

"They don't tell you *everything* in the paper. Especially our paper. This isn't exactly New York."

Darla glared at Frank. "Nobody tells me *anything*."

Frank slapped his hand to his chest. "What are you giving me the devil eyes for?"

"Oh, you *knew*."

Frank looked away with a tiny shrug.

The last thing Charlotte wanted to do was tell Darla everything that had happened to her the day she found Jason Walsh dead. Darla would lock her in her house and never let her outside again if she knew she'd walked in on Stephanie holding a gun in her hand, standing next to a dead assistant D.A. in an abandoned warehouse, and that Stephanie had proceeded to attack *her*. She still had the bruises. Luckily, Declan and Frank had arrived, or she might have ended up as dead as the D.A.

Darla closed her eyes and tilted back her head. "You found a *body*. Mariska would kill you if she knew."

Charlotte nodded, though Darla couldn't see her response with her face pointed at the ceiling and eyes shut.

Darla opened her eyes. "*Moriarty*... That's Stephanie's last name, isn't it? The one on her sign. She's *related* to the woman who did this?"

"Jamie's her mother."

"So we have a whole family of killers in town."

Charlotte looked away. *You have no idea.* Darla didn't know Jamie had once worked for witness protection and had imported dozens of killers for relocation in the area for her own twisted amusement. If she knew that, she'd lock *herself* in her house and never leave.

Darla put both hands on her head as if she were trying to keep it from exploding. "Why would she think *you* can get her daughter out of jail? Because you were there? Does she expect you to take the blame?"

Charlotte sighed. "I don't know."

Darla wagged a finger at her. "Well, you don't do it. Don't *you* take the blame—"

"I won't. Jeeze, Darla, I'm not going to confess to a murder I didn't commit. Do you think I'm *crazy*?"

Frank held up his hands. "Okay, okay, none of this is getting us anywhere." He patted his pockets and pulled out a phone. "I need to get the crime techs here—"

The moment Charlotte saw the phone in Frank's hand, she gasped. "My phone!"

What an idiot.

Charlotte shimmied past Frank and Darla and ran outside, headed for her house. She could hear Darla screaming, "Where're you going?" behind her as she neared her own door.

Jamie had her phone number. She had to. She'd called her at Seamus' party. Of course, she'd call again. The monster hadn't left Mariska and Bob dead in their bed, so odds were good Jamie *wanted* to talk. She'd taken them as some sort of leverage or threat.

Charlotte burst through her door, bouncing it against the rubber stopper she'd had to install on the wall behind it after Abby slammed through too many times. She heard ringing and ran down the hall toward her phone. She saw it glowing, still lying on the table beside her bed.

She lifted it to her ear.

"Hello? Hello?"

Nothing.

Charlotte checked her call history. Two missed calls. Both were from the same number, though *not* the number that had called her during Seamus' party.

Charlotte hit the number to dial back. After two rings, someone picked up.

"Joe's Laundry Service. Can I help you?"

"Joe's..."

Not Jamie. A misdial.

Charlotte slumped to a seat on her bed. "I'm sorry. Wrong number."

"Oh? Were you looking for someone?"

Charlotte was about to hang up when something about the woman's tone caught her attention. It was almost as if she were goading her. As if she knew.

She decided to give it a chance. "I'm looking for Jamie?"

"I see. I'll see if we have that part in stock."

"Part? It's not a part—"

The woman put her on hold, and Charlotte heard elevator music swell on the opposite end of the line. She gripped the phone in frustration. She was about to hang up again when a different woman's voice returned to the line. This voice was lower. Sexier. And *familiar.*

"It took you *this* long to check your phone?"

"I—" Charlotte stopped, mentally berating herself for not adopting a tougher attitude before answering the phone.

Should she be sweet? Butter-up Jamie in hopes of getting Mariska and Bob returned? Or would the maniac take that as a sign of weakness?

"Maybe I've put my faith in the wrong person," added Jamie. Her slow, snarky tone reminded Charlotte of her conversations with Stephanie. It seemed the poison apple didn't fall far from the psycho-tree, but Charlotte had even less time for Moriarty nonsense now.

"Where are they?" she asked, making her voice sound as tough and steady as she could. Inside her shirt, she could hear her heart thumping.

"Who?"

"Don't *who* me. You know who. Mariska and Bob."

"Oh, those two. They're fine. They're not bound and hovering over an alligator pit or anything. Well, at least not the alligator bit."

"What do you want?"

"I told you what I want."

"Am I supposed to take Stephanie a cake with a file in it? You never told me how you expect me to get her out of jail."

"I want you to prove she's innocent. You're a detective, aren't you?"

Touché.

"I'm not doing a *thing* for you until Mariska and Bob are back safe. My friends are off-limits."

"How about your dog?"

"Jamie, I swear—"

"I'm kidding. Take it easy. I think my point's been made. Look out front."

Charlotte rolled to peer through her bedroom window, flipping open the slats of her plantation shutters. By the early morning light, she watched as a golf cart rolled into view, weaving down the street like Pineapple Port's often slightly drunk neighborhood patrol. Mariska and Bob sat in the front, their hands tied behind their backs. Bob was driving the cart with the sides of his arms and his chin, rubbing the wheel to point left or right in a desperate attempt to end up straight in the end.

"Slow down. No, *slow*! You're going to kill us both!" she heard Bob bark. She guessed Mariska was working the gas pedal. It *would* be Jamie's style to tie Frank's feet so the two of them would have to work together to get anywhere.

"I'm *slowing*!" screamed Mariska.

Giant red bows sat perched on both of their heads. Coils of silver tinsel snaked around their bodies. Mariska blew the festive garland away from her mouth when she wasn't screaming at Bob. Christmas balls dangled from her chest, hooked through Mariska's pajamas. One jostled loose and rolled to smash on the street as they passed Charlotte's house.

Cart, Mariska, and Bob all blinked with a smattering of

twinkling multi-colored lights.

"Were the lights too much?" asked Jamie in Charlotte's ear. "I should have gone with white lights. I find the colored ones tacky, don't you?"

Charlotte watched Darla and Frank spill from Mariska's house, running toward the approaching cart. Pushing through Frank's legs, Abby found her way outside and jumped into the back of the golf cart as it rolled to a stop against the curb. She found a spot perched on the back trundle seat, ready for a ride around the neighborhood, oblivious to the trussed Christmas characters in front.

"Aren't they festive?" asked Jamie.

"You're a lunatic."

"I'm not, actually. I've been tested."

"If you're waiting for me to thank you for returning them, it's going to be a while."

Jamie snorted a laugh. "Stephanie told me you were a real drip, but I think she might have you wrong."

Ouch. For some reason, being called a drip—even by someone as odious as Stephanie—hurt a little, and Charlotte was mortified she felt that way.

"Tell me what you want me to do."

"I want you to get Stephanie cleared."

"Right, you said that. But why me? The only person in law enforcement I know is Frank, and he couldn't get Stephanie released in a million years."

"You have more resources than *Frank*." Jamie's tone made it clear she didn't consider a local sheriff an asset or a threat.

"Could you let me know what they are? And while we're on the subject, who could be better at this than *you*? I thought you were some kind of genius?"

Jamie sighed. "It turns out being a genius doesn't make you good at *everything*."

"My heart breaks for you."

"I should rephrase. I *am* good at everything, but this isn't something I can even try."

"Why?"

"Because I *know* who framed my daughter."

"Go tell the police then. Or better still, go *kill* him or her? I thought that's what you like to do best."

"Police. Right. That's funny. And killing him wouldn't get Stephanie out of jail. In fact, it would probably seal her fate. See my problem?"

"This man is the one who really killed the assistant D.A.?"

"More or less, I suspect."

"Then you could just torture him until he confesses."

Jamie laughed. "I like the way you think. But that brings me to my second point; he's been an enemy of mine for a very long time. He'd see me coming from a million miles away. If it'd been easy for me to get to him, he would have been dead a long time ago."

"So you need someone he wouldn't expect."

"Exactly. And who would he expect *less* than the person Stephanie beat the crap out of before being dragged to prison."

Charlotte frowned. "We were pretty evenly matched."

"Don't kid yourself. I'll send you more information. Hang tight for a couple of hours. I'll send you some help to watch your back, too, just in case."

"Just in case of *what*?"

"Don't worry about it."

"What if I can't do this?"

"That's easy. Fail, call in the Feds, do anything I don't want you to, and I'll kill everything and everyone you love."

"Great. Is there a time limit?"

Jamie snorted. "No. Why would I put that kind of pressure on you? I'm not a *monster*."

CHAPTER FOUR

Charlotte shoved her phone into her pocket and slid off her bed. Darting through the house, she burst once more through her front door and ran across the street to the golf cart where Darla and Frank were already helping Mariska and Bob from their bindings. Darla plucked the Christmas decorations from them while Frank worked his pocket knife against the thin clothesline ropes that bound their wrists and, in Bob's case, ankles. As she neared, Charlotte saw silver glitter sparkling on their hair and faces. It looked as though someone had glitter-bombed them.

Charlotte threw her arms around Mariska, not caring for a moment that she'd end up looking like a disco ball herself until she showered.

"I was so worried."

Hands freed, Mariska squeezed back, her big Polish momma's arms crushing the breath from Charlotte's lungs.

"It was all worth it to get a hug from you. You're always so stingy with them."

"Are you okay? Did she hurt you?"

Mariska cocked her head. "She? I assumed it was a man..."

"You didn't see who did it?" asked Frank.

Bob sniffed. "Just woke up tied to the golf cart. Though that's not the first time that's happened." He winked and chuckled. "At least this time, I had my pajamas on."

Mariska slapped his arm. "You're so *stupid*."

Frank smirked, his mustache rising on the right side like a rearing caterpillar. "We should get you two checked out. They probably used some kind of injection to knock you out."

Mariska waved Frank away. "We're fine. But I can tell you if they carried me out of my bed, there was more than one of them."

"That's a good point—"

Frank cut short when Mariska glowered at him. She put her hands on her hips.

"You're supposed to *argue* with women when they say things like that."

"I didn't mean..."

Even in the early light, Charlotte thought she could see Frank's cheeks color.

"I didn't mean *you*. I meant one person couldn't carry either one of you very easily. You're not children."

Bob pulled a chunk of tinsel from his shoulder. "You should probably quit while you're ahead. I can tell you from experience the hole you're digging is already too deep."

Mariska smacked him on the arm again. The movement sent glitter showering from her curls.

Charlotte smiled, but she could feel the sense of dread creeping around the back of her brain like a thief bent on stealing all her sense of well-being.

Nothing is right.

It was wonderful to have Mariska and Bob back, but she had miles ahead of her before she'd feel like they were truly safe.

She caught Frank watching her. He motioned with a nod of his head for her to follow him as he strolled behind the golf cart. She complied, and he spoke, his voice low and whispery when he thought they were far enough away from the others. "Did you find anything on your phone?"

She nodded. "Jamie called again."

"I guessed as much. And? What did she want?"

"Same thing. For me to get Stephanie out of jail. Mariska and Bob were a warning. A taste of what she *could* do if I let her down."

"We need to call the FBI. She's on their list. They can trace that number."

"She warned me not to."

Frank scoffed. "Of course she did. Doesn't mean we have to listen."

"But she's watching. Either she or a minion is. She'll know. And the number she called from was different than the last. There's some sort of middle man, middle woman to be exact, who relays the call."

Frank grunted, and Charlotte worried he'd plow ahead and call the FBI anyway.

"I'm serious. She could kill half the neighborhood before you or me, or the FBI knew what happened. Remember, they've been looking for her for decades, and they never found her."

Frank crossed his arms across his chest. "But this has got to be their best shot. What about just me and you? Can *we* try to find her?"

"She doesn't seem concerned about you." Charlotte winced. *Whoops*. "That didn't come out right—"

"You mean she thinks I'm too incompetent to ruin her plans."

"Maybe. But what does she know?"

Frank huffed. "I'll take it as a good thing. Means I can help, and she won't hold it against you."

"Right. And having your help makes *me* feel better." She tapped him with a playful punch on the arm. "I don't think you're any dumber than any other small-town sheriff."

"Har har." Frank tightened the maroon, terry-cloth belt around his middle. "So what are we supposed to do? Sit around and wait for her to kill everyone?"

"This might seem a little out there, but you *could* have a

little faith in my detective skills."

"But Stephanie's guilty. You were there. You saw it."

Charlotte hooked her mouth to the side, recalling her time in the warehouse. "I *don't* know. I only saw the aftermath. I don't *know* if she killed the D.A."

"So you think she was framed?"

"Jamie thinks she was framed—and Steph's about as charming as her mother, so anything is possible."

"Can Declan talk to her? Maybe get the straight story? I'm sorry to ask..."

"No, that's a good thought. He might have some pull with her. I think she's still a little obsessed with him."

Frank took a deep breath and released a long slow sigh. "Okay. For now, I'll leave this as your operation. It sounds like Jamie just wants you to investigate. What do you want me to do?"

"I'm not sure yet. Jamie said she has info for me that will help. Apparently, she has an enemy, and she thinks he's responsible."

"She thinks someone framed Stephanie to get to her?"

"I'm thinking something like that. Remember, before her cover was blown, Jamie worked for the witness protection program and put all her clients in this area. Maybe someone didn't appreciate being here."

Frank traced his mustache with his thumb and index finger, petting down the wild edges. "She knew who was after each of these guys, right? The people they flipped on—"

Charlotte's eyes grew wide. "That's a good point. She had the power to expose her clients to the people who wanted them dead. She could blackmail them into doing anything she liked. She didn't gather them all here for fun—"

"She built an army of killers and stool pigeons who had to do anything she asked."

"Exactly. And maybe one of them doesn't like being under

her thumb."

"That could be someplace to start. We have the book Stephanie gave you, the one with the fingerprints of Jamie's witness protection clients."

Charlotte pointed at him, excited to have what felt like a solid lead so quickly. "The *book*. You're right. Maybe our guy is in there."

Charlotte turned to watch Mariska and Darla chatting on the front door landing. Darla brushed glitter from Mariska's pajamas. Eyes stared through Mariska's front door, Izzy's white tail wagging behind them.

Abby had lain down on her golf cart seat, the flick of her eyebrows betraying the movement of her own eyes as she waited impatiently for her ride.

Everything felt so normal...

...except *not*.

CHAPTER FIVE

"Is that a tattoo?"

Miles looked up from his beer. A bat-faced girl with a half-grown-out dye job stared back at him, her plump pink-painted lips hanging open like a cow's.

"What's that?" he asked, trying to decide on the fly if she looked like someone with her own house. He needed a place to sleep in town. It was a long drive back to the farm.

"I said, is that a tattoo on your arm? It's *crazy*, dude."

Dude. Miles scowled. He hated being called *dude.*

He glanced down. His short sleeve t-shirt had ridden up, exposing a network of coral-like zig-zag lines on his upper arm. He grunted and took a sip of his beer.

"Sorta. A nature tattoo."

The girl rubbed the back of her index finger beneath her nose and sniffed. "Like henna?"

Miles shrugged. He didn't know what *henna* was but didn't feel like learning either.

The girl leaned closer to him. He could smell her sweet, strawberry-scented perfume mingling with the stench of stale beer.

"How far does it go?" she asked, as flirtatiously as a woman with bad skin and greasy two-tone hair could manage.

Fish on.

Miles put down his beer.

I really hope she has her own place.

He swiveled on his stool to face her. "You live 'round here?"

"Yeah, just over the bridge." She blinked at him. "Why?"

"Just makin' small talk. Live alone?"

"Yeah."

He nodded and looked at his arm. "Tell ya what. I'll show you for a beer."

She grinned with tobacco-stained teeth.

"Deal."

Miles didn't mind the color of her chompers. He didn't trust people with pearly white teeth. They were always fake in every other way as well.

Keeping steady eye contact with the girl, he pulled his *Salt Life* t-shirt over his head.

The girl gasped.

"Oh my god..."

"Hey, you can't—" The bartender took one step toward Miles and then stopped both his momentum and his sentence, gaping.

"Is that a tattoo?" he asked, echoing the girl's earlier question.

In the mirror behind the booze rack, Miles admired his own markings. A red coral reef covered most of his chest, the branches crawling up his neck, across his shoulders, and down his upper arms. He knew a good portion of his back sported the marking as well. He turned so the greasy girl could see the tendrils of it reaching across his spine.

"That's the wildest tattoo I've ever seen. It looks like it's following your veins."

Miles sniffed. "That's 'cause it *is*. It ain't a tattoo."

The girl scowled and traced her finger along his back. Girls always had to trace the pattern. Sometimes he felt a little like a snake charmer, mesmerizing the women with his markings instead of using a pipe.

"Then what is it?" asked the bartender. "You got some kind

of disease?"

The girl snatched away her hand.

Miles shook his head and slipped his shirt back over his head. "Got struck by lightning as a kid."

"No way," breathed the bartender. "And it did that?"

"Yup. Shot through my body and left a trail so I could know where it went."

"That's somethin' else."

The girl's dull eyes widened. "Did it hurt?"

Why do people always ask that?

"Of course, it hurt."

The girl tittered with nervous giggles.

Miles took another swig of his beer. "Some good came out of it, though."

The bartender snapped from his awe and began wiping down the counter. "Yeah. You got a cool tattoo."

"Nah, besides that."

The girl shifted to the edge of her barstool. "What?"

Miles held up a hand. "It burned off my fingerprints." He showed the girl the dark pads of his fingertips. The ones he still had. The lightning had blasted off the tips of his pinky fingers to the first knuckle.

The girl raised her hand to cover her gaping mouth. "Why would you *want* to lose your fingerprints?"

"Makes it easier to steal stuff, don't it?" Miles grinned, and the girl laughed too hard. She reached out and traced the lightning roadmap on his arm, her gaze playing tag with his.

He hoped his blue eyes still had the effect they did when he was younger. As a rule, between his eyes and his unusual markings, he'd never had any trouble getting bar girls to take him home. Of course, that was before he was arrested. Before he flipped on his oxycodone-selling bosses to avoid jail time. Not because he was a snitch, but because he didn't give a rat's ass about them. He wasn't really in the drug-*selling* business and didn't need them. Helping them with "problems" that needed to "disappear" had been a way for him to enjoy his work and get paid. He didn't care if they were selling drugs or timeshares.

But real estate agents rarely needed someone killed.

Then that fake-Fed bitch had sent him here with a new name and the promise of a new life—but only if he did what she said.

Screw her.

She couldn't keep hold of him. He'd lived off the grid his whole life. After a botched attempt to kill her, he'd disappeared into the swamps to reset. When he popped out of his hidey-hole again, he found out she was gone.

He'd lost his chance for revenge.

Until that man called and told him her daughter had opened a law office in town. A man who hated the Fed bitch even more than he did. He asked for Miles' help.

It really was Christmas.

It was all too perfect. And the worst part was done. He'd framed the lawyer. Now all he had to do was wait for her mother to come out of hiding to save her.

Nothin' to do but drink beer and—

He turned and looked at the sloppy girl beside him. He wasn't drunk, but somehow she still looked blurry. She just was...all grease, paint, and fuzz.

Blurry.

"What's your name?" he asked.

The girl dipped her face and looked up at him.

Oh, she's feelin' it. The eyes still have it.

"Fawn," she said, her voice softer than it had been.

"Like a little deer."

She giggled.

I hunt deer.

"You live out in the forest?"

She laughed again. "I don't live in the forest, silly. I live over in the trailer park by the state park."

"And you said you live by yourself?"

"Yeah. Now. Momma moved into her boyfriend's place."

"Huh."

Miles took another swig of beer and eyed her from head to toe while she pretended she didn't know he was looking at her.

Not much to look at. Not too skinny, though, and not too fat.

Eh. Any port in a storm.

And she has her own place.

He leaned toward her. "You want to get out of here?"

She giggled.

CHAPTER SIX

"Where do you want to go?"

Declan appeared on Charlotte's doorstep at five minutes past five. He'd left his best and only employee, Blade, in charge of his pawn shop, the Hock o' Bell, and now stood in Charlotte's kitchen with no idea about the approaching storm.

She was finding it hard to tell him about Mariska and Bob's kidnapping. He was so handsome, standing there in his polo and khaki shorts, a self-imposed work uniform, his swimmer's body filling out the shoulders and chest nicely.

"Maybe Mexican?" she suggested.

In truth, her appetite had left the moment Jamie put the well-being of everyone she loved on her shoulders. What time she hadn't spent grilling Mariska and Bob for details about their early morning abduction, she'd spent staring at her phone, waiting for Jamie to call with the extra information she needed to begin looking for the person who *really* killed the assistant D.A.

Assuming it wasn't Stephanie who remained the best and most obvious suspect. Too bad she wasn't an acceptable target for her psycho mother.

Which brought Charlotte's mind circling back to the most troubling aspect of her new investigation: What if Stephanie *was* guilty? Would Jamie accept her daughter's transgression as an answer? Or would the truth condemn everyone Charlotte loved—

"Hey, yoo hoo..." Declan waved a hand in front of her face. "Mexican sounds fine. But why do I get the feeling you're not thinking about dinner?"

Charlotte snapped from her thoughts and smiled. How could she *not* smile looking at Declan? He was sweet, funny, and one hundred percent supportive when it came to her career as a newly minted private eye. And, as a bonus, she'd recently discovered he was secretly badass to boot. He was almost perfect for her...

If only he hadn't come with a crazy ex-girlfriend and a murderous almost-mother-in-law...

"There you go again. What's wrong?"

Charlotte realized she'd drifted off again, her smile fading from her lips. She jerked it back into place. "I'm sorry. My mind *is* elsewhere. I need to walk Abby before we go. Want to come?"

Declan shrugged. "Sure."

Charlotte grabbed Abby's leash from the wall hook. The moment the chain jingled, the dog leapt to her feet and trotted to her, eager to go. The three of them headed outside, Abby leading the way, as usual. Heaven forbid anyone ever walk through a door before her. She'd nearly taken out Charlotte's legs a hundred times, trying to keep that from happening.

Charlotte stared at the ground as they walked, manufacturing the best way to tell Declan about Jamie's demands. She'd resisted calling him the *moment* Mariska and Bob's crisis had ended. She'd wanted to get her mind around the situation, and she knew he'd think it was all his fault for bringing Stephanie into her life—which was true, *technically*—but Steph was a crazy train no one could have stopped.

"So, how was your day?" she asked.

Good. Keep it simple. Look at you interacting like a person who isn't trying to keep everyone alive. You go, girl!

Declan sighed. "Weird. But every day is weird with Blade around. He showed up with pine needles sticking out of his t-shirt today."

"Pine needles? Oh, wait. What shirt was he wearing? Was it a good one?"

If there was anything that could distract Charlotte from her worries, it was Blade in all his glory. Declan's odd employee always wore the most terrifying t-shirts. Built like a brick wall, the man stood about six-foot-six and claimed his scary name had been blessed upon him by his hippie mother, who'd named him after a blade of grass. And yet, he always wore tees with the names of weapons manufacturers on them, usually knife manufacturers. Charlotte kept meaning to look into Blade's background, but he was such a sweet and gentle giant she'd never found herself motivated to unearth any dark past.

"Today's tee had a picture of a crab holding a knife."

"A crab holding a knife?"

"Yep, a *big* knife. It said *Let's Dance*."

Charlotte laughed. "Is he still a selling machine?"

Declan thrust his hands in his pockets as Abby stopped to do her business. "Yep. He probably sold five things today I never dreamed I'd be able to unload. He sold a porcelain figurine of a woman in a dress holding what looks like an otter. I've been staring at that thing for *years*, wondering where she got that otter."

"What about the pine needles in his tee?"

"Oh, I asked him about those. He said he went *forest bathing*."

"What the heck is forest bathing?"

"Funny you should ask. I Googled it, and it's a term for hanging out in the forest, enjoying the place. But from what I can tell, Blade went into the forest and rolled around in the sticks and pine needles. He had little cuts all over his face and hands."

"He literally tried to take a bath in a forest?"

"Yep. Said he overheard some guy yapping about how great it was."

Charlotte laughed harder as Abby insisted they started walking again. "But he never asked the guy *what* forest bathing was?"

"Nope. Mr. Literal just started rolling. Remind me to never tell him, 'Hey, why don't you take a *stab* at this.'"

Charlotte wiped her eyes where tears of giddy laughter clouded her vision. She had to fight to stop laughing. It seemed the stress of the day had finally driven her mad, and Declan's Blade story had pushed her over the edge.

Abby dragged them toward a woman standing in her yard with a Pomeranian in one hand and a phone in the other. A dachshund sat on the grass at her feet, tied to her lamp post by a leash. It looked almost as if it were pouting.

The woman looked up as they approached and motioned to the dachshund. "Is this your dog?"

"No." Charlotte thought she knew everyone's pets, but she didn't recognize the wiener dog staring up at her with doleful brown eyes. She was usually better with the dogs than the people. For instance, she was pretty sure the woman's name was Wendy but wasn't positive. She knew the Pomeranian's name was Sadie.

The woman-probably-named-Wendy huffed. "He wandered over to say *hi* to Sadie." She held up the Pomeranian as she said her name. "But I don't know where he came from or who he belongs to."

Abby strained to touch noses with the Dachshund, but he turned his head to avoid her. He'd clearly been wandering around, leash-free, out on an exciting adventure, and was now embittered by his capture. She suspected he'd fallen for the oldest trick in the book—the Pomeranian honey-trap. Abby's attention only shined a light on his humiliation.

His little chest rose and fell as he sighed.

"We'll keep an eye out for someone looking for him while we're walking around the neighborhood," offered Charlotte, pulling Abby back to the sidewalk.

The woman raised a phone to her ear. "I appreciate that. I'm going to call the office and see if they have any idea. It must be someone new."

Charlotte nodded, and they continued their walk.

"So, how was your day?" asked Declan when they'd wandered a few feet away from Sadie and her mom.

Charlotte winced.

Oh right. That.

Here we go.

"Um...also weird."

"Did Mariska go forest bathing, too?"

Charlotte scanned the area, searching for anything to distract the conversation from her day. To her surprise, she actually spotted a diversion. "Not exactly. Hold on..."

She stopped, staring at the stoop of a house five doors down from the captured Dachshund.

"There's a clue," she said, pointing.

On the porch of the house sat a clay-colored statue of a Dachshund.

Declan nodded. "Good eye."

Charlotte handed Declan Abby's leash and jogged to the door to knock. Inside, a dog barked in response to her rapping.

Hm. They already have a dog inside. Maybe this isn't the house.

A woman answered. "Yes?"

"Are you missing a Dachshund by any chance?"

A pointy brown nose popped between the woman's ankles as the hot dog threw a final bark in Charlotte's direction for good measure.

The woman shook her head. "No, I have Harry and Sally right here..." The woman glanced down at the two of them to count the faces.

One face.

"Harry?..." The woman pirouetted as she searched for the missing dog.

The Dachshund, once held back by her owner's legs, trotted outside to investigate Charlotte. As she lowered to a squat to say hi, the dog made a sharp left, avoiding her hand. The pink-collared girl instead trotted down the path leading from the door, stopping to sniff every couple of feet.

"I'm afraid you've got some wanderers," said Charlotte, standing.

The woman nodded, her wide eyes betraying her growing panic. "I *am* missing one. Now, where did Sally...*Sally*!" The woman slipped past Charlotte and scooped up her dog. Sally didn't look any happier about being captured than Harry had.

Charlotte pointed down the street. "Five houses down that way, there's a woman with your other dog. You can see her from here."

The woman took a step forward and strained her neck to get a peek. "Thank you *so* much. I swear I don't know how he got out. I should have named him Houdini."

Charlotte felt a strong urge to point out that Houdini's first name actually was Harry but stopped herself.

The woman started down the street, holding Sally over her head, presumably so the woman with Harry tied to her post would see she was looking for the other half of her pair.

Declan grinned as Charlotte joined him to reclaim Abby's leash. "Look at you, solving mysteries everywhere you go."

"It's a gift." Charlotte sighed. She'd delayed long enough. The time had come to Band-Aid the situation—rip it off and get it over with. "Speaking of solving crimes, I need to tell you something."

"Oh no. I don't like the way that sounds."

"Oh, it's *much* worse than it sounds. When I woke up this morning, Mariska was gone."

Declan stopped and turned to her. "What do you mean, *gone*?"

"*Gone*. She and Bob. They were missing from their bed, and mannequins were there instead."

"In their beds."

"Yes. Someone had kidnapped them and replaced them with mannequins."

"You're kidding. This was part of a joke?"

Charlotte tilted back her head and stared up at the sky. "I wish."

"And you still haven't found them?"

"Oh no. We found them. Or I should say, they found us. They drove up, covered in Christmas decorations and tied to their golf cart, not long after I found them missing."

Abby found the spot to do her more *serious* business, and Charlotte pulled a poopie bag from the plastic, bone-shaped container hanging from the handle of her leash in preparation for clean-up duty.

"Please skip to the end," said Declan. "The suspense is killing me."

"You're going to be sorry you said that."

"I figure."

"Well, guess who I got a phone call from claiming responsibility?"

"I can't imagine."

"Jamie."

The blood drained from Declan's face as if someone had left his tap on. *"No."*

"Yup. It was her way of showing me what would happen if I didn't get Stephanie cleared of all charges. She made it pretty clear everybody's a target if I fail."

Words seeming to fail him, Declan put his arms around her and cradled her against his chest. She realized she must have looked like she needed a hug.

She did.

She leaned into him, finding his pecs a lot harder than pillows but twice as comforting. Charlotte felt her defenses slip as tears rushed to rim her eyes.

"I'm so sorry," said Declan.

"What are you sorry about?"

"Without me, Stephanie and Jamie would have never met you."

She sniffed and pulled back to look up at him. "But then life would be so *boring*."

He kissed her on the forehead and hugged her to him again.

"Let's go figure out what we're going to do."

CHAPTER SEVEN

"This it?"

The black Cadillac rolled to a stop in front of the square modular home in the center of the Pineapple Port retirement community.

Andy Sanfasso looked at the piece of paper in his hand. "Yeah, I think so. The numbers are right."

Butch Fermani turned off the Cadillac's engine.

Andy cocked an eyebrow at him. "Whataya doin'?"

Butch held out his hands, palms rotating to the sky. "I'm turnin' off the car. Whaddya think I'm doin'?"

"Shouldn't I just drop off the stuff?"

"You don't think we should introduce ourselves?"

Andy grimaced. "I dunno. I was thinkin' maybe she should get the stuff first, think about it, and then we make ourselves known."

"Nah. Get it over with now."

"Fine."

"Good."

They exited the car and walked up the driveway. Andy rapped his knuckles on the hood of the Volvo parked there as they passed it. "I guess she's home."

Butch tucked the manila envelope under his arm and pointed at a dog bowl sitting beside a pot holding the skeleton of an ex-geranium. "She's got a dog."

Andy grunted. "Good to know. Hey, remember Richter's dog?"

Butch chuckled. "That crazy thing. Thought it was some kinda Pitbull by the sound of it, but I could pick the thing up in one hand."

"Whatever happened to that dog?"

"I gave it to my cousin's kid."

"Oh yeah? That's nice."

"Kid had suhmn wrong with his head. Dog, like, brought him out of his shell."

"That's nice."

"Yeah. Mutt wasn't doin' Richter any good anymore."

They chuckled and released a collective sigh, recalling the good old days. The days before they got arrested. Before they agreed to turn state's evidence against their bosses. The days before they were shipped to Florida to live out the rest of their days as law-abiding citizens.

Andy raised his hand, preparing to knock. "Get ready for the dog."

Butch nodded and pulled a gun from the waist of his pants. Andy frowned.

"You can't *shoot* the dog."

"You said *get ready*."

"I mean, get ready to move so I can run and not end up in a pile at the bottom of the freakin' stairs widju."

"Oh." Butch tucked the gun back into his pants. "I wouldn't shoot the dog anyway."

"Uh huh."

"Seriously. Unless it was gonna bite me. And it was *big*. Like, *Cujo* big."

"Right. Watchu bring that for anyway? You should've left it in the car."

Butch shrugged. "Simone said to stay on our toes. Said the

girl was unpredictable."

"Yeah, well, *I'm* gonna be unpredictable next time you bring a gun to suhmn simple like this."

"Whatever."

"*You* whatever." Andy raised his hand to knock again, and Butch sighed.

"We shoulda got coffee or suhmn'."

Andy left his hand hanging in mid-air and looked at his partner. "Yeah, we *should* have got coffee. That's a good call."

"You wanna go get coffee?"

"Let's talk to the girl first." He knocked, and they waited.

No one came to the door. Nothing barked.

"She ain't home," said Butch.

"Her car's here."

"Dog ain't home either. Maybe she's walkin' the dog."

"Another good call. You're like a freakin' genius all of a sudden."

"So let's go get coffee."

Andy shrugged. "Yeah, why not?"

They turned, Butch's foot already hovering over the next step down. At the bottom of the stairs, a woman with nutmeg-colored, wrinkled skin stared up at them through beady eyes. The hands positioned on her hips acted as a makeshift belt for the loose-fitting dress hanging from her tiny bones. She had a vape pen hanging from the right side of her dark red lips. Her mouth draped in a curve of obvious disapproval.

"What are you two goons doing here?" she asked.

Butch stopped and grabbed the handrail to keep from failing forward as Andy banged into the back of him. When they'd both stabilized, Butch put his hand on his heart. "Jiminy Christmas, Tilly, you almost gave me a friggin' heart attack. Whatta *you* doin' here?"

Tilly's neck telescoped toward them, head tilting like that of a curious turtle. "I asked you first."

Both men were large and round, and they struggled to find

an elegant way to stand side-by-side on the tiny landing, boxed in as they were by Tilly at the foot of the stairs.

"We got business," said Butch.

"What kind of business?"

"For *her.*"

"Her? She's long gone."

"Yeah, well. Only in spirit."

"You mean only in body."

"Whatever."

"What's she want you to do here?"

Andy looked at Butch. "Whaddya think?"

His partner's eyebrows tilted up in the center like seesaws, his mouth twisting into a knot. "I dunno if we should say."

"You scared she'll kill you?" asked Tilly.

Andy scoffed and returned his attention to her. "*Yeah,* I'm scared she'll kill us. Or I'll have to run. I don't have that kinda livin' in me anymore, Tilly. I play golf tree, four times a week."

Tilly pulled the vape pen from her lips, and a large plume of mist filled the air around her. "You here to kill this girl?"

Both men gasped.

"Are you out of your freakin' mind?" asked Andy. "When she makes me do stuff—"

"When she makes *us* do stuff," corrected Butch.

Andy nodded. "Right. When she makes *us* work, we're just muscle. Monkey stuff. We don't kill people no more. Not for her and not for anyone."

"Sometimes we go find her somethin' she needs," added Butch.

Andy jerked a thumb in Butch's direction. "Yeah, sometimes we find something she needs. That kind of work. Little fixer stuff."

"No killin'."

"My wife would kill *me* if I killed someone."

Tilly trained her steely gaze on Butch. "How about you?

You golfing now, too?"

Butch sniffed. "Nah. I'm on a bowling team, though." He motioned toward Tilly's vape pen.

"What is that crazy thing?"

"Vape pen. I'm trying to quit smoking."

Butch nodded his approval. "Huh. Good for you."

Andy shifted, his gaze sweeping the carport area. "Hey, how'd you know we were here, anyway?"

Tilly flicked her wrist at the sky. "I got the place wired."

"The girl's house?"

"The neighborhood."

Butch twisted to look at Andy. "Maybe that's good."

Andy shrugged. "Maybe it ain't."

"Might make our job easier."

"Maybe."

Tilly slipped the vape pen into a large square pocket on the side of her dress. "So, what job did Simone give you this time?"

"She wants us to deliver a package and watch over the girl until she's done doin' whatever Simone has her doin'."

"So you're here to *protect* Charlotte."

The men nodded.

"In a matter of speakin'," added Butch.

"Manner," muttered Andy.

"What?"

"It's *manner* of speakin'."

"You sure?" Butch looked at Tilly.

She nodded her agreement.

"Huh."

Tilly thrust her hand into the pocket of her oversized house dress to twiddle with the pen. "Simone have something to do with what happened this morning?"

"What happened?" asked Butch.

"Someone pulled the people across the street out of their house."

"Beat them in the street?"

"Kidnapped them."

Andy and Butch both shook their heads.

"We don't know anythin' about that," said Butch. "I mean, it wasn't us."

Andy frowned. "It could be Simone, though. I know she likes to mix up assignments, so none of us see the big picture. They still missin'?"

Tilly shook her head. "No. They came back in a golf cart a little while later, tied up and decorated like Christmas trees."

Butch laughed. "Dat's gotta be her. You gotta admit. She's got style."

"Tilly, what's up?" called a female voice.

Andy and Butch glanced at each other as Tilly pirouetted to look down the driveway. An attractive young couple headed toward them, a sandy, wavy-haired dog leading the way. The dog's tail started wagging as Tilly leaned down to pet it. After a few good chin scratches, Tilly straightened and slipped a hand into the other pocket of her house dress to produce a thumb drive.

"I brought you that footage you wanted."

"Oh great," said the girl, taking it.

The couple's attention moved to Andy and Butch, still standing on the landing.

"Can I help you?" asked the girl.

"You Charlotte?" asked Andy.

The girl looked at Tilly.

"Am I?"

Tilly nodded.

Charlotte shrugged. "I guess I am."

Butch lifted his hand to flash the manila envelope. "We got somethin' for you."

"From Jamie?"

Andy scowled. "Jamie?"

"Jamie's her real name. Simone was her cover," croaked

Tilly in her smoky baritone.

Andy nodded. "Oh, yeah. Yeah then. From *Jamie*."

They stood in silence until Butch spoke up, bobbing his head toward the door.

"You got coffee in there?"

CHAPTER EIGHT

Charlotte stared at her brewing pot of coffee, feeling a little as if she'd fallen down the rabbit hole. Here she was, playing hostess-with-the-mostess to two of *Jamie's* flunkies. The woman who threatened her life and the lives of everyone she loved had sent these men to her doorstep, and she was *making them coffee.*

"Cream? Sugar?"

"Black, thanks," said the one sitting on the left side of her sofa. Charlotte thought that one was *Andy,* but she wasn't sure.

"Splash of milk if ya got it," said the one on the right. *Butch.*

"Tilly?"

Tilly waggled her fingers in the air. "I'm good."

Charlotte pulled the milk from the refrigerator.

For all I know, these men were actually sent here to kill me.

She glanced at Declan, who sat stone-faced in a chair facing her new friends, his arms crossed against his chest as if he were holding himself back. She could tell he didn't like the idea of her new friends floating around. Tilly seemed to think the men were safe, but she'd be hard-pressed to convince Declan.

"It'll take a sec," she said, moving into the living room. All the furniture Declan had picked out for her from his pawn shop was finally coming in handy. Tilly, Declan, and the two goons were the most company she'd had all at once in quite a while.

"No problem. Appreciate it," said Andy.

Charlotte put her hands on her hips and turned her attention to the two men on her sofa. Both were in their sixties, with dark hair and tan skin. Specks of gray salted one's impressive coif. The other was shorter, with thinning hair slicked back across his scalp. Both were heavy-set.

"So what do you have for me?" she asked, eyeing the large envelope between them.

Butch looked around until he spotted the package lying beside him on the sofa. He picked it up and held it out to her.

"Simone, er, *Jamie* said this could help you."

"She gave it to you?" asked Charlotte, hoping to confirm her suspicion Jamie was near.

"It was delivered."

Charlotte sat on the leather ottoman that matched the chair where Declan sat. Declan had bought the pair from a Mr. Bing's estate. Most of his pawn shop's inventory came from estate sales held at one of the area's many fifty-five-plus communities.

A lot of her things had come from Mr. Bing.

He'd had good taste.

Charlotte took the packet and slid out a few sheets of paper.

"This doesn't look like much."

Andy shrugged. "We don't get involved in the details. That's what she gave us."

Charlotte scanned the top sheet and read aloud. "Andy and Butch will be keeping an eye on you so you can concentrate on the job at hand." She looked at the men on her sofa.

Andy tapped his finger to his chest. "We're protection."

"Hold on," said Declan, unwrapping his arms long enough to hold up a palm. "Protection from what? Jamie sent you here to be bodyguards?"

Andy shrugged. "Bodyguards, fixers, fetchers, and all-around help."

"You got a spare room?" asked Butch, his eyes flicking from Declan to Charlotte.

Declan chuckled, more with agitation than mirth. "You guys are *not* sleeping here."

Andy frowned. "Whatever. We can take turns sleepin' in the car."

Butch winced, reaching behind himself to touch his back. "I dunno, Andy. I got a little sciatica."

Andy rolled his eyes and turned back to Charlotte. "Look, bottom line is the boss lady wants you alive, and we're here to make sure you stay dat way."

Charlotte sighed. "Let's take this from the top. You guys work for Jamie?"

"Not exactly," said Tilly, who had wandered from the room and now reentered with a cup of coffee in each hand. She offered one to Charlotte, who declined. Next, she walked past Andy and Butch. They watched her like dogs watching a toddler with a hamburger. Tilly offered Declan a mug, and only when he refused did she turn to the pair of goons.

"Here," she said, placing the mugs on the coffee table.

The men both leaned forward and claimed their mugs. "T'anks."

Tilly sat back in her seat and, turning a steady gaze on Charlotte, motioned to the men. "Jamie's got them by the balls."

The men shifted in their seats, looking uncomfortable.

"How do you mean? She was their WITSEC officer?" asked Charlotte.

Andy and Butch glanced at each other and then blinked at Charlotte, seemingly struck dumb.

Tilly snorted a laugh. "Yeah, she knows. They both know."

Andy's eyes grew wide. "What? What're you tellin' me?"

Butch dropped his head into his hands. "I knew it. I knew it when Simone ran we were blown—"

"You're not blown. We won't tell anyone," said Charlotte.

"But if *you* know—" began Andy.

Declan leaned forward to rest his forearms on his knees. "We have a long history with her. We know she abused her little corner of witness protection, and we know she parked a lot of people here in Charity. It wasn't hard for us to put the pieces together if you're here, doing *her* bidding with those accents. You're not exposed on any larger scale."

"I can't say I feel good about this," said Butch.

Charlotte found herself eyeing Tilly. The boys hadn't been shocked to find out *she* knew about their placement in WITSEC. The three of them clearly had a history that included their secret past.

Tilly felt her gaze and glanced in her direction, so Charlotte returned her attention to Butch and Andy. "She's threatened to expose you? That's why you're running errands for her?"

Andy nodded. "Yeah. Though the people mad at us are mostly dead."

"*Mostly*," said Butch. "That's the important part. The men we flipped on have kids. We don't know what they know."

"Why don't you just leave? She's gone now," suggested Declan.

Andy shrugged. "We got families here. And she'd know. She'd still find us."

Butch nodded, looking grim. "No matter where we went, she'd know."

"She always knows."

Charlotte could tell by the expressions on the men's faces they held no love for Jamie Moriarty. They were her unwilling puppets, and she jerked their strings whenever she saw fit.

"Is it fair to say there are *more* people around here who'd like to see this psycho thrown in jail?"

Butch laughed. "Captured? They'd give their left—" he stopped and cleared his throat. "Captured ain't the half of it. If I'm bein' honest, we'd all like to see her *gone.* In a permanent way. If you know what I mean."

"I know I would," muttered Andy. "But none of us tried anything, even when we knew where she lived."

"There was that one guy," said Butch.

Andy rolled his eyes. "If that story was even true."

"What story?" asked Charlotte.

Andy looked away as if he was embarrassed to say, so Butch picked up the conversation. "There was a story some guy tried to kill her with spiders."

"With *spiders*?"

"Yeah, put them in her car or something."

"No one ever heard from him again," added Andy.

Butch looked around the room as if Jamie was hiding behind every chair. "Be honest widcha. I'm not real comfortable talkin' about her now like this. Far as I know, she's got—"

"Cameras. All over the place." Andy looked at Tilly. "Like you."

"Never like *me*," said Tilly with a note of pride. "And you know *I'm* not helping *her*." Tilly muttered something under her breath that sounded like an Italian curse.

Andy and Butch took sips of their coffee simultaneously.

Declan cocked his chin in Tilly's direction. "How do *you* know her then? And these guys?"

Tilly sighed. "I was in witness protection, too, remember."

"As a little girl. Jamie wasn't around then."

Tilly shrugged. "I keep my ear to the ground when things interest me." She hooked a thumb toward Andy and Butch. "And when these two showed up, it didn't take a genius."

"She never asked *you* to do anything, did she?" asked Charlotte.

Tilly snorted a laugh that turned into a rattly cough and took thirty seconds to pull under control. "My problems were long before her time."

"But you still ended up *here* with the rest of them? Isn't that a heck of a coincidence?"

Tilly fingered something in her pocket. "When you want someone to disappear, the middle of Florida isn't a bad place to start. Then and now."

Charlotte nodded. *Tilly had a point.*

She turned to the men. "Would you mind giving us a second?"

They both perked, peering over their mugs at her.

"You want us to go?" asked Andy.

"What, step outside a second?" added Butch.

"If you don't mind."

Andy nodded and set down his mug. "Sure. Sure. You got it."

Butch stood, cradling his coffee against his chest. "You mind if I take this with me?"

"No, that's fine."

"Thanks."

Andy looked at his partner, then at his own mug, plucked it off the table, and headed for the exit.

Abby stood as the men rose and escorted them to the door. Once they'd left, she sat and stared at them through the screen.

"Those two are not staying in your house," said Declan the moment they were gone.

Charlotte shook her head. "No. Not a snowball's chance in hell."

"I hate to say it, but they're sweet guys," said Tilly.

"How well do you know them?" asked Charlotte.

"Well enough. We move in similar circles. They're good guys. Family guys. Grandkids and all that. They don't like this situation any better than you do. What I'm saying is, you don't have to fear them."

Declan frowned. "Unless she changes her mind and decides she wants Charlotte dead. Then they have to do anything she asks, right?"

Tilly nodded her head from side to side. "Yeah, so you might have a point there."

Charlotte rubbed her neck. The day was starting to make her shoulders bunch. “Do you know more like them?”

“Retired hitmen?”

“Not necessarily. Just more of the WITSEC people here in general. More under Jamie’s thumb.”

Tilly held her gaze a moment too long before shrugging. “Maybe.”

Charlotte smiled.

You know a lot of them. Maybe all of them.

Declan cocked an eyebrow at her. “Why do you have that look on your face?”

“Oh, nothing. I was just thinking how handy it might be to know more people who want her gone for good.”

Declan glowered at her. “Please tell me you’re not thinking about trying to take her down?”

Charlotte grinned. “Maybe.”

CHAPTER NINE

"Can you guys come back in now?"

Andy and Butch reentered the house, both their mugs hanging on their index fingers, empty.

"Do you know who else she uses?" asked Charlotte.

Both men's brows knit as they looked to each other for help.

"What're you askin'?" asked Butch.

"Other WITSEC people. People she's threatened to expose, have killed, gets killed, etcetera."

"Um..." Both men looked as if they wanted to turn and bolt back out the door.

"You know, the whole point of the program is to *not* know anyone if you know what I mean," said Butch.

Andy agreed. "Yeah, we're supposed to be quiet-like, blend in." He chuckled. "Though that bank robbery last spring had Tophat written all over it."

Butch laughed. "Yeah, that *had* to be him."

"Bank robbery?" probed Charlotte.

Andy pointed to the east. "Yeah, over outside of Orlando. Little town, I forget the name of it. Some fat guy wearing a tux asked to get in there because his diamond cufflinks were in the vault—"

"And once they let him in the vault, he robbed them blind

and walked right out," finished Andy. "The funniest part is that Tophat's a *skinny* guy."

"You said he was fat," said Charlotte.

"He was wearing a suit for carryin' loot," said Butch, circling his arms in front of him to show the girth of the suit. "He did the same thing back in Jersey City back in ninety."

"Ninety-two, I think," corrected Andy.

Butch nodded. "Ninety-two. I think you're right."

"His name's Tophat? That's his last name?" asked Charlotte.

"Nah, that's what we all called him back in Jersey 'cause he was so fancy," said Butch.

"Nice suits," added Andy.

"Nice suits."

"Do you know his real name?"

The men paused, and Butch looked at Andy. "Donny Topham, ain't it?"

"Yeah, that's it."

Charlotte headed for the back of the house. "Tophat, Topham..."

Behind her, she could hear Andy talking. "Yeah, I guess his last name had something to do with the nickname, too, now that you mention it. But nice suits. It was mostly about the suits."

"Beautiful suits," agreed Butch as Charlotte strode back into the living room with Jamie's fingerprint book in her hand.

Charlotte sat on the ottoman again and set the book on her lap. She flipped through the pages of fingerprints until she found one with the initials D. T. at the bottom.

That has to be Donny Topham.

"I wonder if they lifted any prints from that heist," she mumbled.

"Did you just solve a bank heist?" asked Declan.

Andy held up his palms. "Whoa, whoa. We didn't come

here to rat anyone out. I don't know if Donny did that bank hit."

"Yeah, we're not rats," added Butch.

Charlotte squinted at them. "You're in witness protection. Doesn't that mean you're rats by definition?"

Butch and Andy began talking over each other, both gesticulating with their hands as if they were trapped in invisible boxes and trying to feel their way out.

"That was different."

"Yeah, that's what you'd call extenuating circumstances."

"That's what the lawyers called it."

"Any way you cut it, we did what we had to do."

"And Tony had it comin' anyway."

"He did. With or without us."

Charlotte held up a hand in the hopes of calming them, and they fell silent. "I'm sorry. I didn't mean to worry you. I'm not going after Donny Topham.

Andy laughed. "We know you ain't going after him."

"He's dead," explained Butch. "Heart attack about three months ago."

Andy nodded. "Maybe four. That's why we can talk about him."

Charlotte closed the fingerprint book.

So much for Donny Topham.

She stood to pull the thumb drive Tilly had given her from her pocket and moved to her laptop, where it sat charging on the kitchen table. She plugged in the drive and clicked through the files to pull up Tilly's surveillance of that morning's kidnapping. Declan moved behind her to watch over her shoulder.

The night vision image of Mariska's house showed no activity until the front door opened, and two men came out carrying Bob between them. Bob appeared limp, unaware he was being toted through his front door. Setting him on the ground, one of the men disappeared and returned into the frame with a wheelbarrow. They placed Bob inside and rolled him out of frame. Returning a few minutes later with the wheelbarrow, they repeated the process with Mariska. She slipped as the men dropped her in, and Charlotte saw her legs bounce on the rim of the wheelbarrow.

That explained the two bruises Mariska had on the back of her calves.

One of the men wore shorts, and Charlotte spotted a tattoo on his calf. She stopped the movie at the best moment possible and zoomed in.

Charlotte pointed at the tattoo. "That look like a sailfish to you?"

Declan squinted at the grainy video. "If I had to guess. It isn't a great picture."

"What about your friend with the sailfish tattoo on his leg?" said Charlotte, turning to look at Butch.

"Pollock Johnny?"

Andy slapped Butch's leg, and his partner grimaced.

"Is Pollock Johnny a big guy?" asked Charlotte. The man in the video hovering over Mariska's unconscious body appeared enormous in both height and girth.

Butch looked at Andy, who shook his head. "It's too late now. Go ahead and answer her." Andy glanced at Charlotte. "Johnny's a big boy."

"Yeah, he is. Like all those Chicago Pollocks. He sat next to me the other day at one of the meet—"

Andy elbowed Butch in the stomach, and Butch cut short.

"A meeting?" asked Charlotte, hoping to finish Butch's thought. "You were at a meeting with him?"

Butch shook his head. "Nah, not a meeting. A party. My birthday party. I mean, a meeting to plan my birthday. My birthday's comin' up, and I was thinking about doin' sometin'."

Andy walked over and peered at the computer screen. "Show me a bit of whatchure lookin' at."

Charlotte started at the beginning of the clip and let it play.

Andy pointed to the screen. "What's he doing with those

people?"

"Those are my neighbors. Jamie had them kidnapped this morning."

Andy grunted and wandered back to the sofa.

Charlotte stared at her screen, her finger tapping on the table.

"What are you thinking?" asked Declan.

"There's something here. I need to go through this packet she sent me. There's got to be a way to get her with the help of all these people she's been blackmailing."

Declan nodded. "They flipped once. Maybe one of them can flip on her?"

"Hey," barked Andy from his perch in the other room. "Come on. You're hurtin' our feelings. We're not rats..." Andy's gaze drifted to the fingerprint book. "Except what we said about Tophat."

Butch glanced at him. "And Pollock Johnny."

Andy's shoulders slumped. "Shoot. We're terrible at this."

"Kind of a miracle we lived this long, now that you mention it."

Tilly stood. "Well, if you need anything else, let me know. I think I'll turn on the extra cameras until all this blows over."

"Thank you, Tilly. I really appreciate it."

"Sure." She glared at Andy and Butch and pointed from her eyes to theirs with her forked index and middle fingers. "Remember, I'll have eyes on you two. I see *all*."

Butch and Andy both offered her a goofy grin.

"Whatever, Tilly. See you around."

Charlotte strolled into the living room to address her new bodyguards. "You two do whatever you would normally do. I don't want to endanger you or your family, but you can't sleep in my house."

Andy shrugged. "We'll figure out somethin'."

Butch looked worried.

"Worried about your back?" asked Charlotte.

"Yeah. No. That ain't it. I gotta be honest. That woman scares the crap out of me."

"Jamie?"

He nodded. "I mean, if you could get her out of our lives, I'd be forever grateful, but—"

Charlotte shook her head. "I can't. It was a nice thought for a second, but I need to concentrate on what she asked me to do, just like you do. Maybe that way, we'll all come out of this alive."

Both men appeared relieved. Andy stood.

"We'll go outside. You got some chairs out there?"

"There are some in the shed."

"Great. We'll set up."

Butch held up his mug. "You want me to put this in the sink?"

Charlotte took it. "I'll do it, thanks."

Andy and Butch headed outside. Declan turned to Charlotte, looking expectant.

"So you're not going after her now? That's probably a good—"

She cut him short. "Of course, I'm going after her."

"You just said—"

"To a couple of snitches."

"Ah. Good point. They might tell Jamie everything you said."

"It could be part of their job. Or their *only* real job. That monster can say they're my bodyguards, but chances are pretty good they're *really* here to watch me and report back to her."

Declan nodded and slid his arms around her waist. "I know what my job is."

"Oh yeah?"

"Yep. I'm your real bodyguard."

Charlotte grinned. "Oh, that goes without saying. But I have another job for you, too."

"Yes? Personal masseur?"

"Nope." She pulled him close and whispered the answer in his ear.

She felt his shoulders slump, his weight suddenly heavier. She held him up until her knees started to buckle.

"Wait, wait, you're crushing me," she said, laughing.

He straightened and held her at arm's length to stare deep into her eyes.

"Please tell me you're kidding."

She shook her head. "I really need you to go talk to Stephanie."

CHAPTER TEN

Declan sat at the plastic picnic table waiting, his leg bouncing with nervous energy. He'd never been in prison before. It wasn't something on his bucket list. Around him, boyfriends, fathers, husbands, and kids sat chatting with women wearing orange jumpsuits.

Though some of the women were pretty frightening, they didn't scare Declan. Nor did the visiting family members, some of whom were pretty shocking to look at as well. Not even the guy two tables over with embedded-fishhook tattoos all over his arm.

That one fascinated him.

Did the guy get a tattoo for every fish he hooked? And if so, why did he keep fishing?

He'd made some dubious choices, but Fishhook Guy didn't scare Declan either. The person who had his knee bouncing with anxiety was walking through the door now, wrapped in her very own orange jumpsuit.

Stephanie.

Charlotte had begged him to go talk to his ex. She thought Stephanie might be more inclined to share important information with him than with *her*—the girl who could testify she'd discovered Stephanie next to the body of a dead assistant district attorney.

She was probably right.

There was no love lost between Charlotte and Stephanie, and because he and Stephanie had been childhood friends long before they dated, she tended to share more with him than probably anyone else in her life. He knew her past. He knew she'd been a mercenary after working for the government in a shadow ops assignment.

He knew killing people didn't cause her to lose a moment of sleep.

He'd been in the shadow program too, but he'd left. For him, the training had been a way to focus on the free-floating rage left behind by his father's abandonment and mother's disappearance. He'd been a troubled kid, and his uncle Seamus had thought the program might be a way to channel his anger into something useful. It was. But when it became clear to him the program had an agenda far darker than he ever imagined, he'd left.

Stephanie had stayed and let her bloodlust run wild. She'd also had a tough childhood, but he suspected her more violent tendencies were inherited from her mother. When Jamie abandoned her as a baby and left her with a neglectful foster mother who was only interested in regular payments—it didn't help Stephanie's overall demeanor.

Smart and ruthless, Stephanie had been a perfect team asset. When she'd finally quit and returned to Florida, he'd tried to help her, tried to set her straight, but he'd known from the start it was a losing battle.

They'd clung to each other during their darkest times as adolescents, but he'd grown up and found a way out of his shadows.

She had not.

In his heart, he knew he wasn't *really* scared of Stephanie. He was scared of the person he'd been when he was with her.

Stephanie scanned the room, and Declan remembered to start breathing again. She walked to the table and slid into the bench seat across from him. She seemed almost awkward, walking in flat slip-on shoes instead of stilting it over in her trademark high heels.

He smiled. "You look good in orange."

She raised her middle finger in his direction.

"Making friends?"

Stephanie scoffed. "Oh, sure. I had to break one girl's nose. I'm sure I'll be on her Christmas list forever. Mom sent you?"

"In a roundabout sort of way, yes."

"What does that mean?"

"It means your mother kidnapped Charlotte's friends and told her if she didn't find a way to get you out of jail, the kidnappings would turn into murders."

Stephanie's eyes grew wide. "She's putting my fate in goody-two-shoe's hands?"

"Backed with a good dose of threats. She isn't counting on Charlotte's good nature."

Stephanie's lip curled. "Well, we all know what a good nature sweet Charlotte has."

Declan crossed his arms against his chest. "*Not* being a psychopath doesn't make her a goody-two-shoes. If your mother hurts anyone, I promise you'll see another side of Charlotte."

Stephanie raised her hands and wiggled her fingers. "Ooooh. *Angry* Charlotte. Scary."

Declan sighed. "Look, I've got places to be—"

"Oh, me too. By all means, get to the reason you're here so I can get back and play another round of Shower Before They Find You."

"I'm here to pull everything you can remember out of your head. We need to know *everything* if we're going to prove you didn't kill the Assistant D.A."

"Let me start by telling you I didn't kill Jason. I *swear*."

"You didn't kill him? Or you don't remember killing him?"

Stephanie frowned, her shoulders slumping. "Maybe a little of both. I lost some time between arriving at the warehouse and waking up. But I know I didn't have any *intention* of killing him. I was trying to decide whether to blackmail him or report him. Execution was never on the table."

"He was making life difficult for you, wasn't he? Sabotaging your cases?"

"Sabotaging cases that could have gotten me killed. It's not like I represent people unwilling to take their frustrations out on me."

"So that's a great reason to kill him."

"Maybe, but I'd already had Charlotte follow him. She had proof he was tampering with my witnesses. I didn't *need* to kill him. He was going down anyway. And—"

Stephanie fell silent.

"And what?"

She looked away and then turned back to him. "And I'd told you I was going to be a better person. I meant it."

"So you shifted from murder to blackmail? Wow. Big leap."

"It is, actually." Stephanie sighed. "Anyway, he was the one breaking the law. I was just trying to survive."

"Fine. Fine. What else? Why were you in the warehouse?"

"He texted me. Said to meet him there."

"And you brought a gun?"

"I always have a gun. But yes. I also have a policy of packing when I show up at abandoned warehouses."

"Did you tell him you had evidence of him breaking the law?"

Stephanie closed her eyes. "No. He was already sitting in that chair when I got there. Already still and...he didn't look *right*."

"But maybe he knew. Maybe he pulled a gun on you, and you shot him in self-defense?"

Stephanie dipped her head to rub her temple. "It's possible. But I did see something. A gun. And it was near him, but I swear Declan—I don't think it was *his* hand."

"What do you mean?"

"It was like someone was hiding behind him. They raised the gun to make it look like it was Jason, but..."

"But it *wasn't*. You think someone else was there?"

She nodded.

"Okay, good. That's something. Who?"

Stephanie tilted her face to the ceiling. "You think I haven't been trying to remember? I feel like it's in my head, but I just can't get it out."

"Did you see anything?"

"I think just a hand, an arm? There was a beam of light shining on something."

"Like a flashlight?"

"No. There were holes in the ceiling. Rust spots or whatever. The sun came through in beams."

"And then what?"

She sighed. "I saw the gun, and I grabbed mine as I was diving out of the way. There was gunfire."

"Whose? The mystery gun or yours?"

"The mystery gun. No, both. I shot back. Once."

"You're sure, *once*?"

She nodded. "I'm pretty sure."

"What happened next?"

"My head. I hit my head on something."

"What?"

Stephanie squinted. "A carpet?"

"You knocked yourself cold on a carpet?"

"Yes...no? I know it doesn't make any sense. But that's what was there when I woke up."

"And that's when you realized Jason was dead?"

"Yes. And then your girlfriend walked in and..." She trailed off.

"And you tried to kill her."

"I was a little out of my head at that point."

"Sure. We'll go with that. Totally out of character for you."

Stephanie chuckled. "Do you know you're the only person in the world I can be myself around?"

Declan sighed. "I'm the only one who knew you as a kid."

She nodded. "Before the world corrupted me."

"I'm not sure it was all the *world's* fault."

She giggled.

Declan leaned back in his chair. "I can't remember the last time I saw you really laugh."

Stephanie sniffed. "Yeah, well, I tried to go straight and ended up in jail. If you can't laugh at the irony of that, what can you laugh at?"

Declan nodded, trying to remember if there was anything else he'd been instructed to ask. He straightened. "Oh, Charlotte said she'd like to look around your office."

"Why?"

"If someone set you up, they might have gotten in there at some point. You might have a client who was up to no good. She thought she should at least look around."

Stephanie hooked her mouth to the right. "If she's going to root through my office looking for information about dirtbags, she's got a long weekend ahead of her. I've got drawers and drawers of dirtbags."

"Anyone you think might hold a grudge?"

"Maybe. But I thought Jamie knew the person who framed me. Isn't he really after her?"

"Seems like it, but it bears asking."

Stephanie traced a figure-eight on the table with her index finger. "I don't think so. I've been lucky so far. Haven't lost any major cases. My clients are happy in their miserable little lives."

"Okay. Where's the key to your office?"

Stephanie thought for a moment. "In my purse, which was

in my car. Which I imagine the police have now."

"Do you have a spare?"

"I do. Under the flowerpot in the front. Dig through the sand there about five inches down."

"Good. How about your apartment?"

"My what?"

"How do we get into your house if we need to look around there?"

Stephanie sighed. "I live in the office."

"What?"

"In the back. I live in the office."

"There's an apartment there?"

"There is now."

"Is that even legal?"

"Probably not."

"Why wouldn't you just get an apartment?"

"I work weird hours." Stephanie huffed. "What do you care? I told you how to get in."

"Okay, okay."

Stephanie crossed her arms on the table and rested her chin on her forearms. She looked tired.

"I should tell you I have the whole place wired with cameras. There's a false wall in my room that goes into the office space next door. You'll find all the surveillance equipment in there."

Declan squinted at her. "You have a secret command center hidden in your office?"

"You could call it that."

"You know you're starting to sound more and more like Batman, right?"

Stephanie laughed and lifted her head. "He was crazy, right?"

She rapped on the table with her knuckles and stood. Declan followed suit.

"Well, see you," she said. "I'd shake your hand, but no touching in the visitors' room. And it would be weird anyway."

"Agreed."

Stephanie winced as if she were in pain.

"What's wrong?"

"Tell your girlfriend thank you for this. Even if Mom's making her do it."

Stephanie's seemingly genuine appreciation struck Declan as so unusual his head jerked back as if she'd slapped him.

"Really?"

"Really."

"It's nice of you to recognize she really *will* do all she can for you."

"Tell her I'm sorry I tried to kill her."

"I'm sure she'll be happy to hear that."

"And tell her if she *doesn't* get me out of here next time, I won't just *try*."

Declan rolled his eyes. "*There* she is. The Stephanie we all know and love."

Stephanie offered him a little wave, her hand hovering by her hip, before wandering back toward the guard, watching the door leading back to the cells. Out of questions and feeling dismissed, Declan was nearly to the exit when he heard her call out behind him.

"Declan!"

He turned as the other prisoners, and their guests looked up in unison. Stephanie stood in the doorway, flanked by a guard, straining to keep the door open as the guard dragged her from the room.

"There's a bouncing betty under the key," she yelled.

"What?"

The door shut, and he could see her through the glass, pantomiming an explosion as the guard jerked her down the hall.

CHAPTER ELEVEN

"See this hole?"

Charlotte stood behind the abandoned carpet warehouse where she'd found Stephanie near the body of the dead A.D.A. A small, perfect circle had been punched through the back wall of the building. She pointed at it so Mariska and Darla could see. The pair had wanted to help her with her investigation, so she thought she'd let them try and locate Stephanie's missing bullet. Stephanie had admitted to firing once, and when Charlotte checked in with Frank, he reported the bullet had yet to be located. If they could find Stephanie's bullet in the pine forest behind the warehouse, they could clear her of shooting and killing Jason Walsh.

"Flimsy walls," muttered Darla.

"That's probably why they abandoned it. The carpets were getting wet," suggested Mariska.

"Or the critters were getting in and eating the fluff."

"I think the building was in better shape when they were actually in here," said Charlotte.

Darla shrugged. "You can't stop critters when they want that fluff."

Mariska gasped. "Oh, that reminds me. We have to keep an eye out for the coyotes while we're out here."

Charlotte frowned. "Coyotes?"

"Didn't you get the Port o' Call?"

Charlotte rolled her eyes. She *had* received Pineapple Port's newsletter, the Port o' Call, in her mailbox, but she hadn't taken the time to read whose daughter was getting a promotion at work and who was trying to sell broken exercise equipment or used medical paraphernalia.

"I've been a little busy. I must have missed it."

Mariska pursed her lips. "Oh, you can't do that. It's very important."

"*She* was *kidnapped* and found the time to read it," mumbled Darla as she put her finger through the hole in the wall.

Mariska nodded. "Exactly. If you'd read it, you'd know we're being overrun with coyotes."

Charlotte wrapped her fingers around Darla's wrist and pulled her finger out of the hole. "Don't touch anything. *Who's* being overrun?"

"Pineapple Port. Maybe all of Charity, I'm not sure."

"So you're not *personally* being overrun by coyotes."

"No." Mariska's gaze drifted. "I don't think so..."

"How did this happen? I've never heard of coyotes around here before."

"They think there are a couple of jackasses feeding them," said Darla.

Charlotte scowled. "In the neighborhood?"

"Yes. They probably think they're wild dogs. But now they're packing up."

"The neighbors are leaving?"

"No, the *coyotes*. They're roaming in *packs*."

"They're attacking small children," added Mariska.

"Really?"

"No, but they could. That's the point. When they pack up

like that, they can take down an elephant."

Charlotte chuckled. "Has anyone warned the elephants?"

Mariska ignored her and continued, the tone of her voice growing increasingly urgent. "The Port o' Call said to carry a bag of rocks whenever you're out walking so you can throw them at the coyotes."

"You're going to fend off a pack of elephant-eating coyotes with a bag of rocks?"

"You bet your life. I'm worried about Miss Izzy when we take our walks. She doesn't do well with stress."

"Shouldn't Izzy be protecting *you* from the coyotes? Did you get her a bag of rocks to wear around her collar?"

Mariska shook her head, appearing saddened by her own dog's anxiety levels. "She's tough with the cartoon birds on the television, but Izzy freezes when she sees the Sandhill cranes. She gets one look at those giant birds and shoots between my legs and won't come out. I have to turn around or drag her past them."

"So you don't think she'll rise to the challenge of wild coyotes."

"No. Not a chance."

Charlotte could feel a fit of giggles coming on and covered her mouth with one hand. "Sorry. I'm imagining you, standing there with Izzy between your legs, throwing rocks..." She snorted a laugh.

Mariska huffed. "It's not funny. Some of the locals are terrible at throwing things. What are they going to do? The rocks are no help if you have bursitis in your shoulder."

Charlotte raised her other hand to help the first hold back her amusement.

Darla pretended to shoot from her hip, clicking her middle digit on the imaginary trigger. "I've been taking Frank's gun with me when I walk Turbo."

Mariska's jaw dropped. "Oh, Darla. You're going to *shoot*

them?"

"If it's me or them, yes. If they have me cornered—"

Charlotte snorted another laugh.

"It isn't funny," said Mariska.

Charlotte sniffed and wiped her eyes. "Come on. It's pretty funny. You two are talking about Pineapple Port like you live in the forests of Transylvania."

"Well, you can laugh all you want, but remember when we had that feral cat problem?"

"Yes?"

"Not anymore," said Darla grimly.

"The coyotes got the cats, and they're moving their way up the food chain."

Charlotte dragged her hand over her face. "Okay, okay, let's get back to business and forget the coyote problem for a second."

"Fine. But I'm going to get you a bag of rocks."

"Thank you. Now, back to this hole in the wall. The walls are too thin to easily tell the trajectory, but we should follow where we think the bullet would have gone and check the trees. It had to hit one of them."

"So we're looking for a bullet embedded in a tree?" asked Mariska.

"Right. Oh, but the bullet probably won't look like a bullet anymore. It'll be flat like a pancake if it hit a tree."

"So we're looking for tiny silver pancakes. I can do that."

Charlotte imagined she'd be getting silver dollar pancakes for breakfast the next day. You couldn't say food in front of Mariska without her running off and making it.

Darla slid the long, black bag draped over her shoulder to the ground and unzipped it. From it, she pulled a metal detector.

"That was a good idea," said Charlotte.

Darla nodded. "This isn't the first time I've had to find a bullet in a tree."

Charlotte opened her mouth to ask about Darla's bullets-in-trees history but decided she didn't want to know. Darla had a bit of a shady past. After all, she'd been the one who taught Charlotte how to pick locks. It shouldn't be a complete shock. She'd also spent time looking for bullets in trees.

Charlotte had to get back to corralling Mariska, who'd wandered down the side of the building.

"Mariska, where are you going? I don't think the bullet went through the wall and made a hard left."

Mariska glanced over her shoulder. "There's a pile of little carpet squares over here. I couldn't tell what they were. Hey..." Mariska turned to face the outer wall of the warehouse. "Are you sure that's a bullet hole down there?"

"What do you mean?"

"There's more of them here." Mariska stuck her finger into the side of the building as Charlotte moved in to investigate. She squinted at the new hole.

"You're right. That looks like a bullet hole, too."

"And this one down here," called Darla from farther down the wall. "And another."

"Hmm."

Charlotte took a step back. What did that mean? Did Stephanie shoot at Jason *multiple* times? The new bullet holes were farther away from where Jason had been tied to a chair. It didn't make sense. They couldn't have had a whole *firefight*. The early reports she heard from Frank were that Stephanie's gun had been fired once. She thought if she could find the bullet, it would clear Stephanie, but now she was starting to understand why the cops had apparently given up trying to find it themselves.

Charlotte sighed. "I'm going to have to go inside and see what I can see from there. You guys keep looking for bullets."

Mariska fished in her purse. "Do you want to take some coyote rocks with you?"

"No. I think I'm good."

Jogging around the building, Charlotte located the bullet holes Mariska had found from the other side. Two holes, maybe two feet from each other diagonally. They didn't fit Stephanie's story at all. She said she'd found Jason tied to the chair and shot once after someone had shot at her. She'd dove for safety and hit her head, ending the firefight.

But Stephanie also said she thought someone might have been hiding behind Jason. Maybe that person had run, and she'd shot twice more at him? Maybe after hitting her head, she forgot the additional shots?

Charlotte pulled out her phone and called Frank.

"Frank here."

"Did you get the official ballistics report back on Stephanie's gun?"

"Hello to you, too."

"Sorry, *hello*."

"Hello. And yes, I did get it back. Hold on."

She heard papers rustling on Sheriff Frank's desk.

"Here it is. Her gun was fired once. The bullet was recovered from Jason's body."

Charlotte gaped. "It was? This morning you said they hadn't found the bullet yet."

Frank grunted. "Sorry. Got the report right after I talked to you. Hadn't had a chance to get back."

"Oh. That's bad news. I've got your wife and Mariska out here looking for bullets in the trees. I was hoping to find Stephanie's far from Jason's body."

"Nope. Inside his body, as it turns out."

"But Stephanie's gun was still only fired once, right? We found a couple other bullet holes in the wall here."

"Eh, that place has been abandoned for years. I wouldn't be surprised if kids shot it up once or twice."

"Ah. Makes sense. Anything else?"

"Yep. Hold on, let me see..." She heard Frank's pen tapping on the desk as he read the report. "Ah. Here's something good for you. Seems Jason was already dead. They didn't see the bullet hole right away because there was no blood."

"What do you mean?"

"He didn't bleed after being shot. He was shot post-mortem, so he didn't bleed, and the bullet just sort of sunk into him like he was soft cheese."

Charlotte's lip curled. "Yikes, Frank. *Cheese*?"

He sniffed. "Probably about right."

"But that means she didn't kill him!" Charlotte heard the excitement in her voice as she forgot about Frank's graphic description and realized her troubles were over if Stephanie didn't shoot Jason.

Frank didn't let her remain excited for long. "Hold on there, missy. As the person in the warehouse with him and the one who put a bullet in his dead body, Stephanie's still the best suspect for the murder. She's not going anywhere fast."

Charlotte slumped. "Shoot. What about the bullet that Stephanie says was shot at her?"

"Can't find any real evidence *anything* was shot in her direction. The wall behind her is half holes as it is and leads across the road. They looked and couldn't find anything."

"Okay. Well, I guess I got *some* good news anyway."

"Tell you what. If you want to keep Darla searching for the bullet, be my guest. It stops her from shopping online."

Charlotte chuckled. "I'll take that into consideration. Thanks." She hung up and walked back around the warehouse to the ladies.

"Bullet-hunting has been called off. Seems the powers that be have them all."

"But Darla just found one," said Mariska. She stood beside her friend, who had a pocketknife in her hand. With it, Darla pried at the side of a pine tree. Mariska held a zip-lock sandwich bag beneath the spot, and a moment later, something heavy dropped from the side of the tree into the bag.

Charlotte lined up the path from the tree to the warehouse. This bullet had to be what caused one of the mystery holes Mariska had found.

"Frank thinks those are probably from kids shooting up the place."

Mariska zipped the bag and thrust it toward her. "Well, you might as well keep it."

"Do you want me to look for the other one? This is fun. It's like looking for treasure."

Charlotte considered the offer and smiled, remembering Frank's joke. "Nah. Let's get out of here before the coyotes find us."

"Or the bobcats," added Mariska.

"Or the panthers," said Darla.

"Bears."

"Gators."

"Pythons."

Darla pouted. "Why the hell do we live here anyway?"

CHAPTER TWELVE

"There's some kind of weird bird on your roof," said Mariska as they approached Charlotte's house.

Charlotte squinted toward the top of her house as the ladies left her ancient Volvo to return to their own homes. She spotted a flash of movement on the opposite side of her roofline before the creature Mariska had seen moved into better view.

"That's no bird. That's Blade."

The enormous man sat crouched on her roof, fiddling with some small contraption. As she pulled into her driveway, he glanced down at her and waved, grinning wide enough she could spot the gaps where he was missing one lower tooth and one upper. Charlotte chuckled to herself, remembering what Darla called a smile like that: Summer Teeth. Some'r there and some'r not.

Charlotte turned off her ignition as a Cadillac pulled to the curb and parked behind her. Andy and Butch peered out at her through the Caddy's tinted windows. Butch's window lowered, and he pointed up at Blade.

"He supposed to be up there?"

Charlotte glanced up at Blade. "I'm not entirely sure."

Declan appeared from behind her house and held up a hand. "It's okay, guys. He's with me."

Butch nodded and remained in his air-conditioned car. Charlotte thought she'd seen the black Cadillac lurking outside the warehouse while she, Mariska, and Darla were bullet-hunting. She'd been right. It seemed Butch and Andy were officially watching her. A fast food paper sack appeared in Butch's hand, and he rooted through it in search of lunch as his window slid back up.

Charlotte smiled at Declan. "Where did you come from?"

"I was around back helping with some of the wiring."

"Wiring? I assume that has something to do with why your ginormous employee is crawling around my rooftop?"

Declan nodded. "Blade decided you needed motion-triggered cameras around the perimeter of your house. He brought six. I think he's almost done setting them up."

Charlotte glanced up, but Blade had moved to another corner of the roof, out of view. She lowered her voice, leaning toward Declan. "You told him about my troubles?"

"He—" Declan pressed his lips into a tight line, the muscle in his razor-sharp jawline bulging. "I'm afraid he overheard me talking to Seamus. Then he couldn't stop worrying about you. It was either let him install the cameras or watch him wring his hands until the bones broke."

"So you told *Seamus* about Jamie?"

"It's always good to keep Seamus in the loop when it comes to people like Jamie. He knows how to think like a criminal."

"True. I wonder why that is?" She elbowed Declan in the ribs, and he smiled.

"Yeah, yeah."

Charlotte heard clattering above her, and she shaded her eyes to peer up at Blade. She felt a little ashamed that more people knew she was tucked under the thumb of a murderer.

"Hi, Blade."

"Hi, Miss Charlotte. I hope you don't mind. But I told Declan

I'd like to do this for you. Just in case."

"It's sweet of you. I appreciate it."

Blade grinned beneath his droopy mustache.

Charlotte returned her attention to Declan. "So Blade had six motion cameras sitting around his house? Or he went out and bought all this stuff?"

"I didn't ask."

"Who's going to be on the other end of these cameras?"

"You. Me. They work off an app on your phone, so anyone with access to the app can be notified of motion and watch the clip."

"So I'll get a ding every time a possum waddles by or Butch walks over to pee in my bushes."

Declan's gaze darted to the Cadillac. "Butch is peeing in the bushes?"

"No. I was just kidding. But I can imagine a world where that might happen with them sitting outside my house all day. Unless they have the bladders of blue whales."

Declan sighed. "I wish you'd just move in with me for a bit."

Charlotte shook her head. Declan had suggested the night before she come stay with him, but she didn't feel *moving* would solve her problems. If anything, it dragged scrutiny to a spot they might need as a safe house and put Declan and Seamus under Butch and Andy's surveillance. She didn't want those two keeping an eye on any more people than necessary.

"I want to stay near Mariska and Darla, just in case Jamie decides to mess with them again. And anyway, with all these cameras and ex-mobsters around my house, it's safer than Fort Knox."

Declan didn't seem happy, but he shrugged and nodded. "I hear you. For the record, Seamus sometimes sleeps in the little apartment over his bar, so he isn't *always* on my sofa watching soccer. If you need a quiet place to think, my house is not a bad option for the first time in a long time."

"You must be enjoying that."

"You have no idea."

Blade clomped his way down the ladder propped against the side of her house. "I think you're all fixed, Miss Charlotte. No one will be able to *look* at this house without you knowing."

"Thank you, Blade. I feel safer already."

Blade's attention shifted to the two men sitting in the idling Cadillac, his eyes narrowing.

She nodded her head toward Andy and Butch.

"I'm told they're harmless."

Blade nodded. "Sure." He flashed another smile and wandered off to retrieve his ladder and tools.

"So, how's it going so far?" asked Declan.

"I went through the papers Andy and Butch delivered about a hundred times. There isn't much there..." Charlotte trailed off as a strange thought bounced through her mind.

There are two of them.

"What is it?" asked Declan.

Charlotte paused a moment longer while her suspicions gelled. "She thinks the person who framed Stephanie did so to get back at *her*. But it just occurred to me there might be *two* people involved."

"Two people working together to frame Stephanie and trap Jamie?"

"Yes. I'm thinking the one who does the dirty work is probably the one who rigged the warehouse scene for Stephanie. But there could be another person who *orchestrated* it—Jamie's true enemy."

"Why do you think that?"

Charlotte rubbed the collar of her t-shirt between her fingers, snapping the hints in Jamie's packet together in her mind like puzzle pieces. "In her pathetic collection of *helpful* notes, it feels like she's describing two different personalities. One person she suspects sounds like a bit of an animal. She said to look for him where *swamp people* hang out but then went on to say the man she wants has been hunting her for years. Anyone capable of staying alive that long when she wants them gone *has* to have a certain level of sophistication. That doesn't sound like a swamp person."

"But why wouldn't she tell you there are two people?"

"I don't know, but I can tell you it's making me angry she'd throw all this in my lap and then play games."

"That's sort of her specialty."

"Yeah, I know. Great, isn't it?" Charlotte kicked at a tangled ball of wire laying in her driveway and watched it bounce against her steps. "For some reason, she doesn't want me to know who the mastermind is. The only vaguely useful information she gave me was to say the man I'm looking for isn't in the fingerprint book but should be."

"What does that mean? Maybe he came too late, and she hadn't had time to add him before she had to run?"

"Maybe."

Declan crossed his arms against his chest. "Is it possible *Jamie* is the mastermind?"

"That she's screwed her own daughter?"

Declan nodded. "Either to test her or you."

"But why test me?"

"You know who she is. The last time she came up against you, her cover was blown, and she had to leave town."

Charlotte laughed. "Maybe I'm the secret enemy. Maybe I'm hunting myself."

"Being on Jamie's radar isn't funny."

Charlotte waved away his concerns. "I don't think this is about me. If she found me threatening, she'd try to kill me, not ask me to solve mysteries for her."

"I guess." Declan stared at the ground, rocking back and forth for a moment before looking back up at her. Charlotte could tell he didn't like the open ending of her exchanges with

Jamie. All the loose ends felt particularly loose, and he liked neat, tight knots.

"Nothing else useful?"

"Not really. She ended with *watch out for spiders*, which was odd, to say the least."

"Spiders? Does she mean there are a bunch of other people involved?"

Charlotte shrugged. "I don't know."

Just another loose end.

CHAPTER THIRTEEN

Stephanie sat up, her head grazing the bunk above her.

Where am I?

She looked around the concrete room, half in a dream.

Oh right. I'm in prison. Fantastic.

"Bitch, you're crying in your sleep again."

Stephanie cocked an eye toward the woman in the bunk above her. "Mind your business, Beatty."

Beatty leaned over her bunk to peer at her. "It *is* my business when you're keeping me awake—"

Stephanie grabbed the woman's greasy hair and jerked her throat against the edge of her bed. Standing, she pressed harder with her opposite hand, dodging as her cellmate's right arm flailed. Beatty used her left to push against the bed frame, trying to keep her windpipe from crushing against the metal.

"Okay! Okay!" she croaked.

Stephanie released her, and Beatty scrambled back into her bed, holding her throat. She glared at Stephanie, and Stephanie held her gaze until she looked away.

"You're crazy," muttered Beatty, rolling on her side to face away.

Stephanie sighed.

You have no idea.

Stephanie sat back on the edge of her bunk and wiped her hands on the edge of her sheet. She was pretty sure killing a cellmate didn't play well with juries, or they'd be dragging Beatty's greasy, dead body out of the cell.

No. The perception of juries didn't matter.

I don't kill people anymore.

Right?

But everyone *thought* she'd killed Jason. And even *she* wasn't one hundred percent sure she hadn't. Each night as she went to bed beneath Beatty, she struggled to remember every detail of her moments in the warehouse.

Jason had been tied to a chair.

Tied?

She assumed he was. *His arms were behind him, weren't they?*

She closed her eyes and tried to picture him. So still as he sat there. His posture was *unnatural.*

Jason *had* to already be dead. His head hung down...

Or unconscious. He might not have been dead.

Did I shoot him? Did I kill him after all?

No. Something was up. How had she knocked herself unconscious on an old roll of carpet? She'd jumped out of the way of all sorts of things over the course of her life, and she'd *never* knocked herself out doing it.

It had all happened so fast.

And if Jason was dead or unconscious, it didn't matter. She was sure he'd never moved, and yet someone had shot at her. It couldn't have been him, so there *had* to be someone else there.

Then there was the coral.

She took a deep breath to slow her beating heart.

Since arriving in prison, she'd had a reoccurring dream of herself swimming underwater through a giant, red coral forest. She picked her way through the coral branches, inching through the murky darkness of the water and getting more and more lost. A growing panic built until she looked at her air meter and saw she was nearly out, with no exit from the coral jungle in sight.

She'd take a breath, and although she could feel the air entering her lungs, there was no oxygen.

She was drowning.

That's when she'd wake up, gasping for air, nearly clipping her head on Beatty's bunk every time.

And every other time, she then had to shut Beatty up because *Beatty didn't learn.*

What did she expect? Statistically, most people in prison have been in prison before. *Learning from mistakes* wasn't a strong suit of the prison population. *Smart* people didn't get caught in the first place—

Whoops.

What does that say about me?

Stephanie put her head in her hands.

But I didn't do it. I couldn't have. Why would I shoot Jason? Who was shooting at me?

It didn't help that Charlotte had walked in a moment later. Stephanie was confused and angry at the time, and who should walk in but her romantic rival? Miss Goody Two Shoes.

Bad timing on Charlotte's part.

Outside Stephanie's cell, there was a loud pop, and the lights on the cell block sprung to life.

"Morning, sunshines," said Gina, the morning guard. The doors unlocked, and prisoners began groaning and yawning, then shuffling toward breakfast.

Stephanie stood and stepped out into the hall. The moment she'd cleared her cell, someone pushed her from behind. She stumbled, her hand dragging along the wall in search of something to grab.

Nothing.

She hit the floor knees-first and winced as her bones pounded the hard polished cement floor.

Someone snickered behind her.

Stephanie flipped around and stood, squaring as MuuMuu stopped to smile down at her.

Great. The moving mountain had noticed her.

MuuMuu was an enormous woman of Tongan descent. Her large, rounded shoulders and thick features had put her at the top of the food chain moments after entering prison, and she'd never looked back.

Stephanie stared at the woman's hanging lower lip and small, pig-like eyes as she straightened and forced a smile to her lips.

"Out of the way, blondie."

"Good morning, MuuMuu. Didn't anyone tell you bullying isn't fashionable anymore?"

MuuMuu's expression didn't change. She wasn't known for her great sense of humor. Except for the time she dipped Beatty's head in the toilet for being late paying her for protection. That was *hilarious.*

Protection. Duh. That's why MuuMuu pushed her. Beatty had ratted on her for roughing her up.

When all she had to do was stop talking.

MuuMuu reached out to club Stephanie on the side of her head with her monstrous bear paw of a hand. Stephanie dropped and swung her leg, her foot striking the side of MuuMuu's knee with all the force she could muster. The giantess roared, her knee buckling and arms flailing to grab Stephanie and keep her from falling. Stephanie barely scrambled out of the way of that falling redwood in time, and MuuMuu hit the ground with a thud they probably could feel way over in cellblock B.

A collective gasp escaped from the inmates gathering to watch the fight.

MuuMuu lay on her back like a stranded turtle.

Stephanie had an idea.

This is an opportunity.

She didn't have time to work out the entirety of the plan percolating in her brain but felt solid enough to leap on top of her fallen foe. Knees pinning MuuMuu's limbs, she pushed her fingers neatly into the notch of the woman's throat. MuuMuu tried to lift a meaty arm to push Stephanie away and then stopped as the pressure at her throat intensified.

"If I crack this windpipe, there's a good chance you're going to die, understand?"

MuuMuu nodded as best as she could.

Stephanie leaned down to whisper into her opponent's ear. "Listen to me. I'm going to let you knock me off you. Okay? You save face, and I walk away. I've got a business opportunity for you. We'll talk later. Blink if you understand."

MuuMuu blinked, her face growing more crimson by the second.

Stephanie eased her pressure, and MuuMuu clapped the side of her head to knock her from her perch. Stephanie threw herself away from the woman as if she'd been hit by a train.

A deep *ooooh* rose from the crowd.

MuuMuu lumbered to her feet, assisted by several of her more beefy sycophants.

"Next time, I'll kill you," she said, stabbing a finger at Stephanie.

Stephanie rubbed her head where she'd purposely knocked it against the wall and nodded, appearing defeated. MuuMuu walked on with her circle hooting around her.

The Tongan's lumbering gait seemed even more labored than usual. She'd picked up a noticeable limp.

Stephanie turned and had to stop short from walking into Morning Guard Gina. The woman stood staring at her, her hands on her hips, disapproval stamped across her expression.

Nice timing.

"You alright?"

Stephanie nodded. "I need to make a phone call."

"About MuuMuu? I would let it go. You'll only make it worse. I can't always be here."

You weren't here.

"No. I need to talk to my lawyer. Totally unrelated to the Pillsbury Dough Girl."

Gina laughed. "Girl, you crack me up. Sure. I'll get you a phone."

Gina turned and led the way to the bank of phones located just outside the visitors' area.

Stephanie took the least grubby-looking receiver of the four available and called Declan. She made a mental note to look for hand wipes at the commissary. It was the little things you missed in prison. Easy access to hand sanitizer, being able to Google every question that popped into your head, edible food...

Declan answered after the first ring. At least the first ring *she* could hear. She suspected he'd already had to agree to accept a call from prison.

"Stephanie?"

"You know other people in prison?"

Declan sighed. "No. What do you need?"

"Tell me, am I your little jailbird?"

"Don't start. What do you need?"

"Spoilsport. Fine. Be that way. I called because I keep having this dream about coral."

"Coral? The color or the reef?"

"The reef. And I think it means something, but I don't know what."

"Means something for your case? What could coral have to do with your case?"

"I don't know. That's the point. I wanted to bounce it off you and see if it rings any of your girlfriend's bells."

"Okay. I'll ask her about coral."

"Maybe tell my mother, too, if she calls. I, of course, don't have a phone number for her, and she only blesses me with a call once every decade or so."

"Okay."

"Actually, I *did* get a call from her the other day before I realized the coral dream wasn't just prison anxiety."

"What did she want?"

"She wanted to know if I did it. I told her I didn't and that I wouldn't even if I *wanted* to because I was going straight for you."

Declan sighed. "I hate it when you say things like that. *Going straight* can't depend on me."

"No. I know. I'm not thinking of you as the piece of chocolate cake I get at the end of my death diet."

"Uh, good."

"She didn't like it either."

"Your chocolate cake metaphor?"

"No, the idea of you influencing me to be good."

The line went quiet.

"Declan?"

"I'm here. I'm just wondering how worried I should be that your psycho mother is angry with me."

"Eh. She probably won't kill you."

"Great. Is that all?"

"I think so. Tell Bopeep about the coral."

"Right. Thanks for probably getting me killed."

Stephanie chuckled. "No problem."

CHAPTER FOURTEEN

Miles heard his phone buzz against the egg crate the woman he'd picked up at the bar had serving as a nightstand table.

The girl beside him still wore her clothes. She lay tangled in musty, cartoon racing car sheets, one cellulite-puckered leg jutting from the side of the bed like a crane's beak.

He'd asked her why she slept on kids' sheets after she dragged him into the end of the trailer that served as her bedroom. She said she'd lost a son, and sleeping on his sheets made her feel close to him. She'd started crying then. He got out of bed and fetched her another shot of Wild Turkey to tip her over the edge. She was a lot quieter when she passed out.

Miles grabbed his phone and stepped over the clutter to move into the main section of the trailer.

"Miles here."

A man started talking without saying hello. Jim, the man who'd asked for his help taking down Jamie.

"There's a girl working to get Stephanie exonerated."

Miles scowled. "What? Speak English."

"I need you to take care of a girl."

"That I understand. Whudya need?"

"I'll text you the address. She's got two bodyguards sitting outside her house in a Cadillac and motion cameras around the perimeter of the house."

Miles snorted. "Why don't you just put her in a bank vault and call it a day?"

"Are you saying you can't handle this?"

"No. I can handle it." Miles spun the lid off the bottle of Wild Turkey and took a swig.

"Alright then. Do your job and keep her from getting Stephanie freed. We need her in jail."

"Got it. Text me the info."

"Done. And Miles..."

"Yeah?"

"Don't get near her boyfriend. His name's Declan. Don't let him see you."

"Why not?"

"He's not someone you want to mess with. There's no reason to complicate things."

Miles shrugged. "Whatever. I'll handle it." He hung up. A second later, his phone dinged, and he read the name and address.

Charlotte Morgan.

He grunted and scratched at his belly with his stubby, print-less fingers. *Too bad.* He liked the name Charlotte. He might have had an aunt by that name, but he couldn't remember.

Miles heard the girl waking up behind him in the bedroom. She blasted an exaggerated yawn and called for him using the nickname she'd christened him with the night before.

"Hey, Lightning, you out there?"

He looked back into the bedroom and saw her beckoning to him.

Those damn sheets.

He shook the empty Wild Turkey bottle, finding his liquid courage gone.

"You got any beer?" he called back to her, pulling open the

mini-fridge.

CHAPTER FIFTEEN

Miles parked in the Publix parking lot and pulled the large canvas bag from the back of his mud-splattered pickup truck.

There was no one around to see how the bag moved on its own when he wasn't touching it.

He felt good. In his element. He'd spent half the day at the trailer getting buzzed on beer he'd talked the girl into picking up at the corner store and then taken a nap. When he woke up, the girl was still asleep, so he sneaked out and drove to his farm to gather the equipment he needed to run his errand for Jim. He'd pulled the canvas off his old pickup, and it had *started.*

It was like God was on his side today.

Now it was nearly three a.m., and he had everything he needed to stop *Charlotte Morgan* from freeing Simone's daughter.

Ain't nothin' but a thang.

Illuminated by the parking lot lights, Miles jogged to the road and crossed without pause. No cars whizzed by at three in the morning.

He slipped through the unmanned gate of the Pineapple Port neighborhood and strode briskly toward his goal, keeping his head low to avoid any personal cameras that might spot him from the doorways of the homes he passed.

He made his way to the house next to his target's and slipped into the back yard. Peering around the corner, he pulled down his night-vision goggles and stared at the two men sitting in a Cadillac outside Charlotte's house.

Just like Jim said.

He'd driven by earlier in the day to check out the situation. Two older men were stationed in the car. By the tilt of their heads, he suspected they'd fallen asleep.

The girl might have more people guarding her than the President, but if they were all as good as these two, he'd be okay.

Miles set down the bag and fished for the mask in his pocket. Finding it, he removed his goggles and pulled the specialized balaclava over his head, covering every inch of his face, including his eyes. Clear plastic windows stitched into the high-tech fabric of the hood would allow him to see.

The stealth clothing would protect him from the thermal imaging he felt confident the cameras mounted on Charlotte's home possessed. He couldn't be sure, of course, but he guessed if someone was smart enough to rig all those motion detection cameras, they were probably smart enough to use *good* ones, ones with thermal imaging that would make his body heat trigger their sensors. Luckily, there were things he could wear to hide his heat.

Motion was trickier.

He'd planned for a long night.

Miles had looked up the style of modular home Charlotte owned and figured out where her bedroom was. Fortunately, it was at the back of the house where he wouldn't have to go far. Still, moving slower than a camera could detect took patience.

Miles reached into the side pocket of his gym bag and pulled out a Bud Light. Whipping the butterfly knife from his belt, he poked two tiny holes into it and drank it dry without the loud *Psssh!* The tab opening might have caused. When he was done, he tossed the can into the thicket behind the houses and picked up the canvas bag.

Then he began to move.

Slowly.

One tiny step at a time, each step taking a minute or more. This way, he inched the fifteen feet to Charlotte's bedroom window.

He'd reached the window when he realized his bladder was full.

Damn beer.

He grit his teeth and tried to ignore the gentle ache in his lower abdomen.

How can I spend all day planning my attack and then forget beer makes me pee?

Miles pushed the thought out of his mind. Bending ever so slowly, he pulled the glass cutter from the side pocket of the bag. He straightened and stuck the suction cups to the window pane. Beneath the soffit of the house, he suspected he was no longer in camera range, but he couldn't be sure. He'd tried to spot the location of *all* the cameras during his afternoon reconnaissance, but he couldn't be sure he'd clocked them all. There might be more in the trees. He had to continue assuming one pointed toward him at all times.

Miles worked the glass cutter, carving a perfectly round, eight-inch hole in the window. The suction cups attached to the center allowed him to pluck the glass from its spot without a sound.

When he wanted to be quiet, there was no one quieter.

Miles bent down to the bag and slipped the glass cutter back into the side pocket. He was about to unzip the bag when he spotted two glowing eyes at the edge of the thicket lining the back of the house.

Crap.

Possum, he guessed. If the critter came out of the thicket, it would trigger the sensors. If he tried to wave it away, it would trigger the sensors. Who knew what alarms that might set off. Even if they saw it was just a possum, it would wake the watchers and put them on alert.

"Git," he hissed.

The possum stared back at him.

"Git now."

A standoff ensued. The possum stared at him. Miles stared back.

The need to relieve his aching bladder grew stronger.

Stupid, stupid possum. He had half a mind to kill *it* instead of the girl, blow his cover and just go home.

Inside his stealth clothing, he felt a drop of sweat slide down his neck.

Go away, you ugly cur.

The critter seemed to have heard his silent plea. It turned and waddled back into the undergrowth.

Miles heaved a sigh.

He gripped the zipper of his bag and took another deep breath. This would be the tricky part. Finding the head from the tail and grabbing it without moving so fast, he set off the cameras.

Miles slid his hand into the bag and felt the head of the beast within. He'd velcroed its head to the right side of the bag so he'd know where it was and the Velcro had held.

Thank Jesus for little favors.

With his hand around the creature's head, he unfastened the Velcro with his other hand. The snake wasn't happy. He could feel the body writhing in the bag. He pulled the seventeen-foot-long reticulated python from his case and fed its head into the hole he made in the window.

Perfect.

His job was done.

Now the snake just had to be a snake.

He hadn't fed the snake for weeks. That girl sleeping in her bed was going to look like a turkey dinner to it. He might not have time to digest her before someone realized she was missing, but the life would have been squeezed out of her by then. Of that, Miles was certain.

Time to move.

He couldn't be sure he hadn't triggered an alarm. There'd been no way for him to keep the snake from moving.

Miles grabbed his bag as the last of the tail slid into the house and moved himself through the darkness. He took the shortest path that would move him out of the view of the cameras. Once away from the house, he broke into a jog toward the nearest hunk of scrub forest to relieve himself.

CHAPTER SIXTEEN

"Abby, don't," mumbled Charlotte, unsure if she were dreaming or awake.

Abby barked again and stepped back, placing a paw directly on Charlotte's cheek. She jerked her head out from under the dog.

"Come on. What are you doing?" She put her arms around the dog to keep her from crushing her face.

"What are you—"

Something moved near Charlotte's feet.

Hm.

It took her sleepy mind a moment to piece together what bothered her about that movement.

The dog is right here...

That was it. The *dog* was usually the thing that moved at her feet at night.

And if the dog is up here with me...

Something moved again.

Faster.

Abby skittered out of her arms and yipped as she fell off the side of the bed.

Before Charlotte could react, something flopped across her hips, and she froze, her breath caught in her throat.

The nightlight she kept on in the hallway provided just

enough light for her to see the heavy thing sliding across her legs. The pattern, the shape, the way it moved. All these things told her it could only be one thing.

A snake.

An enormous snake.

How can a snake be that big?

She would have thought it was a dream, except she could feel her heart pounding. No way could she sleep with what felt like a rhinoceros repeatedly slamming into her ribs.

The snake began to move.

Charlotte glanced to the left and saw its tail, much too far away. The thing had to be twenty feet long.

She wanted to slide out from under the weight of the creature but feared any movement would signal her presence. If the head turned back for her while she was pinned beneath its weight...*that had to be a bad thing.*

Abby barked from the hallway. The snake had eyes on her. It was moving across Charlotte's legs on its way toward the yapping morsel in the hall.

Charlotte wanted to scream for Abby to get away from the approaching reptile but, again, feared noise would bring quick retribution from her slithering guest. She wasn't entirely sure she could scream. It felt as if her throat had closed for the foreseeable future.

Slowly, she reached out her hand and grabbed her phone from the nightstand. The snake remained on her, but it paused.

Oh no.

She froze.

Did it pause because it felt me move? Or because...I dunno...whatever snakes pause for?

The snake remained still. Abby remained barking in the hallway, a regular staccato yap. Surely, Andy and Butch would come busting in any second with all the racket Abby was making, but Charlotte wasn't sure that's what she wanted. Once those two oafs were in the house, who knew what might happen? There weren't a lot of—

Um.

What is this?

A python?

Probably.

There weren't a lot of *pythons* in New Jersey, she guessed.

She raised her phone and dialed Declan. The snake remained still. It seemed unhappy about chasing after the yapping Abby but not *so* unhappy it had changed its mind. If it started forward again, Charlotte judged she had about three or four feet before she'd have to grab the tail to keep it from reaching her dog.

She wasn't looking forward to that part.

What do I know about pythons?

They're destroying the everglades' ecosystem.

Okay. True, but not helpful unless a team of conservationists burst through her door right now to kill it.

She didn't think pythons were poisonous, but she didn't relish the idea of being bitten by a face bigger than a dinner plate, either. And if the thing started wrapping around her—

"Hello?"

Charlotte pushed a whisper from her dry throat. "Declan, there's a snake in my room."

"What? Charlotte?"

"Snake."

"There's a snake in your room?"

She nodded and realized he couldn't see either her head bobbing or the *size* of the snake in her room.

"Yes. Big. Help. Now."

"How big?"

"Twenty."

"Inches?"

"Feet."

"*What?* I'm on my way."

"Thank you."

She hung up and called the number Andy had given her in case of emergency. She guessed a twenty-foot python constituted an emergency, though she still didn't know if alerting the city kids was the best idea.

"Hello?"

She couldn't tell if it was Andy or Butch on the other end of the line, but whoever he was, he sounded sleepy.

The snake began to move, and Charlotte held her breath. It dropped another foot over the edge of the bed and then stopped again. Now she could see the front of it in her doorway. Its head wagged back and forth with agitation as Abby backed another two feet and continued barking.

"Andy?"

"Charlotte? What's wrong? You okay in there?"

Andy definitely sounded bleary. The boys had apparently fallen asleep.

"Listen to me. Do not come flying in here, but there is a very large snake in my bed."

She winced. That just didn't sound right.

"A snake?" Andy sounded a little sharper.

"Yes. A python, I think."

"A python? They're real?"

Charlotte sighed.

City boys.

Andy's going to be a *big* help. He thinks pythons are like dragons and unicorns.

"Yes. Very real."

"Uh..."

"Listen. Come in, normal. Grab Abby. Take her outside. Do you hear me?"

"Uh, sure, is the snake—"

"The snake is in here with me. You're safe at the front door. Just get Abby before the snake does."

I think. In reality, she really didn't know how fast a twenty-foot snake could move. She'd seen Black Racers slither like they'd been shot from a cannon. If this snake was anything like those jerks...

"Okay. Yeah. Right. Comin'."

Andy didn't hang up. She heard him waking Butch and chewing him out for falling asleep on his shift. She heard them get out of their car and then heard Andy's heavy breath on the other side of the line.

"Wait. What about you?"

"Just take care of Abby."

"But we're here to protect *you.* Not the dog."

"You didn't sign up for pythons."

"No, dat's true, but—"

"And if something happens to Abby, I swear I'll feed myself to the snake."

"Oh jeeze, Charlotte—"

"Could you hurry, please?"

"Yeah, sure. Hey, you want me to shoot it?"

"Maybe. Let's start with Abby."

"You want me to shoot Abby?"

"No, come *get* Abby."

"Right. Right. I gotchu."

She heard her front door opening. Butch appeared in the hallway behind Abby and grabbed the dog's collar. He pulled her out of the house, the Wheaten fighting him the entire way.

Andy appeared as Butch disappeared with the dog. His jaw hung low as he stared at the serpent partially in the hall and partially still lying across Charlotte's lap.

He pulled his gun from a holster strapped to his body.

"Charlotte, I'm going to have to shoot that thing."

"How good a shot are you?" she asked as quietly as possible.

By the hall nightlight, she could see Butch grimace.

"I used to be alright..."

Charlotte frowned and shook her head slowly. She held up

her index finger, asking him to wait.

"Let me think a second."

Charlotte ran through the scenarios in her mind. If Andy missed the snake, the sound of the gun might send it into a frenzy. It could retreat and bite her, wrap around her in fear and squish the life out of her...

She lifted her chin to peer down at the head in the hallway. It already seemed lost and restless now that the dog had disappeared. The head began to twist to the right as if it was thinking about turning around.

Crap.

Outside, she heard tires screech to a halt. She heard a voice that sounded like Declan's shout something to Butch.

Thankyouthankyouthankyou, you big sexy ex-soldier boy. Please tell me you brought your gun.

Declan appeared at the end of her hallway, moving Andy aside.

Andy looked at him. "She told me not to shoot it unless—"

"I have my gun," said Declan, staring down the hall and locking eyes with Charlotte.

Yay!

His gaze dropped to the floor in front of her bed. "Holy—"

He sees the snake.

Declan pulled out his pistol and fired. The python's head stopped moving and flopped to the ground. Disturbingly, the body stretched across her legs began to *move.* Charlotte scrambled out from under her sheets and rolled to the opposite side of her bed as the tail thunked to the floor.

Declan strode forward, stepped over the dead snake, and pulled Charlotte into his arms.

"You scared me to death," he whispered into her ear.

"*You* were scared to death?"

She held on to him, gripping his body against hers. She liked to be tough and not so damsel-in-distressy, but sometimes a pair of strong arms wrapped around you were exactly what you needed when you were almost crushed by a giant python. She hoped pressing herself against him would keep her heart from pounding through her chest and escaping on its own.

Charlotte opened her eyes and spotted Andy squatting over the snake, poking at it with the tip of his gun.

She looked up at Declan.

"Nice shot."

He took a deep breath and released her. "How did this happen?"

"I have no idea."

Declan glanced around the room and quickly spotted the missing glass in Charlotte's window.

"Someone did this on purpose. They cut your window."

"Someone tried to murder me with a snake?"

"It looks like it."

A fog of fear slowly began to lift from her brain, revealing a few things that didn't make sense. "How did you get here so fast?"

"I was down the street."

"Why?"

Declan shrugged. "I was watching. Apparently, not well enough."

"You were watching Andy and Butch, and they were watching me, and someone still managed to try and kill me with a twenty-foot snake?"

He frowned. "Mm."

"What about the cameras?"

"Nothing set them off."

"A python being shoved through my window didn't trigger the cameras? You're going to have to talk to Blade about the quality of his equipment."

Declan nodded and pulled his phone from his pocket. "That's actually my next call."

Charlotte walked down the hall and outside to find Abby

there, Butch still holding her collar. She lowered and hugged the dog.

"My little watchdog."

"Is it dead?" asked Butch.

She nodded.

Butch heaved a sigh. "I didn't sign up for none of this."

Declan walked outside. "Blade's going to see if he can find anything on video."

Charlotte nodded. "In a few hours, I'll call Tilly and see if she has anything on *her* cameras."

Declan ran a hand through his hair and heaved a sigh.

"Why can't I ever just date someone who works in an office?"

CHAPTER SEVENTEEN

"Tell me you're kidding."

Miles felt like a child being scolded by his father. He didn't like the feeling as a kid, and he didn't like it now. Jim's voice had that same tone of deep disappointment that usually came before his father backhanded him.

"I didn't know she had a dog."

"Knowing if someone does or doesn't have a *dog* shouldn't be the deciding factor on whether or not you decide to *kill them with a python.*"

Jim sounded frustrated. The dude talked funny. If he knew where he lived, he'd put a python in *his* window.

"I told you to stop her from investigating what happened in the warehouse. Not to try and kill her with a *snake.*"

"Same thing."

"It is not at all the same thing!" Jim was yelling now.

"I got it. Jeeze. They killed my damn snake. I got expenses."

"Are you saying you want me to reimburse you?"

"Well, yeah, it'd be nice. They don't grow pythons that big on trees, you know."

"Don't pythons, in fact, often live in trees?"

Miles sucked on his tooth.

There's going to be one livin' in your bed if you keep talking to me like that.

Jim didn't wait for an answer. "Look, we're only working together because you said you could find Jamie."

"Who?"

"Simone."

"Yeah."

"You said you'd tried to kill her once already and almost done it."

"That's true."

The last bit. I don't have any idea where she is now. I told you that lie, hoping you could find her for me.

"You said you came so close to killing her that you had to become a recluse—"

"*Become* a recluse?" Miles laughed. "How can I *become* a spider?"

"What? What are you talking about?"

"I didn't say I'd *become* a recluse. I said I tried to kill her *with* a recluse."

Jim fell silent for a moment. "Come again?"

"I said I almost killed her *with* a recluse. *Recluses*, actually. A whole jar of brown recluses. I put them in her car, but somehow they didn't bite her."

"You...your assassination attempt was made with brown recluse spiders?"

"Uh huh. Someone said they saw her outside her car with a high heel in her hand stompin' and slappin' them all dead. She knew that sort of thing was my style of killin', so I had to skinny out of town after that."

"You have got to be kidding me. How did you end up in witness protection in the first place?"

"I tricked my boss into a room with a brown bear."

There was another long pause.

"Jim?"

"Just don't do anything."

The line went dead.

Miles hung up and stared at the cheese puff sitting beneath the sofa across from him. He wasn't sure what he was going to do. Killing people with animals was his thing. He'd forgotten how much he loved it, and he didn't want to stop.

He'd never liked shooting people. It was so, well, just not *natural.* Some people hunted with bows and arrows because shooting didn't seem fair to the animal. He hunted with his bare hands and other animals. There was a nobility to it.

Miles stooped to pick up the cheese puff and popped it in his mouth, chewing on it thoughtfully. He strolled out the back door of his Daddy's home and headed for the large barn. His Daddy had been dead for years, and the home was barely fit to live in, with all the holes in the roof and the rotten floorboards, but he still kept his pets in the back barn and slept most nights in the bedroom, which he'd patched enough to keep dry.

Some nights, he went to town and found a friend with a better house and a better bed, even if the sheets were for kids.

He passed his pickup truck. The logo painted in fat, bubbly lettering declaring "Wild Party" had nearly faded from view. The "a" in *party* was a lion's face, but in fact, he hadn't had a lion in a long time. His one-time partner in the wild-animals-for-parties business left him when he was sent to jail, and the bastard took most of the best animals. The lion, the tiger cub, the parrots...all gone while he rotted in a cell. It had been Miles' idea to create an exotic animal rental company, but that hadn't kept L.J. from taking all his animals and running off to Orlando with them. Even now, he sometimes saw L.J.'s wild animal rental ads. His old partner was making a fortune.

I should go kill him...

Miles had been forced to start over. He caught a few gators and stumbled on to the biggest python he'd ever seen in his life during a trip to the Everglades. He could have made money killing the snake and turning it in for the bounty, but instead, he'd taken it to his daddy's land to use as an attraction. The damn thing was too big, though. That's why he'd used it to try and get Charlotte. He knew as soon as the police showed up and found Knuckles slowly digesting a woman, they were going to shoot her, but the fact was, he couldn't afford to feed her anymore anyway.

He'd still miss her.

Miles rapped on his truck and moved toward the barn.

Is Jim gonna fire me? When the guy called about taking down Simone, he'd been happy to help. To be paid for taking down a woman he hated with every bone in his body, well, that was just too good to be true. Sure, he might have lied a little to seem more useful to Jim, but who didn't lie about their resume?

Miles opened the barn door and walked to the gator moat he'd dug in the corner. Badboi's eye rolled toward him, and his inner eyelid—the one that slid back to front—flicked.

He needed to take care of Charlotte and get back in Jim's good graces. He had to stay on the team until he found Simone. Badboi could do the job. He was an aggressive little bastard, especially when he was hungry.

"I don't think you're getting fed tonight, Badboi."

The gator grunted.

CHAPTER EIGHTEEN

"Midge's Donuts, can I help you?"

Charlotte rolled her eyes at Declan, who sat staring at her expectantly as she began her phone call.

She doubted the number Jamie last called her on now belonged to a donut shop.

"Someone tried to kill me with a snake."

The woman on the other end of the line paused. "Just a second please."

There was a delay, and then Charlotte heard Jamie's voice.

"Did I say you could call me?"

"Oh, sorry, were you busy making the crullers? And you wouldn't have left this line usable if you didn't think I might call, *Midge*."

"What do you want? Have you made any progress?"

"No, I haven't made any progress. It's only been a day, the *helpful packet* you sent me didn't contain anything useful, and someone tried to kill me with a snake. How was I supposed to make any progress?"

"That's not my problem. Wait, did you say snake?"

"Snake. Python, to be exact. And all this is kind of your problem. Killing my whole family upon my failure might give you some sense of satisfaction, but your daughter will still be rotting in jail."

"You think I don't have fallbacks? Do you really think I left Stephanie's fate in *your* hands alone?"

"I'm sure you have your bases covered. But wouldn't it be easier to help me a little?"

Jamie huffed. "Possibly. Tell me about the snake."

"Someone slipped a giant python through my window while I was sleeping. If Abby hadn't started barking, I'd be wrapped in a snakeskin jacket the hard way right now."

"Hm."

"It wasn't you, was it?"

"Me?" Jamie nearly shrieked the word. "Why would I try and kill you with a snake? Why would I try to kill *anyone* with a snake?"

"You like to kill in creative ways."

"*Clever* ways," stressed Jamie, sounding genuinely offended. "What's clever about throwing a snake at someone?"

"So, is this your swamp man?"

"I think so. I know someone who uses animals as assassins. He tried to kill me by releasing a troop of brown recluse spiders in my car."

"A pack of spiders is called a *cluster*," said Charlotte before she could stop herself. She hadn't meant to say it out loud.

Jamie snorted a laugh. "*Nerd.*"

"Whatever. Got a name for this weirdo?"

"Miles Davis."

Charlotte frowned. "The trumpet player?"

"No. Coincidence. Believe me. His family never heard of Miles Davis when they named him. He was Kyle Brown in the WITSEC program, but he still rolled around calling himself *Miles* like an idiot. I doubt he's using Kyle now."

"Is he in the fingerprint book? Maybe we can match the prints outside my window."

"There won't be prints outside your window."

"Why? He always wears gloves?'

"No, he has no fingerprints."

Charlotte gaped. "So he *is* the same person you said wouldn't be in the book but should be?"

"Yes. The snake confirms I was right to suspect him but framing Stephanie...I don't know."

"Not his style?"

"Not his brain power."

"So you admit there might be someone else."

Jamie grunted in the affirmative.

"Who?'

"There are a few possibilities. I need to look into some things and get back to you."

Charlotte sighed. They'd hit another wall, but at least she felt like Jamie was *trying* to help her now. She returned her thoughts to the swamp man. With a little more information, he might be within her grasp. It could be one down and one to go.

"How does this guy have no fingerprints?"

"Hm?" It sounded as if Jamie, too, had been letting her thoughts wander. "Oh. They were burned off when he was a child. Lightning. Zapped him and escaped through his fingertips, taking more or less of them with it."

"Yikes... Can you help me find him?"

"I don't know where he is *yet*. I can work on that, too, now that he's crawled out of the swamp he ran to after trying to kill me. I can tell you he's got a grade school education—"

"Great. I won't waste time combing through Nobel prize winners."

"You didn't let me finish. He has a *doctorate* in *redneck*. Actually, saying that isn't fair to rednecks. He's a genuine swamp creature. Oh, and he's got an amazing tattoo left by that same lightning strike. It flash-burned the image of his veins on his skin. His chest and upper arms are all covered in a map of his veins."

"Wow. That's some important information you could have shared earlier."

"Don't get too excited. He can cover it pretty easily with a long sleeve shirt. Might peek up out of a crew neck collar. I don't remember. I didn't like to be near him. He smelled like low tide."

"Okay. So I'm looking for a smelly guy named after a famous trumpeter with no fingertips and a crazy vein tattoo."

"Bingo."

"Great. That should narrow it down."

"Exactly. You should be grateful. I couldn't have found you a more distinctive target if he had two heads."

"Want to share more information about your *real* target? The smart one?"

Jamie fell silent for a moment before muttering one last phrase.

"Not yet."

The line went silent, and Charlotte lowered the phone. She looked at Declan.

"What? What did she say?" he asked.

"How do you find a guy with a crazy tattoo who loves snakes?"

"Huh?"

Charlotte tapped the edge of her phone against her teeth.

He has to feed the snake.

She held up an index finger. "Two seconds. I have to make a call."

She dialed Frank.

"Hey, did they autopsy that snake?"

Frank snorted a laugh. "Why would they autopsy the snake? It didn't eat *you*. Did you have a guest sleeping over you forgot to tell us about?"

"*No*, but I'd like to know what it's eaten."

"Why?"

"If its belly is full of nasty-looking wild rats, then this guy probably pulled the monster from the everglades. But if it's full of white, *fancy* rats—"

"Then he's buying them from a pet store, and we can track him that way."

"Exactly."

"You know what, you're pretty smart for a lady who almost got eaten by a snake."

Charlotte snickered. "Gosh, thanks."

"I'll see what they did with the carcass."

"Thanks. Declan has Blade checking the cameras. Maybe we can figure out why this guy didn't trigger them."

"Also a good idea."

"I also have a name and partial description."

"Of the snake fella? How could you? I thought you were asleep."

"My guardian angel, Jamie, reckons this M.O. fits a man named Miles Davis."

Frank grew quiet for a moment. "Isn't he some sort of jazz man?"

"No. I mean, *yes*, but not this time. We're looking for a white man with some sort of crazy tattoo on his chest, back, and arms. He was struck by lightning as a kid, and it tattooed a map of his veins on him somehow."

Frank scoffed. "She's pulling your leg."

"No, he also has no fingerprints, so don't bother trying to look him up that way."

"He burned them off?"

"The lightning did."

Frank grunted, sounding impressed. "Hm. I guess when lightning burns off your prints, why not be a bad guy?"

"Does feel a little like destiny. Oh, and that's his real name. In WITSEC, he was Kyle Brown, but Jamie says he never warmed up to his new identity."

"Hm. I'll see what I can do."

Charlotte said her goodbyes as Declan moved beside her at the kitchen table and pointed to her open laptop screen.

"You're not making another call until you talk to me. What

is that?"

She looked at the picture she'd Googled while talking to Frank.

"Crazy, isn't it? It's a woman who was struck by lightning, and somehow the electricity tattooed her veins on her skin."

"So you decided to give up on the case and start a freak show?"

"*No*, Jamie thinks the guy involved is a man named Miles Davis—"

"I heard you say that to Frank. *The* Miles Davis?"

"No, he's dead."

Declan nodded. "That *would* make it harder for him to be involved."

"Right. *Our* Miles Davis has no fingerprints and a tattoo like this one on his chest, back, and arms."

"From lightning?"

"Yep. Hit as a kid."

"Huh."

Declan fell silent, and Charlotte looked at him. She could tell by the expression on his face his mind was whirring.

"What are you thinking?"

"That branching tattoo looks like coral."

She studied the screen. "It does, doesn't it?"

"I hadn't had a chance to tell you, but Stephanie called me with a message for you. She said she keeps having this dream about being underwater and swimming through a giant red coral reef."

"You're kidding."

"She thinks it has something to do with what happened in the warehouse, but she doesn't know what. She just swims, sees the reef, panics, feels like she's drowning, and wakes up."

"I almost feel bad for her."

Declan nodded. "Every once in a while, she admits to being human, as hard as that is to believe."

"That she's admitting it or that she's human?"

"Both."

"So, you're thinking she must have seen this guy without realizing it before she knocked herself out."

"Exactly."

"So there's a good chance Jamie is right."

"So this is the guy out to get her?"

Charlotte shook her head. "Yes and no. I think Miles *works* for the real enemy. And so does she. She just either doesn't know or won't tell me who she suspects yet. But if we can find the swamp creature, maybe we can follow the thread from there."

"Hm." Declan kissed her on the side of the head. "I'm going to run out and check in with Blade for you. Are you going to be alright here?"

"I'm in my house with two ex-mafia hit men sitting in the car outside and surrounded by cameras in the daylight. I'll be fine."

"Says the girl who was almost eaten by a giant snake."

"Yeah, yeah," she slapped his hip. "Get out of here."

Charlotte found herself staring at Abby, who lay sleeping on the cool kitchen floor after her harrowing evening. She lowered herself to the ground and slipped her head under the dog's front leg, so it felt as though Abby were hugging her as they slept.

"Tough night, huh?" she asked.

The dog yawned and moved her foot to press against Charlotte's shoulder, stretching.

Charlotte closed her eyes until the dog shifted again and put her paw directly on her face.

"Okay, this tender moment isn't working for me anymore," said Charlotte, sitting up.

Her phone rang with the tone that said *unknown number* and she stood to grab it. She didn't recognize the number.

"Hello?"

"I know who you're lookin' fer."

The male voice on the other side of the line was low with a rough southern twang.

"You do? Who?"

"The man huntin' Simone."

Simone. The person on the other end of the line had to be one of Jamie's witness protection clients. They were the only ones who'd known her as Simone.

Charlotte suspected she was talking to Miles Davis, but she didn't want him to know she was zeroing in on him.

"Okay. Who's after Simone?"

The voice dropped an octave lower. "Come to the Riverwalk, and I'll show ya. I've got stuff that will lead you right to him."

"Can't you just tell me his name?"

The man sniffed. "It's complicated. I don't rightly understand what I'm lookin' at here, but I think you will."

Nothing about Miles' invitation felt right, but Charlotte couldn't risk missing a chance to end the case. She was familiar with the Riverwalk, a paved walking trail lining a nearby river. It ran about five miles long and served as a favorite path for joggers.

Why would he pick such a public place to set a trap? It's worth a shot.

But she needed better directions.

"*Where* on the walk?"

"Near the condos."

In her mind, Charlotte pictured that spot on the walk. It was one of the more public areas, with single-story condos on one side and the river on the other. It seemed like a relatively safe place to meet. It would be a bad place to choose if he intended to murder her. And she'd be able to see him carting a giant snake from a mile away.

Maybe old Miles *had* decided to turn in his boss. Maybe he'd be willing to testify that Stephanie didn't kill Jason Walsh.

"Okay. I can be there in twenty minutes. Does that work?"

"Yeah."

"Okay. I'll see you there."

She was about to hang up when she heard him speak again.

"Charlotte?"

He knows my name.

She raised the phone back to her ear. "Yes?"

"Don't bring your dog."

CHAPTER NINETEEN

Cormac glanced at Blade's sofa. Every dark red cushion was covered in white cat hair, and Blade, noticing this for the first time, suffered a moment of embarrassment. He hadn't been expecting company, or he would have vacuumed.

Cormac remained standing in his dark suit pants. He was a tall man, not as tall as Blade but impressively large, barrel-chested, and fit for a man in his mid-sixties. When he spoke, it was hard not to listen. He seemed like a man fully in control of the world around him at all times.

At least that was the side of him he allowed Blade to see. Blade knew he wasn't always in control of *everything.*

For one thing, he didn't know how to dress for the heat.

Who wears dark pants in Florida anyway? You have to go with the tropical flow...

"You want a kitchen chair?" asked Blade.

Cormac shook his head. "No. So there's nothing on the cameras?"

"No. Your man did a good job avoiding them."

Cormac grimaced. Blade was grateful he didn't plan to deny his involvement. He was barely keeping himself from throttling the man for endangering Charlotte as it was. If he started lying—

"I didn't tell him to kill her. He misunderstood me."

"I'm pretty angry at myself for not doing a better job on my end with the cameras. He should have never got that close."

"How'd you know it was me?"

"You asked me too many questions about the cameras and about Charlotte, though I'll admit it didn't hit me until after the snake."

Cormac nodded. "And you're *sure* she's not working for Jamie?"

"Yes. Miss Charlotte is wonderful." It made Blade smile just thinking about her.

"She's trying to get Stephanie out of jail—"

"Jamie threatened her family. You should have asked me before you had that idiot try to kill her. Miss Charlotte is on *our* side. Always. You only needed to talk to her."

"I'm not ready to do that." Cormac sighed and nearly lowered himself to the sofa. At the last second, he realized his mistake and sprang back up, lifting his hand into the air. "Who's to say she isn't a *plant* to kill Declan?"

"Do you think I didn't check her out when I got here? She grew up with her grandmother in Charity after her mother died. Jamie didn't orphan her just so she'd move in with her grandmother ten minutes from Declan in the hopes they'd meet and fall in love and Charlotte could someday *kill* him. She's not some kind of Russian sleeper agent. Not even Jamie's that good."

Cormac grunted. "Sometimes I wonder. And so what if she grew up here? It doesn't mean she wasn't recruited."

"She *wasn't.*" Blade said the words through gritted teeth and saw Cormac's eyebrows raise with what looked like surprise.

"I haven't seen you get that upset in a long time."

"I don't usually let myself feel harmful emotions like anger anymore, man, but you're making me mad. Miss Charlotte is sweet. She's the best thing that ever happened to Declan. I won't let you kill her."

Cormac sighed. "Fine. If you're so sure."

"I am. You should have checked with me first. I've been here for months. I know stuff."

"Have it your way." Cormac tapped his fingers on the table. "So, how's Declan been?"

"Good. Fine. He's been in a really good place."

"And he didn't recognize you? Has no idea you're here to protect him?"

"No. He was too young to remember me. And it turns out I'm a *really* good salesman. I like the people around here. I sold a chair he'd had on the floor for *three years* yesterday. The top knobs were carved to look like squirrels. Really unique. I'll be honest. I almost bought it myself."

Blade noticed Cormac staring toward the other side of the living room.

His boss cocked his head. "Did I just see a little white head walk by behind that box?"

Blade tilted his body to look around Cormac. "Probably." He spotted the cat's head as it popped up from behind the box and then disappeared again.

Cormac scowled. "What *is* that?"

"It's Johnnie Walker Cat."

"It's too tall."

"He only has his back legs."

"He, you mean he *walks* on his back legs?"

Blade nodded. "He belongs to my neighbor down the street, but I watch him when he needs me to."

"And his name is Johnnie Walker Cat?"

"It is when he's here."

Cormac sighed and rubbed his face with his hand. "Okay. Well, I called my man off regarding Charlotte. But we have to slow her down. I can't have her getting Stephanie out of jail before—"

"Hold."

Blade stood and peered through the front window of his home. Outside, a man climbed the stairs to his porch.

"It's Declan."

Cormac's head swiveled toward the door. "Where?"

"Outside."

There was a knock on the door.

Blade hooked a thumb behind him. "Get in the back."

Cormac moved briskly toward the back of the house. Johnny Walker Cat strode after him, and as Cormac disappeared into the guest room, Blade heard him yelp with surprise as the cat followed him in.

Blade gave Cormac a moment to settle in with Johnny Walker Cat and then moved to the front door.

The knocking came a second time, and Blade opened the door.

"Hi, Declan. How can I help you?"

"Hey, big guy, do you mind if I come in for a second? I wanted to talk about making my house secure and bringing Charlotte there."

Blade frowned. "I'm kind of in the middle of something, working on some improvements to the cameras."

"Oh, you are?" Declan's neck stretched, and Blade could tell he was trying to see inside. He shifted to the right to block his vision. "That's also what I came to talk to you about. I don't understand how someone could move through all those cameras, cut a window and slip a snake into it without triggering *something*."

"I think the snake man was moving slowly and wearing some sort of thermal shielding. Clothing like that can block the heat sensors."

Declan nodded.

"So, what do you think about me moving her to my place?"

Blade shrugged. "I can reinstall the cameras there later today if you want."

"Okay. I, uh, well, let me know if you see anything."

"Will do."

Declan took half a step back, and Blade closed the door. Blade waited until he heard Declan walk on his creaky stairs and then moved back to the kitchen.

"You can come out now," he said.

Cormac's voice came from the back room. "Come here. Did you see this?"

Blade walked into the guest room, which he'd been using as a command center for his cameras. The far wall was lined with video monitors. Some flickered with images of the area around Charlotte's home, some from around the Pawn Shop, some around his own house. He'd only recently added the pawn shop cameras after a gang of men in gingerbread man costumes had barged in and held a gun on Declan and Miss Charlotte. He still kicked himself for not doing it sooner. He hadn't seen the cookies coming.

"Watch this truck," said Cormac.

Blade peered at the image of a dark pickup truck as it pulled off the curb and drove away.

"What about it?"

"I think it was following Declan. It parked while he was here and then followed him when he left. Call the office and have them run the plate."

Blade nodded. "Do we have an understanding about Charlotte?"

Cormac nodded. "If you're sure. For now."

"I'm sure."

Cormac turned to one of the monitors and cocked an eyebrow.

"Looks like she's up to no good, though."

Blade leaned in to get a better view of the monitor that had caught Cormac's eye. In it, he watched Charlotte sneaking from the back door of her house, out of view of Andy and Butch, who, in another monitor, still sat out front in their Cadillac.

Blade put his hands on his hips.

"Now, where is *she* going?"

CHAPTER TWENTY

Declan frowned as he drove away from Blade's house. It wasn't like Blade to not invite him in.

Should I be suspicious of Blade?

There'd been a time when he was *always* suspicious of Blade. The gigantic man had always been a bit of a mystery, with his passive demeanor, terrifying t-shirts, and ominous name.

But over the past two months, he'd come to count on the man, who seemed as gentle as he was large. Blade's kind-hearted personality shone like the sun whenever a customer entered the store, and he *fawned* over Charlotte like a protective big brother. Little of the big man's warmth ever seemed to point in Declan's direction, which, Declan had to admit, sometimes made him feel like a flower on the shady side of the garden. He chalked it up to professionalism. Maybe Blade didn't want to be too chummy with the boss.

It was hard for Declan to imagine what part Blade could play in Jamie's manipulations of Charlotte, but—

Declan's phone rang, and he answered as he pulled to a red light. He didn't recognize the number but sometimes received calls from random people who'd been referred to him by past pawn shop customers.

"Hello?"

"Come to the address I'm texting you, and you'll have your man."

Declan scowled. He caught a fair amount of robo-dial spam calls on his phone, but this was the oddest one he'd heard. Something kept him from hanging up. The air on the line didn't feel like a recorded message.

"Who is this?"

"You want to get Charlotte out of her jam? I'll give you everything you need."

Declan's eyebrows shot toward his hairline at the sound of Charlotte's name.

This is no robocall.

"Who are you?"

The barely audible hiss of the live line had disappeared, and Declan found himself holding a dead phone to his ear.

A car behind him honked, and Declan's attention shot to the light hanging in front of him.

Green. Whoops.

He hit the gas and raised a hand of apology. He'd barely made it through the intersection when his phone dinged, alerting him a text message had arrived. He pulled over in a food store parking lot to read it.

1000 Airstrip Road. Go to the center of the field.

Declan tapped on his phone, thinking.

Who could this be?

Someone working for Jamie, probably. She never did anything straightforward. She'd told Charlotte she would help her find who really killed the A.D.A. Maybe this was part of it. She was getting him information.

But why contact him instead of Charlotte?

Declan leaned his head back and sighed. He didn't have his gun. It might have been nice to have a weapon handy for whatever clandestine meeting this was.

Because he *had* to go.

He already felt frustrated and helpless, with Charlotte embroiled in a mess spawned by his ex-girlfriend. Without him, Stephanie and Charlotte would have never met. If he could take care of the situation and get Charlotte out of Jamie's blackmail...

Looks like the shop will be opening a little late today.

Declan pulled up a map on his phone to find the location the man had given him. He spotted it a little farther inland from Charity. Airstrip Road. It seemed to be a small, probably defunct airport. He couldn't find a phone number for it online, but the satellite map clearly showed a runway running perpendicular to the road that led to it.

Declan put his car in gear, pulled out of the parking lot, and headed toward the airport. He had no reason to trust the man on the other end of the line, but if he kept his wits about him, he might gather new information capable of ending Charlotte's entanglement with Jamie.

Should I call Charlotte?

No. Telling Charlotte about the clandestine meeting with an anonymous caller would have her on her way to the airstrip before he could hang up.

On the other hand...

What if she received a similar message?

He decided to call and fish for information without revealing any of his own. He didn't like the idea of keeping secrets from her, but he couldn't risk putting her in further danger.

A white lie. A protective lie.

He dialed, and she answered on the second ring.

"Hey, you still safe?" he asked.

Did that sound weird? No, probably not. She was nearly eaten by a snake. It isn't odd I'd be more worried about her than usual.

"Yes, I'm good." She answered effortlessly and without

guile.

Good.

"Did you talk to Blade?" she asked.

"Yes. He thinks snake-man was wearing some sort of gear to block the motion detectors' thermal cameras."

"Sounds high-tech for the way Miles was described to me."

"Well..." Declan thought about her comment for a moment. "Doesn't have to be a high-tech person using those things. Maybe just a soldier or a hunter. I could see both of those demographics using gear like that."

"So I'm *not* looking for a nerd."

"No. Blade didn't see anyone wearing a Yoda mask."

"Ha. Maybe Miles was a merc."

Declan laughed. "*Merc.* Listen to you. I don't think hired mercenaries generally try to kill people with snakes."

Charlotte giggled. "Probably not."

Declan detected something different about his connection with Charlotte. The air on the phone sounded more *airy* than usual.

"Are you still at home?"

"Huh? Oh, uh-huh."

"It sounds a little like you're in a car."

"No. I'm outside. Out back. With Mariska."

"Oh. Okay. Well, be careful."

"I am. You heading to the shop?"

"Hm? Oh, yep. Call me if you need me."

"Will do."

Declan hung up, feeling guilty. He'd wanted to tell her where he was headed so badly he could feel the words pounding on the back of his lips during their entire conversation.

You're doing the right thing. Keep her safe.

Declan drove for twenty minutes before he spotted the old sign marking Airstrip Drive. One of the bolts holding it in place had come loose, and it hung at a cockeyed angle. The road was clear but unpaved. He turned onto it and drove another six minutes over crunching gravel before the forest around him cleared, and two rusted plane hangars revealed themselves in the distance.

He parked in a large, unlined lot in front of a small, flat-roofed office with broken windows. In front of the two hangars beside the office, an airstrip led toward the edge of a scrub-pine forest flanked by a large field of brown grass.

Declan stood outside his car, hands on his hips, scanning the area from behind his Aviator sunglasses. There were no other cars and no people to be found.

Go to the center of the field.

Those had been the instructions. They didn't make a ton of sense when he heard them the first time, and now, as he strolled out toward the airstrip, they made even less.

Why would I go to the center of the field?

Maybe they'd left a package there for him. Someone who didn't want to be identified might have planted everything he needed to know in the field.

Declan started toward what he guessed would be the center of the property, taking a moment to glance into the buildings as he passed them. The office had been stripped bare, but a quick twist on the door knob revealed it locked. Graffiti marked the walls where kids had probably crawled through the broken windows to party.

They'd probably been the ones who broke the windows in the first place.

The cement-floor hangars stood empty, peppered with holes where people had shot through the corrugated steel. The aerated walls reminded him of the rug warehouse where Charlotte had had her showdown with Stephanie. In the corner, he spotted a smattering of beer cans, backing his theory the abandoned airfield had been used as a party spot.

As he strolled farther from the buildings toward the center of the field, an uneasy feeling crept around the base of his neck.

He felt exposed.

Declan stopped and scanned the area.

I feel like a sitting duck.

The memory of bullet holes in the corrugated metal building walls brought to mind how easy it would be to perforate *him* from the surrounding tree line.

Someone had already tried to kill Charlotte. Probably because she was trying to clear Stephanie. Could it be someone knew he was helping her toward that goal? Having tried to swallow Charlotte whole, had they moved their attention to him?

He dropped his gaze and studied the brush, searching for movement.

I'd rather be picked off by a sniper than eaten by a snake.

Declan strolled to the outer edge of the strip, his head bouncing and swiveling like a bobblehead doll as his gaze swept the surroundings near and far.

Snakes. Snipers. Snakes. Snipers.

Clumps of dying weeds sprouted from cracks in the asphalt, and he kicked at a crumbling edge, sending pebbles bouncing into the scrub grass.

The low hum of an engine in the distance reached his ears.

A plane?

Maybe a helicopter? Was someone going to land and talk to him?

Somehow, the idea made him feel better. If the arranger of the meeting was arriving by air, meeting in the middle of an airfield made sense. It meant his location wasn't contrived so someone could snipe him dead from the tree line. They just wanted to hop out of the plane, meet with him, and then return to the air where they felt safe from whomever didn't want them to talk to him.

Sure. That makes perfect sense.

The sound of the engine grew closer and more sputtery. He could tell now the engine was small. Maybe too small.

That doesn't sound right.

It definitely wasn't a helicopter. He thought the sound better matched the engine of a small prop plane, but as it grew closer, he felt less and less sure. He'd seen and flown in some pretty small planes during his time in South America, but this noise sounded almost *tinny*. Almost like a child's toy.

Maybe a drone? Maybe they were standing what they felt was a safe distance away and sending him a package of information by drone.

Also possible.

Something colorful appeared above the tree line to his right. He turned to squint in that direction.

What the—

A kite? An air balloon?

Who schedules a clandestine meeting in a field and shows up in an air balloon? Phileas Fogg?

Declan chuckled to himself. Since when did he know the characters from *Around the World in 80 Days?* Charlotte's penchant for old movies was beginning to affect the way he thought.

The colorful dome rose higher above the pines. The arc of rainbow fabric looked like a parachute, but it seemed to be going *up*.

The engine grew louder.

That's when he saw him.

There's a man floating in the sky.

Hanging from beneath the striped parachute, a pilot, for lack of a better term, appeared to be sitting in a chair, strapped to a plane propeller, heading in Declan's direction.

Hm.

Declan wasn't entirely sure what to do with this new information. If showing up to a meeting in the middle of a field in a plane or a helicopter had seemed odd, showing up to a meeting in a flying chair seemed absolutely *insane.*

He shielded his eyes from the sun and watched the man weave his way toward him, bouncing off invisible walls of air. Something rested in his hands. It was long and thin and felt familiar. It looked like a—

Declan turned and began to sprint toward the hangers.

It looks like a gun.

He'd only taken a few steps when he heard the first shot.

The man hanging from the flying rainbow, sitting in a propeller chair, was *shooting* at him.

Declan's arms and legs pumped as fast as he could move them, his swimmer's lungs expanding with each gulp of air. He corrected his angle toward his car as the second shot zinged by his ear and hit the ground beside him with a dull, dusty thud. He swerved to make himself a more difficult target.

The motorized paraglider passed overhead and circled around for another pass.

Declan realized it would be too easy for the airborne sniper to hit him in his car or to take potshots at any building he entered. He'd already seen that the hangers couldn't take a bullet.

I have to reach the forest's edge.

He shifted direction again. Another bullet hit the ground nearby, and Declan raised his arms to shield his head.

Fifty more feet.

A bullet stuck the tree in front of him as the paraglider made a sharp turn to loop again.

Declan ran past something shiny on the ground as he plunged into the trees.

Shielded by pines, he stopped and leaned his palms on his knees, puffing as he caught his breath. His gaze rose to inspect the objects he'd passed on the way into the trees.

A bucket of balls and an old golf driver.

Someone had been shagging balls into the field around the airstrip.

He heard another shot, and somewhere to his left, he heard

the bullet strike a tree. The paraglider turned to make another pass.

Safe for the moment, Declan strode from the tree line and dumped the bucket of balls out into the field. Grabbing the driver, he twirled it in his palm. The club didn't feel too bad. It had clearly been outside for a while, but its synthetic shaft had weathered well. He positioned a ball away from the others with his foot and swung.

The ball arced into the sky, missing the paraglider by a good ten feet.

Not too shabby.

Declan pulled out another and another, smacking them in the direction of the paraglider as the sniper turned for another pass.

He heard the ding when one hit the engine block strapped to the man's chair.

Gotcha.

Something tumbled from the sky. A dark stick, tumbling end over end.

The gun.

The golf ball had startled the man, and he'd dropped his weapon.

Declan had been hoping to knock his foe out of the sky, clog his engine or something, but that might have been optimistic for a guy with a nine handicap. He'd take disarming the man.

Let's hope he doesn't have a spare weapon.

Declan dropped the driver and bolted for the fallen gun.

Above him, the paraglider leaned forward and strained to see where he'd dropped his weapon. Declan recognized the very moment the sniper spotted him running across the field. The moment it occurred to the man that soon Declan would have a gun.

The sound of the engine grew stronger, and the paraglider headed back the way he came.

Declan reached the gun and pointed it at the engine as it headed away from him. He fired and heard the *ping*! as it ricocheted off the metal.

The motor revved again, and Declan pulled the trigger. Another *ping!* and a puff of smoke escaped the engine.

"Ha! Got you!"

Engine gasping and sputtering, the paraglider barely made it over the tree line before Declan heard the engine no more.

There has to be a clear spot on the other side of the trees the man used to take off.

Declan bolted toward the scraggly forest separating him from his would-be assassin. He wove through the pines, heart pumping and sweat collecting in his work shirt.

I'm going to have to get changed before work now.

He rolled his eyes as he wove past a tree.

What a thought to have.

How he had changed from his youth. He remembered a time when an attack would have shrouded any logical thought in his head. He would have been filled with rage and a thirst for revenge.

Now he was worried he'd sweat through his work shirt.

Branches scratched his arms and face as he pushed through. He had to face his attacker and discover the meaning of the assassination attempt. Certainly, not knowing who wanted him dead was more dangerous than confronting an unarmed paraglider who'd just hit the ground the hard way.

Declan burst through the trees in time to see a black SUV take off down a dirt road. He cursed, a luxury he'd trained himself to not indulge in a long time ago. Retirees at his shop didn't want to talk to a swearing ex-soldier. They wanted to talk to shiny Declan, the one who smelled good and never had a hair out of place.

The one who worried about sweating through his polo.

He looked down at his shirt. One of the grabbing branches had torn a hole in his sleeve.

Shit. I mean, shoot.

Dirt and pine needles clung to every inch of fabric. He looked like Blade after his forest bathing experiment.

This is not shiny Declan.

Declan inspected the abandoned paragliding contraption. The parachute sat in a tangled ball beside it.

Declan pulled his phone from his pocket and dialed Sheriff Frank.

"Frank here."

"Do you have a fingerprint kit?"

"Who is this?" Frank's voice grew gruffer and deeper, laced with suspicion.

"It's Declan."

A deep silence radiated from the other end of the line.

"Charlotte's boyfriend?" prompted Declan.

Frank grunted. "Right, right, I knew that."

"We've met about a hundred times."

"Yeah, I know who you are. I'm doin' something here. I was distracted. What did you ask me? Do I have a fingerprint kit?"

"Mm hm."

"Why do you sound like a steam engine?"

Because someone in a motorized paraglider just tried to shoot me while I was standing in the middle of an abandoned airstrip field. There was running away involved."

Silence again.

"Is that something you kids do in your spare time now?"

"Nooo. Someone was trying to kill me."

"What were you doing out *there*?"

"Are you implying I deserved to be shot at for being in the field?"

"Now that you mention it."

Declan took a deep breath and released it. "I chased him down, and I have his equipment here. I need it dusted for prints."

"How did you chase down a plane?"

"It wasn't a plane. It was a motorized parasail, but it's a long story. I'm going to send you the address. Can you get someone out here?"

"Yeah, can do. Sit tight. Stay out of the fields."

"Right."

No sooner did he hang up than his phone rang. He recognized the number as Blade's.

"Hey, what's up?" he asked.

"Did you notice anyone following you on the way to the store?"

"Uh..." Declan looked around the field. "No."

"We, uh, I mean *I*, thought I saw someone pull off after you when you left my house."

"Really?" Declan had to wonder if it had been the paraglider.

"Black SUV?"

"Yeah, you saw him?"

"Maybe." *He shot at me from a flying chair.* "Could you open the store for me? I got waylaid a bit."

"With Charlotte?"

Declan straightened. "No. Why do you ask?"

"I saw her on the video cameras. She sneaked out the back of her house. It looked like she was avoiding Butch and Andy."

"Hm. She said she was with Mariska. Maybe she just wanted to go visit without eyes on her. I'll check in."

"Okay. I'll head to the store."

"Great. Thanks."

Declan hung up and dialed Charlotte. She was going to be excited the fingerprint book might finally come in handy. He just had to figure out how to explain why he hadn't mentioned going to the field in the first place.

CHAPTER TWENTY-ONE

Charlotte walked down the Riverwalk, her gaze sweeping in every direction, searching for the man who had called her.

Miles, more than likely.

And not only him, but snakes, too.

The Riverwalk felt both secluded and urban, and with her heightened state of awareness, she wasn't sure if she should feel isolated or safe. The walk had been built to flank a local river on one side and civilization on the other. On her right, a head-high wall blended into a grassy hillside ending with rows of small retirement homes. On her left, a barred fence that looked like the lower section of a misplaced jail cell door kept her from wandering down the muddy slope into the river. Above her, Alexander laurels and Madagascar olive trees provided a shady arched canopy.

Wouldn't it be great if Miles Davis had decided to turn on Jamie's nemesis?

Charlotte accepted she might not have her quarry captured *today*, but if Miles delivered on his promise to provide her with the mystery man's identity, she'd be a giant step closer to satisfying Jamie's demands. She wasn't sure Jamie even knew her pursuer's name. The woman went squirrelly every time she asked for more information, and her reticence to share didn't make a lot of sense.

Why would you hire someone to find someone and then do everything you could to make the job more difficult?

Lost in her thoughts, Charlotte almost didn't notice the man hiding in the greenery flanking the path. He crouched there, just past the row of small square retirement homes watching over this portion of the Riverwalk.

It was just past the part that had made her feel safe.

Charlotte stopped and stared at him.

He didn't move.

Does he think he's invisible?

"I can see you," she said loudly, though short of a shout. She glanced at the last home just behind her. *Was anyone home there? Would they hear her if she screamed?* Her chest tightened with nerves.

Somehow, her clandestine meeting with the man who'd tried to kill her with a python felt like an even *worse* idea upon spotting him squatting in the shrubbery.

Charlotte wasn't sure what she'd expected. Should she have had high hopes for the mental stability and manners of a man who pushed man-eating snakes through women's windows? For some reason, she'd pictured strolling the Riverwalk until she found herself talking to a clean-cut man in a nice white suit. Why, she had no idea. She'd watched *Casablanca* earlier in the week. That could have been it.

Now, faced with the reality of a man in torn jean shorts and a dirty t-shirt skulking in the bushes, she realized the chances of Miles looking like a modern-day Rick Blaine had always been pretty slim.

And I didn't bring my gun.

She hadn't gotten used to the idea of carrying her gun, and her everyday uniform of shorts and a shirt didn't make it easy to properly conceal a weapon.

This might have been one of those times when dressing for the gun would have been a good idea.

"You Charlotte?" asked the man.

Charlotte looked behind her again to see if any walkers or joggers were coming. Now would be a great time to see another human being. *Any* human being.

Nothing stirred behind her except a curly-tailed lizard scurrying across the side of a tree trunk.

You're no help.

She straightened, trying to look more in command of her nerves, even if she couldn't *feel* in charge of them. "Yes."

"I have information fer ya." His voice was gravelly, with the hint of a true Floridian southern drawl. Charlotte had grown up around too many northern transplants and had little accent of her own. This man sounded as if he'd come from a less tourist-laden part of the state.

"I know. You said on the phone. Could you stop hiding in the bushes? Couldn't we maybe meet at the coffee shop down the path there?"

Miles sniffed hard, and she heard the resulting rattle dislodge something gooey in his throat. He spat. "Com'ere. I have to give it to ya."

Charlotte almost laughed out loud.

Nooo, that doesn't sound threatening at all.

She shifted her weight from one foot to the other, considering her options. If she clawed her way up the hill to Miles and he killed her, she was going to feel like an *idiot. "Come here, I have to give it to you in person..."* was the kind of thing cartoon characters said before snatching their prey. It would be like getting caught by the witch in Hansel and Gretel. She'd always wondered how those two little morons hadn't seen *her* coming. A house made of candy? Come *on.*

Charlotte took a step forward. It was time to shake things up a bit and throw him on the defensive.

"Look, just tell me what you want me to know, *Miles.*"

She heard the man grunt at the sound of his name, and Charlotte braced herself for another round of loogie production.

Instead, Miles stood. He wasn't a tall man, but he was built thick and sported an impressive beer belly beneath his filthy shirt. An emblem was printed above his left breast, but Charlotte couldn't make out the words.

"How'd you know my name?" he asked.

Charlotte felt grateful for the confirmation. At least Miles hadn't tried to hide his identity. If this meeting went south, and it felt like it was heading there as sure as a flock of migrating birds in winter, it would help to have confirmation of his name.

"I know lots of things. But I could know more. Tell me who framed Stephanie."

He shook his head. "Nah. Forget it."

Miles turned and scrambled up the hill behind him like a monkey.

Shoot. Calling out his name had spooked the man.

"Wait!"

Charlotte jumped on the retaining wall and grabbed the branch of a bush to haul herself to the hill. Standing as best as she could, her new vantage point enabled her to see what looked like a parking lot at the top of the slope. Miles reached for a chain that dangled between two posts there to pull himself up to the flat pavement.

Palms down and toes digging in the dirt behind her, Charlotte began to climb.

"Wait!"

Miles disappeared over the edge of the hill.

Charlotte had nearly reached the crest when she heard a creaking metallic sound. Heavy. It didn't sound like a car door. She didn't hear the roar of an engine. The sound felt familiar. Where had she heard it before? Her mind raced to associate the sound with an action as she reached for the same chain Miles had used to assist his ascent. She pulled herself upright and stood at the top of the hill.

Miles stood six feet from her at the back of an old pickup. The tailgate was down.

That was the noise. The creaking of a tailgate being dropped. You couldn't live in Florida your whole life and never hear the sound of a pickup truck tailgate dropping. It was practically the state song.

Miles had his right hand on something large and dark, just peeking out from under a tarp in the back of his truck. His left arm crossed in front of his chest.

Something flashed in his hand.

Scissors. He held a huge pair of shears in his left hand.

Snip!

Something snapped as he clipped it with the shears. He leaned into the truck and hauled what was in there out from under the tarp, roaring with the effort. He half-slid, half-threw what looked like a giant log toward her.

The log kept coming, so long Charlotte couldn't process how it had fit in the back of the truck. The thing was huge. A giant hissing, angry log.

Charlotte froze, her hands out to either side, unsure of what direction to move.

Are those teeth?

The thing landed on the ground, took a moment to get its bearings, and then bolted toward her. Four claw-tipped feet were paddling forward with purpose.

Charlotte didn't need any more time to piece together what was happening. She could see what was barreling toward her just fine.

A word lit up in her mind like someone had flipped on Broadway lights.

Alligator.

Left and right didn't seem like good directions to run. The way the gator's head whipped back and forth as it high-speed-waddled toward her, she felt like it could adjust to either of those directions without trouble. Instead, Charlotte turned, forgetting the chain looped low behind her calves. One leg managed to clear it. The other caught, and she fell forward down the hill.

Charlotte yelped and twisted her body, trying to keep from tumbling headfirst into the bushes below. She heard the weight of the enormous creature behind her as it slid, crashing through the low vegetation.

Charlotte directed her fall well enough to avoid the worst of the bushes. Her feet hit the top of the retaining wall, and she jumped, attempting to gracefully dismount to the Riverwalk below. She landed on one foot and one knee, which had not been her preferred plan.

Hot pain exploded across her kneecap, but she didn't slow. She knew the reptile coming at her like an Olympic luge wouldn't be slowing. She felt the breath of the creature and heard the snapping of its jaws as she stood to propel herself forward.

Charlotte took a few steps and then looked down the Riverwalk in both directions. To her left, the path led back to her car, but it was a narrow path. She knew there was some trick to running away from an alligator—something about zig-zagging back and forth—but thanks to the retaining wall, there wasn't much room to maneuver on the path. She knew alligators ran faster than most people thought they could, and the one behind her seemed like a natural-born sprinter. Just her luck to be chased by the Usain Bolt of reptiles.

She crossed off the path to her left as an option.

She could jump back on the retaining wall, but she didn't know how agile an alligator was when it came to climbing short walls. She'd missed that episode of *Wild Kingdom*. And if she started up the hill and slipped back into that maw...

The wall was not an option.

To the right was what appeared to be a baby dragon, sliding off the side of the retaining wall in its single-minded pursuit of her. Its dark green, bumpy skin glistened as if Miles had polished it for its big debut. In a moment, it would be on all fours again. It would come charging at her.

He looked both hungry and angry.

Hangry. That would be a good name for an alligator.

No.

Stop it. Charlotte shook her head, amazed her mind could wander in a crisis. *Don't get distracted naming the beast about to bite off your leg.*

The alligator let out a low, long groan and blinked its eyes sideways at her. For the first time, she noticed one eye was milky blue, the other dark.

How about that.

Instinctively, Charlotte looked in the direction the creature's blue eye faced, guessing the milky blue coloring meant it was blind in that eye. She wasn't sure how much of an advantage it would be to stay on the gator's blindside, but as she looked in that direction, she spotted the iron fence that separated the walk from the river.

She hadn't considered heading toward the river. Her first thought had been to *avoid* water when confronted by an alligator. It was one thing to be eaten and a whole other to be death-rolled in the shallow water, her drowned body carried away and stuffed under a rock somewhere in the depths.

She'd always assumed the Riverwalk fence was there to keep the alligators from coming *out* of the water and snatching poodles for breakfast. Hangry's whole family might be on the other side of that fence.

But if the fence can keep gators from coming up, couldn't it keep them from going down?

There *might* be alligators on the other side of the fence, but Hangry was *definitely* on her side of the fence.

And he was finding his feet. The gator's claws curled, nails digging into paver stones as he prepared to launch himself toward her.

This is crazy.

Charlotte jumped for the iron fence, mounting it and swinging her legs to the opposite side. The drop behind the fence led to shallow water, where she feared other gators or snakes might be waiting, so she clung to the top spikes of the fence, dangling, separated from her scaly pursuer by spaced iron bars.

She screamed as the gator slammed his nose into the bars. The fence shuddered, but she held on as the animal rammed itself against it again, unable to fit its nose through. She hung on the opposite side, a tasty morsel so close but unreachable.

Charlotte braced her feet on the wall below the fence to push her torso farther from the barrier, fearing Hangry would find a way to push his bumpy snout through. She smelled swamp and rotting meat as the dragon propped his face up on the fence and clawed at her with his stubby legs.

Please stop. Please give up...

"Oh!" Thirty feet away, a woman in exercise shorts and a bright pink tank top walked briskly around the corner only to stop dead in her tracks.

The alligator turned to look at her. She was on the side of his good eye.

"Run!" screamed Charlotte. The woman was far enough away and young enough that she could make good progress before the gator reached top speed.

The woman turned and bolted.

The gator began to move in the walker's direction, but he seemed to lack the enthusiasm and sense of urgency he'd enjoyed during his pursuit of Charlotte.

Hangry's head turned back and forth a few times as he tried to decide which direction led to dinner.

Charlotte's arms were getting tired.

The alligator gave her one last lingering stare with his blue eye before turning to slowly walk away in the direction the walker had run. He strolled down the length of the fence, intermittently banging the bars with his snout as he tried to find a way to enter the water.

Too much excitement for one day. He'd settle for fish now.

When the beast had moved far enough away, Charlotte scrambled up the fence and swung her leg over, unable to hang on any longer. She sat there perched on top and waited for her heart to stop banging out of her chest. Her shoulders throbbed. Blood dripped from her skinned knee and ran in ever-thinning rivulets down her shin.

Sirens filled the air, and Charlotte heard cars screeching to a halt in the parking lot above. She hoped Miles was still there waiting to collect his gator, but she suspected he was long gone.

He hadn't stuck around for the python.

The walker must have called the police. Charlotte thanked the heavens the woman had decided to exercise that day. She wasn't sure how much longer she could have held on to those bars.

Soon men with lassos on sticks and guns swarmed over the hill. Others came jogging down the path.

She pointed down the walk.

"He went that way."

A man in a t-shirt that said *Gator Getter* nodded and ran off in that direction as an officer strode forward and helped her off the fence.

As Charlotte found her footing, she heard a commotion coming from somewhere around the bend. A few minutes later, three trappers approached, carrying the alligator between them. Its mouth had been wrapped shut with duct tape, and it hung in their arms, either tranquilized or resigned to its fate.

Charlotte pulled out her phone, grateful it hadn't ended up in the river. She needed to call Declan. She just had to figure out how to explain why she hadn't mentioned she'd left the house.

CHAPTER TWENTY-TWO

"Someone just tried to kill me with an alligator."

Declan's eyes grew wide. He was watching crime techs dust the paragliding contraption for prints while another group folded the chute into an oversized evidence box. Well, they were folding the chute into a box, *in theory.* In reality, Deputy Daniel had been wrestling to cram the billowing silk into an oversized evidence box for fifteen minutes as if the chute were a sentient creature who'd sworn never to be captured.

Declan had stepped further out so he could hear Charlotte over the swearing, but he regularly glanced over his shoulder to be sure the chute hadn't finished with Deputy Daniel and started toward him.

"An alligator? Are you hurt?"

"No. Well, I think I might have pulled something in my shoulder, and I scraped my knee pretty good, but I'm not drowned and tucked under a rock in a lake or anything, so there's that."

"Why were you in the water?"

Charlotte giggled the way she did when she realized she'd been nerding out. "Oh, I wasn't. That's just what alligators like to do."

Declan felt a pang of jealousy that Charlotte's news trumped his own. He thought he'd finally win a game of "who had the weirdest day" with her, but once again...

"How did *this* happen? Did they slip it in your bath?"

"No, I—" Charlotte cut short abruptly.

"Charlotte?"

He heard her sigh. "I'm here. I'm bracing myself to reveal a tiny fib I told you earlier."

Declan closed his eyes. He knew what she was about to say. He'd always known and simply pushed aside the little voice telling him because he'd been on a mission of his own. Blade seeing her sneaking out of her house had confirmed his suspicions.

"You weren't home when I talked to you earlier, were you?"

"No. I was on my way to the Riverwalk."

"Why?"

"Because Miles Davis called and told me to meet him there. He said he was going to flip on his boss."

"And you believed him?"

"Not really. But hope springs eternal. I had to *try*."

"No, you didn't. Or you could have gone with backup. Like *me*. Why didn't you tell me?"

"He said to come alone. I had to go then. I didn't have time."

Declan shook his head, aware he was about to use one of the old-timey sayings Charlotte often used, thanks to her upbringing in the retirement park. "If he'd told you to jump off a bridge, would you have?'

"*No*. But there was another reason I didn't tell you."

"What's that?"

"Because you would have tried to stop me."

True.

"Like I could stop you from doing anything," he muttered.

"What?"

"Nothing. Did they catch Miles?"

"No. He got away. I'm almost glad. I'm fascinated to see

what animal he tries to kill me with next."

Declan sighed. "I guess the important thing is that you're not hurt, but we really need to come up with a plan for situations like this. It's too dangerous for you or *anyone* to meet crazy people on your own."

"Fair enough. What are you up to? Is that someone cursing I hear in the background?"

Declan turned to find Deputy Daniels stuffing the last of the sheet into the box. His face glistened with sweat as he grinned and pointed a thumb to the sky.

"I got this son of a—"

"Yes," said Declan into the phone, feeling his cheeks grow flush as he realized what a hypocrite he was about to sound like to Charlotte.

"Did you get a T.V. in the shop? Or are the old ladies fighting over a particularly exquisite throw pillow?" she asked.

"Neither. I have a confession to make, too. Someone called me and asked me to meet them at an abandoned airfield."

"What? Who? Why?"

"I don't know who. Anonymous. But I went in the hopes I could help you."

"*Ah ha!* And you went by yourself and didn't tell me?"

"Yes. To keep you out of harm's way. I didn't know you were on your way to wrestle an alligator."

"So, during our last conversation, we were both lying to each other?"

He nodded on his side of the line, grimacing. "Yes."

"I don't know if this bodes well for our relationship."

"Last time we'll do it."

"Last time," she echoed. "Deal. Any alligators where you are?"

"No. A man in a motorized paraglider tried to shoot me."

"*What?* Are you okay?"

He glanced down at his tattered shirt. "I'm fine. I tore my

favorite white polo running through a forest."

"What the heck is a motorized paraglider?"

"It's what I'm calling a guy in a chair hanging from a parachute with an airplane propeller strapped to his back. I'm not sure what the official name for that contraption is."

"I think *death machine.*"

He chuckled. "Sounds about right."

"So what happened?"

"I hit golf balls at him until he dropped the gun."

"Golf balls?"

"A club and a pile of balls were abandoned near the woods, so I used them." He chuckled. "I was a real Tiger *woods*."

Charlotte groaned. "Yikes."

"Sorry. Anyway, I went running for the gun, but he got away before I could get him. Frank sent guys out to dust his *death machine* and gather it for evidence. They're here now. Deputy Dan just spent half an hour trying to pack up the chute. You would have been hysterical."

"I'm sorry I missed that."

"Me too."

"Why is someone trying to kill *you*?"

"For helping you, I guess."

Charlotte grew quiet. Declan could almost hear her thinking. He had an idea of his own.

"You sneaked out?" he asked.

Charlotte responded with a grunt, still firmly in her own thoughts. "Hm?"

"Do Andy and Butch think you're still in the house?"

"Oh. Yes. I sneaked out the back."

"Don't go back to your place. Go to my house," he suggested.

"I don't know that your house is any safer. Seems they're after you now, too."

"We know Andy and Butch are Jamie's eyes, right? Maybe Jamie isn't trying to keep you alive as hard as we thought. This guy trying to kill you with animals sounds like her sense of humor. Maybe Andy and Butch aren't there to protect you but to spy on you and tell her where you are."

"Jamie told me it wasn't her. She said she wouldn't use snakes to kill people because it wasn't clever enough."

"And she never lies."

"Hm. Good point. Though I'd hate to think Andy and Butch were trying to kill me. I mean, I always knew spying on me was part of their mission, but—"

"I know. But Jamie's threatened them, and they have to think of their families. And they *are* in witness protection. We don't know what they're capable of or what they've done in the past."

"I guess that's true."

"At least maybe at my house, we could try and work some of this out under the radar for a bit. I'll tell Seamus to meet you there, and I'll be there as soon as I can get out of here."

Charlotte chuckled. "Now Seamus is my bodyguard?"

"Seamus is a bit of a wild card, but he's also trained. You'll be safe with him."

"I need to get Abby."

"I'll grab her. I'll pretend I'm visiting you and then sneak out the back with Abby, the same as you did. Then I'll sneak back and go out the front like I'm leaving."

"Okay." Charlotte paused. "Be careful. I've sort of grown accustomed to you being alive."

He smiled. "I'll try and keep it that way. You be careful too."

They hung up, and Declan glanced over at the deputies loading the machine into the back of an open-bed truck.

"Are you finished with me?"

Deputy Daniel nodded and puffed out his chest, seeming very officious for a man who'd just been rolling on the ground with a rainbow parachute. "We're good. We'll be in touch if we need anything else."

"Thanks." Declan nodded and headed through the woods toward the airport parking lot where he'd left his car. As he broke from the tree line, his phone rang, and once again, a voice asked him if he was willing to accept a call from prison.

He agreed.

CHAPTER TWENTY-THREE

"Have you been in contact with your mother?" asked Declan.

Stephanie frowned. She'd called Declan to ask *him* things, not to have him ask *her* things.

"You don't say *hello* anymore?"

"Someone just tried to kill me and Charlotte, and I'd like to know if she knows anything about either attempt."

"Someone tried to kill *you*?"

"Yes. A man in some kind of flying contraption tried to shoot me."

Stephanie felt her face prickle as the blood drained from it. "What kind of flying contraption?"

"Some kind of motorized paraglider."

"Huh." Stephanie rubbed her eye with her opposite hand.

"Huh? What?" asked Declan.

"It's just strange."

Stephanie looked away to keep him from reading her expression.

Mother.

During the brief time she'd spent catching up with her

mother—before Jamie had disappeared once more—her mother had told her about a sniper she'd used to kill a man from a paraglider in Oludeniz, Turkey. There were no mountains in Florida for paragliding, but Declan's story was too similar to be a coincidence. It had to be the same man. A sniper specializing in paraglider potshots. How many of those could there be?

"Hey, I need that phone," said another voice, a little too loudly, on Stephanie's side of the line. Stephanie turned to find an angry Latina woman pointing at her.

She smiled. "Mariana, isn't it?"

The woman's face twitched at the sound of her name. "Yeah. So? I need that phone. That's all you need to know."

"Just a second, Declan, darling." Stephanie lowered the phone from her ear, her gaze never leaving Mariana's.

"Well?" barked the Latina, but Stephanie could see her growing uneasy. She'd begun to subtly rock back and forth with nervous energy.

"You may have the phone when I'm finished."

Mariana thrust out a hand. "I need it *now*."

Stephanie raised the phone back to her ear.

"Sorry. The natives are restless. Just one more second."

"Just ask your mother for info if you get a chance, will you?" said Declan.

"Of course."

"Oh, what did you call for?" asked Declan.

"Just looking for information—"

"Bitch, I told you I need that phone."

The Latina now stood so close to Stephanie that she could smell on her breath the hamburgers they'd had for lunch. The meat was rotting between her teeth.

Stephanie put a hand over the lower half of the receiver. "You should consider flossing."

"What? What you say to me?" Mariana grabbed the chest of Stephanie's shirt, balling it in her fist.

Stephanie lolled her head to the right and made eye contact

with MuuMuu, who sat nearby on a bench. If Mariana tried to swing at her before MuuMuu could lumber over and shut the nuisance up, her plan was to break the phone receiver across the bridge of the Latina's nose, but she really didn't want to do that. She needed to finish her conversation with Declan.

MuuMuu stood and moved toward Stephanie. Mariana was too busy screaming to notice. When MuuMuu tapped her on the shoulder, she whirled, raising her fist, ready to strike. When she saw MuuMuu staring down at her, her fist lowered.

"Hey, MuuMuu," she said, her voice sticking in her throat.

MuuMuu poked a sausage finger into Mariana's chest. "You have a problem with Blondie, you have a problem with me."

Mariana glanced at Stephanie. Stephanie smiled and shooed her away.

"Go on now."

The Latina's expression darkened. Deciding against a confrontation, she walked away to flop dramatically into a chair, grumbling in Spanish.

Stephanie winked at MuuMuu. After her earlier scuffle with the enormous woman, she'd found time to find out what the Tongan *needed*. MuuMuu had a sister—a terrifying thought—desperately in need of legal advice. Stephanie agreed to take care of the sister in return for MuuMuu's help during her time in prison. The arrangement was already working well.

"Thanks, girlfriend."

MuuMuu nodded and lumbered back to her seat.

"What's going on?" asked Declan from his end of the line. The side where people didn't threaten you when you were on the phone, and you didn't have to befriend sasquatch to cover your ass.

Well, at least not as often.

Stephanie straightened her crumpled bright orange top with her free hand and lowered a steady gaze on Mariana, doing her best to telegraph a message with her eyes.

Please try that again on the outside, Miss Thing. I won't need MuuMuu out there.

Mariana looked away.

"Stephanie, are you there?"

Stephanie returned her attention to Declan. "Sorry. Yes. Little disturbance. It's been dealt with."

"Sounds as if prison agrees with you."

"It's almost better than a South American jungle. *Maybe.* The food's worse."

"We were living on rations and jungle bugs."

"Exactly."

Declan chuckled. "So why did you call?"

"To get an update. Are you and your girlie making progress when people aren't trying to kill you?" Stephanie paused. "Did someone try to sniper her from a paraglider too?"

"No. A man your mother identified as one of her WITSEC clients, Miles Davis, tried to kill Charlotte with an alligator."

"Miles Davis, the musician?"

"No. Different one. We think that's who slid the python through her window."

"Naturally."

"And speaking of Miles Davis, did you tell your mother about your coral dream?"

Stephanie felt a flush of heat rise to her cheeks. She *hadn't* told her mother about her dreams of drowning in a field of coral, and she never would. Jamie would see her nightmares as a sign of weakness, and nothing was more dangerous than revealing your weaknesses to Jamie. Declan was different. Declan was the only one who could see her.

"No. I haven't had a chance to tell her yet."

"Well, I don't think it's just a dream."

Stephanie perked. "What do you mean?"

"Your mother told Charlotte she suspects Miles is doing the dirty work for someone else. She said Miles was struck by lightning as a child and had the image of his veins flash-fried onto his skin."

"His veins..." Stephanie closed her eyes and tried to picture what such a thing would look like.

It looks like coral.

"*The coral.* It has to be him. I saw him there. He shot at me from behind Jason."

"That's what I'm thinking."

Stephanie balled a fist. "*Ooh.* I'm going to *kill* Miles Davis."

"Please don't kill him before he leads us to his boss. And anyway, I thought you were a changed woman?"

Stephanie smiled. "Everyone gets a hall pass once in a while, don't they? Anything else? I have things to do now. Revenge to plan."

"Ask your mother if she knows who the guy in the paraglider was and why the hell they're after me all of a sudden. It can't be Miles. He was busy releasing alligators when I was dodging bullets."

"Right. Will do. If she blesses me with a phone call."

"Thanks. That's it."

"Okay. Hey, Declan?"

"Hm?"

"Thanks for letting me know about the lightning tattoo. Now that I know what it is, maybe..." Stephanie fell silent.

Declan finished her thought for her. "Maybe you won't have the nightmares anymore."

Stephanie's eyes felt strange. She raised her fingertips to her cheek. *Wet.* She turned her body away from the crowd of inmates behind her and wiped her face with the back of her hand.

Stupid.

"Sure. Right. I guess. I was going to say maybe I'll be able to remember more. To help you and Charlotte."

"Hey, you called Charlotte by her *name*. She'll be thrilled."

Stephanie laughed. "Don't get too excited."

"Never. Take care, Stephanie."

She nodded. "Of course. You know me."

She hung up the phone and wandered away from the phone banks. Mariana, who'd been so eager to get to the phone, eyed MuuMuu, who nodded her head to let her know she could make her call without the threat of bodily harm.

Stephanie sat beside MuuMuu and rested her head on the enormous woman's shoulder. She was tired. She found the matronly shape of the giantess' cushiony body comforting. MuuMuu patted her knee.

"You know I don't swing like that, right?" she said.

Stephanie chuckled. "Shut up and hold still."

MuuMuu laughed, making Stephanie's head bounce until she had to straighten.

She leaned her head against the wall behind her and stared across the room at nothing. Some sense of dread gnawed at her guts like a hungry rat.

Mom wants Declan dead.

Why? Because Declan inspired her to be a decent human being? She'd told Jamie as much.

That was a mistake. She could see that now.

Her mother had been encouraging her more vicious side since they reconnected. She'd found it flattering to have Jamie's attention, no matter how warped the delivery system. Everyone craves their mother's attention, don't they? Part of her reveled in the idea that her mother might be grooming her as a protégé.

Part of her didn't.

Jamie didn't want Declan undermining her work.

But was that enough to kill him?

Well sure. That's what Jamie did. When Jamie didn't like something, that *something* had a habit of disappearing.

Stephanie sighed.

I should have warned him. He needed to know. What had kept her from blurting out her suspicions?

Betraying her mother wasn't the best way to stay alive.

And she couldn't be sure about the paraglider...

But I can't lose Declan. He's my only connection to the part of myself my mother doesn't own...

"I think I'm going to have to make another call."

"You want me to make her move?" asked MuuMuu locking her gaze on the Latina. Mariana noticed and turned away, talking hurriedly to whomever she'd called.

"Nah, give her a second." Stephanie sat up and eyed her protector. "You know, I never asked you why you were in here."

MuuMuu smirked. "Tax evasion."

Stephanie's brow knit. "In *this* prison? For tax evasion? Shouldn't you be someplace a little more white-collar?"

MuuMuu shrugged her rounded shoulders. "I evaded them by breaking four of the auditor's ribs."

Stephanie nodded.

"Ah. That makes more sense."

CHAPTER TWENTY-FOUR

Seamus opened the door of his bar, The Anne Bonny, and watched his last patrons stumble over his threshold.

Literally.

I should probably fix that.

His new bar had been an instant hit with the locals, and he didn't want them to kill themselves on the way out. Or on the way in, but on the way in, they were a little more nimble. He worried less about them then.

"And ye don't come back until you learn some manners!" he called after his last two patrons. They roared with laughter.

It wasn't hard to make drunk people laugh, which was one of the reasons Seamus loved drunk people so much.

Seamus watched his customers ping-pong off each other as they made their way down the street, both talking much too loudly about the difference between salami and pepperoni. Chuckling to himself, Seamus was about to shut the door when he noticed a man standing on the sidewalk across the street. The street lamp above him cast long shadows across his face. Seamus couldn't see him, and yet something felt very familiar about the figure.

"If it's a drink yer wantin', I'm afraid you've come a bit late," called Seamus, letting his Irish accent play thicker than it needed to. He'd been in America long enough he could sound as American as apple pie, but the bar patrons seemed to like being served by a true Irishman. In recent days he'd been falling back into an accent he thought he'd lost.

The man across the street shifted from one foot to the other, silent, as if trying to decide if he wanted to leave or remain staring.

"Your accent hasn't changed," he said after an uncomfortable silence.

Seamus straightened and gave his pants a yank over the bulge of his midsection. "Do I know ye, er, *you?*"

"I don't know anymore," said the man.

Seamus sniffed. It was too late for games. "We're closed."

"Ye wouldn't even stay open fer me?"

The man suddenly had an accent very much like his own.

That voice.

Seamus stepped forward, careful to avoid the uneven threshold. He let the door close behind him. A name was bouncing around his mouth. He didn't want to release it, but he opened his lips and spat out as if it had been held prisoner.

"Cormac?"

The man beneath the light pulled his hands from his pockets and started across the street.

What little Seamus could see of the stranger's features melted into darkness as he left the domain of his lamp post, only to be illuminated again by The Anne Bonny's own garishly throbbing bar sign. Overhead, a neon pirate wench grinned from dusk to dawn, and her red and yellow glow cast a sickly pallor on the man approaching.

The man's features slowly knit into a recognizable shape.

"No," said Seamus.

The man smiled. "Yes."

"It isn't you."

Seamus gaped in awe as his long-lost brother's face

appeared before him.

Cormac opened his arms. "It's good to see you again, Seamus."

Seamus threw out his own arms and wrapped them around his brother. He squeezed him tight against him.

"I thought you were dead."

Cormac scoffed. "Nah. You know you can't kill me."

Seamus pushed his brother back to arm's length, his fingers grabbing the fabric of Cormac's suit jacket as he shook him.

"You're *alive*."

"I am."

Seamus looked down at the pavement, shaking his head. He stood like that for a moment, one hand on his brother's shoulder, the other hanging at his side, before he swung that hanging arm and cracked his brother in the jaw with every ounce of mustard he had in the jar.

Cormac spun to his right and caught himself on a car parked in front of the bar. The vehicle's alarm blared, filling the darkened street with hoots and whistles.

Cormac steadied himself and raised his hand to his battered jaw. "What the hell, Seamus?"

Seamus was already striding toward him, his vision white with rage.

"You abandoned your *son*."

Cormac threw up his arms to block another blow and returned with his own, connecting against Seamus' ribs.

"Declan had Erin to take care of him," spat Cormac as Seamus stumbled back.

Seamus squared up as his brother pushed himself away from the blaring car and did the same, both men raising their fists to square off.

Seamus popped Cormac in the nose as the car alarm stopped ringing.

"Erin disappeared not long after you did. The boy was

orphaned."

Cormac stumbled back and bounced off the lamp post to return with a hard left to Seamus' skull, only partially blocked.

"You were here."

Seamus shook off the blow.

"You don't leave a kid with *me*," he screamed, swinging and missing as Cormac dipped under him. "You think it's an accident I didn't have any of my own?"

The sound of a window lifting reached Seamus' ears as he stumbled forward and caught himself on the car. The alarm started again.

"You two stop making all that racket!" a man screamed from a second-floor apartment across the street.

Cormac and Seamus both turned to him.

"Piss off!" they screamed in unison, flashing their middle fingers like a synchronized swimming team with anger management issues.

The man slammed his window shut, and Cormac took advantage of the distraction to tackle his brother against the wailing car.

Wind knocked from his lungs, and Seamus grappled, peppering Cormac's stomach with a series of rabbit punches.

"I know Jujitsu. I could knock you unconscious with a tap of my finger," grunted Cormac as the brothers grappled with each other, rolling along the side of the wailing car.

"Try it, and you'll spend the rest of your life sleeping with one eye open."

The two men twisted and fell to the ground, rolling across the pavement.

"Ow! You're on my throat," croaked Seamus as Cormac rested his forearm on his Adam's apple.

"Sorry." Cormac moved his arm and bounced a glancing blow against Seamus' left cheekbone.

"Why are you here?" asked Seamus, taking advantage of

Cormac's shift to smack him in the jaw.

"Jamie Moriarty. And I'm trying to protect Declan, whether you believe it or not."

Seamus stopped struggling, and Cormac rolled him over to pull his brother's arm behind him. Seamus struggled to keep his face from digging against the pavement.

"What do you mean *protect* Declan?"

"His girlfriend's mixed up in this."

"She's on his side, you eejit. Charlotte's trying to keep Jamie from killing everyone she knows, including Declan."

"I know that now. Blade told me."

"Blade?"

Seamus rolled to his back as a *whoop! whoop!* cut through the racket of the honking car alarm. Blue lights flashed around Cormac's head.

"Stop it!" Roared a voice as the cruiser's door opened.

Cormac froze in mid-punch, and Seamus lifted his head to look past his brother, who straddled his middle. One of Sheriff Frank's deputies stood over them, his hand on his gun. Seamus recognized him as the officer who'd broken up a fight outside The Anne Bonny a few nights earlier.

"That's enough. Get up," said the deputy.

Both the brothers' tensed muscles went slack, and they rolled their eyes in unison.

"This has got nothing to do with you," said Seamus from his supine position beneath his brother.

The deputy arched both eyebrows. "He's about to pound your face in. You should *want* me here to break this up."

Seamus snorted. "He's going to do no such thing."

"Sure I am." Cormac turned and slapped his brother's face on both cheeks, left, then right. Seamus slapped at his hands, doing his best to block the blows while he tried to land his own.

The deputy stomped his foot on the pavement. "Stop it!"

Seamus got a slap in of his own before Cormac caught his left wrist and blocked his right as it attempted a second strike.

"I said *stop it*." The officer pulled his gun. He left it pointed at the ground, but his frustrations were made clear.

Cormac sighed and looked down at his brother.

"We'll continue this later."

Seamus scoffed. "You bet your sainted Aunt we will, you deadbeat dad."

Cormac had started to stand and now paused to stare down angrily at his brother. "I am *not* a deadbeat dad."

Seamus grabbed his brother's leg and pushed him forward, causing Cormac to rise at an accelerated pace. He stumbled against the wall of the bar.

He whirled as Seamus scrambled to his feet. "You sonova—"

The deputy raised his gun. "No! Right now. Both of you, *stop*."

Both on their feet, Cormac's and Seamus' hands hung at their sides as they glowered at the officer. The car alarm stopped screaming. All three of them looked at the vehicle and huffed a sigh of relief.

"About time," said Seamus.

"No doubt," agreed Cormac.

The deputy slipped his gun back into his holster. "Okay. Good. Now tell me, what's going on?"

Seamus huffed. "Oh, I'll tell you what's going on—"

Cormac cut him short. "We're brothers."

The officer nodded. "I have two of my own, so I understand. But you can't wrestle in public in the middle of the night. You're disturbing the peace."

"Yeah!" screamed the man from his window across the street. "*My* peace!"

Seamus pointed at him. "I'll deal with you later, ya snitch."

The deputy raised a hand to the man in the window. "Sir, please go back to bed."

The man slammed his window and disappeared inside.

The officer returned his attention to the brothers. "Do you both have a home to go to?"

"I'm not homeless," muttered Seamus.

Cormac nodded. "Yes."

"Both of you go home. *Now.*"

Grudgingly, Seamus made his way to his car, parked behind the one whose alarm had gotten them in trouble. Cormac started across the street toward his own.

Seamus paused as he put his leg in the driver's side to sit.

"Do you know where I live, Cormac?" he called.

Cormac turned, the key in his hand ready to open his door.

"Sponging off my son?"

"Yeah, whatever. I'm going to go home to tell him what a shite you are."

Cormac turned. "Wait—"

Cormac started back across the street as Seamus flopped in his seat and turned the ignition. He pulled from his spot just as Cormac grew near, and his brother had to jump out of the way to keep his toes from being run over.

Seamus hung his hand out the window as he drove away, his middle finger held high.

CHAPTER TWENTY-FIVE

Still breathing heavily, Cormac waved at the officer, who was now driving away, smiling. His tongue probed the corner of his mouth. He could already feel his lip swelling.

Well. Good to know Seamus hasn't changed.

His phone dinged in his pocket, and he pulled it out to check, his eyes flicking from the road to the phone and back. Someone at the home office had texted him a story about an alligator chasing a woman.

A woman named Charlotte Morgan.

And the toxicology had come back on Jason Walsh. He'd been poisoned by Tetrodotoxin.

Pufferfish.

Cormac grit his teeth and then released it when it made his jaw ache.

Son of a...

He dialed Miles.

"What you want this time a night?" asked Miles, who answered after the first ring.

Cormac checked his watch. It was nearly one a.m.

"I heard a report about an alligator chasing a particular girl."

"Yeah..."

Miles sounded as if he had half a cheesesteak in his mouth, and the sound of his spit smacking made Cormac's lip curl with disgust.

"What are you eating?"

"Canned meat."

"Gah." Cormac pressed his lips together tightly and pushed the picture of Miles eating canned meat out of his head. "Did you hear what I said? I told you to abort mission. Do you not understand me?"

"I lost my best gator to her. He almost had her 'fore she skinnied over that fence. Champ couldn't get his snout through, and then the cops came and took him."

Cormac lowered his forehead into his hand. "Why do I feel like you're not hearing me?"

"I tole you. It's what I do."

"Well, it isn't what you do anymore. Stop it. She's *not* a target. We had that one wrong."

"I didn't have *shit* wrong. You're the one givin' the orders."

Cormac grimaced. He'd almost gotten his son's girlfriend killed by a hillbilly and his circus of reptiles. He already had enough to apologize for—killing Charlotte would destroy any hope of reconciliation with his son. Somehow, he had to make this moron understand it was time to *stand down.*

"Do not, under any circumstance, try to kill Charlotte Morgan again."

Miles sniffed. "I wish you tole me that 'fore I lost my best gator."

"I did!" Cormac heard his volume rise and took a second to calm down. "Look, I've got a final payment coming to you, and then I expect you to slip back into the swamp from whence you came."

"What?"

"Piss off."

Miles grunted. "What about my gator?"

"I'll add extra for the gator."

"What about Knuckles?"

"Who?"

"My python."

"Fine. That too."

Cormac heard a metal utensil clatter into what sounded like a sink.

Great. More details for his brain to picture. *The man is eating canned meat over a sink.*

Miles sputtered, punctuating every other word of his sentence with an invisible finger poke. "You know what? You better believe you will. Unless you want to wake up with a wolverine in your Jeep."

Cormac scowled. "I don't have a Jeep."

"It's a figger of speech."

"I'm pretty sure it isn't."

Cormac heard Miles swallow.

My god, he picked the spoon up out of the sink.

Cormac could only imagine how dirty a sink in Miles' world might be. Again, he tried hard not to picture the meat being spooned into the man's mouth. For some reason, he pictured it with little webbed *feet.*

"Look, Miles. We're done. You told me you had intel. You said you've been *years* collecting it."

"I have."

"Notes scribbled on the back of a half-used napkin aren't intel. I asked you to do me a favor and waylay Charlotte, and then next thing I know, you're throwing a zoo at her."

"Ain't no zoo. I work with *wild* animals."

"That isn't the point. You were supposed to slow her down, hell, even kidnap her for a bit. You weren't supposed to try and *kill* her with a snake."

Miles chuckled. "If Knuckles had got her, it *would* have been a kidnapping. She just woulda been wrapped up in snake belly."

"I know you killed Jason Walsh too, *idiot*. They found pufferfish toxin in him. You haven't done a damn thing I've asked you to do right since the beginning."

Miles grunted.

Cormac sighed and turned on his car to get the air running. Miles had him sweating with agitation. "You have some really deep-seated issues, Miles. We're done."

"You still gonna put my money in that account?"

"Sure. I'll give you nine hundred." Back when he'd first located Miles, Cormac had been about to offer him ten *thousand* dollars for his information. Before he could even mention a price, Miles had pounded the table and demanded five *hundred*.

Miles cleared something rattling in his sinuses with a pig-like snort. "Make it a thousand."

"Sure." He wasn't going to give him a penny anyway. The only thing worse than a psycho was a psycho with a little cash.

He heard Miles suck his tooth with his tongue.

You don't want to miss a morsel of that sweet, sweet canned meat, do you, buddy?

"I'm gonna head back then," said Miles.

"Back where?"

"If I told you, it wouldn't be *back* there."

Cormac shook his head. "That doesn't make any sense."

"Back where Simone can't find me. That's all you need to know."

Cormac closed his eyes.

Stupid. He should have known when Miles kept referring to Jamie as *Simone*. It meant he couldn't have any useful intelligence on her. How much could he have uncovered if he didn't even know her real name?

He was about to hang up when Miles spat one last thought at him. "I'll tell you whut, though, Jim. If you don't catch Simone, I'll be back for her, you, and everyone around here."

Cormac put his car in gear and pulled from the curb, following in Seamus' tracks. He didn't like being threatened by anyone, let alone the sorry sack of flesh on the other end of his phone. His patience had finally ended.

"I'll tell you *whut*, Miles," he said, imitating the man's accent. "If I so much as see a *lizard* around here, I'm going to take you out. And I can promise you my gun is more reliable than your animals."

CHAPTER TWENTY-SIX

The prison guard jerked open the barred door and threw a cardboard box into the middle of the cell.

"Alright, Beatty, put all your crap in there. You're moving."

Beatty stared down at the box, blinked at the guard, glanced at Stephanie, and then looked back at the box. She stabbed a finger into the center of her own chest. "Me?"

"Yep. You're moving down the hall."

Beatty's eyes grew wide. "Why *me?* I've been in this cell longer than she has." She pointed at Stephanie, who leaned against the wall with her arms crossed against her chest, watching the drama unfold.

The guard motioned to the box. "Just move it."

Beatty jumped down from her bunk, glaring at Stephanie.

"This is *your* fault. You did something to get me moved."

Stephanie picked up the car magazine she'd borrowed from the prison library and flipped through the pages. She'd been learning how to replace a carburetor.

"I'm sure I don't know what you're talking about," she said without raising her gaze. When she did glance up, she spotted MuuMuu hovering behind the guard, just outside the cell door.

MuuMuu smiled and waved. Stephanie waved back.

Beatty watched the exchange as she began tossing things into the box. "Her? You got *her* moved in here?"

Stephanie returned to flipping the pages of her magazine. "Get your stuff in the box before I feed it to you."

Beatty gasped and addressed the guard. "You heard that. You heard her threaten me."

"And I'm going to *let* her feed it to you if you don't pick up the pace. Let's go."

Beatty huffed and reached for a roll of toilet paper.

Stephanie put a hand on the roll to keep her from taking it. "That's mine."

Beatty's face turned a shade of red Stephanie hadn't seen before as she bent to pick up the box. "You're going to pay for this."

"I doubt it," mumbled Stephanie.

The guard led Beatty out, and MuuMuu entered, carrying her own box of things.

Stephanie smiled. "Hey, girlfriend."

"Hey. I think you have a better window here," said MuuMuu studying the two-by-two square of light above Stephanie's head.

"I imagine they're standard, but we are south-facing."

Stephanie climbed into the top bunk.

"You've got bottom, MuuMuu. I can't spend the rest of my time here wondering when that seven-wonders-of-the-world body of yours is going to come crashing down on my head.

MuuMuu laughed. "You're funny."

Stephanie flopped back on the bed. "I'm just happy to have you here. You know, in case I get audited."

MuuMuu scoffed. "Worse part is, it wasn't even my audit."

"You broke the ribs of someone else's tax collector?"

"My mother's. She's a terrible person."

"The tax lady?"

MuuMuu shook her head. "My *mother*."

"Then why did you help her?"

"Because she told me to." MuuMuu sat on her bunk, and

Stephanie heard the bed groan.

"Even though she knew you'd get in trouble?"

"Uh huh. She was always doing things like that. She had me buy drugs for her from the time I was little. She—" MuuMuu cut short. "She did a lot of terrible stuff."

Stephanie hung her head over the edge of her bed to peer down at MuuMuu. "So even with all that, you tried to help her?"

MuuMuu shrugged. "She's my mother."

Stephanie rolled back to stare at the ceiling. "We have a lot more in common than you think, Muu."

MuuMuu stood again and stacked another roll of toilet paper from her box on top of the one Stephanie hadn't allowed Beatty to take. They had three rolls now. They were practically millionaires.

"When I got in here, I started counseling, and the group helped me realize I don't have to do what my mother says. Doc said she's a toxic person and what I did wasn't my fault. Said she doesn't control me, and even if she *made* me, I don't have to be made in her image. She isn't God."

Stephanie rolled on her side and propped her head up on her elbow. "They told you that, huh?"

"Yep."

"And it worked?"

MuuMuu grinned and held her arms out at her sides. "I feel free for the first time in my life. I feel like the world's off my shoulders."

Stephanie snickered. "You could probably hold the world on those shoulders."

MuuMuu laughed. "You're crazy."

Stephanie squinted at her new cellmate.

"Tell me more about what they told you in therapy."

CHAPTER TWENTY-SEVEN

Declan and Charlotte sat up in bed in unison, both with eyes wide. Somewhere a dog was barking, and a man was begging for the animal to stop.

"Abby," said Charlotte, sliding from beneath the sheets. She wore Declan's boxers and one of his t-shirts as makeshift pajamas. She and Declan had spent a good part of the evening speculating on who might have tried to kill him and where Miles might strike next. When it got late, it seemed silly to try and sneak her back into the house past Andy and Butch.

Who knew what sort of deadly animals might be strewn around her yard in the dark?

Declan stood and beat her to the door, striding toward his living room, Charlotte on his heels.

"It's Seamus. I can hear him," she muttered, recognizing the voice as they grew closer.

Declan flipped on the light and found his uncle with his hands outstretched in front of him, the door open wide behind him. Abby held him at bay, punctuating a never-ending growl with the occasional bark.

Charlotte scurried past Declan and grabbed the Wheaten by her collar.

"What are you doing here so late?" asked Declan. "You usually sleep at the bar on late nights."

Seamus looked at Charlotte, amusement lighting his expression. "Am I interrupting something?"

Declan rolled his eyes. "Charlotte's house isn't safe. It seemed a better idea to keep her here."

Seamus glanced down at Abby. "I think she'd be safe anywhere with this devil dog by her side."

Something about the shifty way Seamus kept glancing behind him made Declan uneasy. "What's going on? Why do you look so shifty?"

Seamus hung his head and ran his hand along the top of it from front to back, smoothing his fuzzy hair. "There's something I have to tell you. Something that couldn't wait."

"About Jamie?" asked Charlotte.

"No—"

Outside, someone closed a car door, and Seamus turned to shut the front door behind him. "I wanted to warn you—"

"What's going on?" Now Declan *knew* something was up. As Seamus' head turned, he noticed a mark on his uncle's cheek. "Why is your face red? You look like someone punched you."

"That's just it. Someone *did*—"

Someone outside knocked on the door.

"Who is that?"

Seamus held up his hands as if he were begging. "Listen, I need to tell you I didn't know—"

"Who is it?" Declan pushed past his uncle and flung open the door.

A man in a suit stood in front of him. His lip looked swollen, and his jacket hung at an odd angle. It took Declan a moment to realize the lapel had been torn. The man's dark hair flopped across one eye.

They stood staring at each other, silent.

The man looked a lot like him.

The visitor was older, but even in the dim light spilling from the living room, Declan could sense the truth.

"How...?"

The man's eyes rimmed with tears, and he opened his arms. "Declan. It's Dad..."

Declan took a step back to avoid the embrace. He whirled to face Seamus. "What is this?"

Seamus sighed and dragged his hand across his injured cheek. "I don't know. He showed up at the bar, and we, we didn't exactly get a chance to *talk*."

Declan turned back to his father and stood there, blocking the man's entry. He couldn't imagine a story that would explain why his father had disappeared, why he hadn't come back to claim his son when his wife went missing, or why he would show up *now*, nearly twenty years later.

"Please, let me come in and explain." Cormac looked past Declan to Seamus. "To both of you."

Declan took a deep breath and expelled it. He took a step back to make way.

"This oughta be good."

"I'll take Abby to the bedroom," said Charlotte.

Declan shook his head. "No. Stay here. You're part of my life now." He glanced at his father and muttered, "More than he ever has been."

Declan felt ashamed as soon as he said it. Not because his father didn't deserve his venom but because he'd sounded *childish*. Bitter. He could feel his childhood hurt and resentment swirling in a maelstrom in his chest. He took another deep breath to try and calm the storm.

I need to approach this like an adult. Don't lash out.

Charlotte let Abby sniff Seamus' and Cormac's shins and released her collar when the dog had decided the two men posed no threat. Bored with the guests and annoyed at being awoken, the Wheaten found a spot on the living room rug and flopped down to drop her head on her forepaws. The bruised brothers found places on the sofa beside each other, and Declan sat in a single chair, Charlotte in another.

"Talk," said Declan.

Cormac took a deep breath and held his hands out in front of him as if he were showing Declan how wide a loaf of bread was.

"Look, there aren't a lot of excuses for how I left you and your mother. I could say it was because I worked for the FBI and that the undercover work made it too dangerous to have a family. And that would be the truth. But the greater truth is I wasn't ready to be a father. I threw myself into my work until I'd convinced myself I had to leave you both to do my job."

"Did Mom know you worked for the FBI?"

"Yes, of course—" Cormac tilted his head. "Yes and *no*. She knew, but she didn't know the kind of work I did."

"Which was?'

"Undercover mostly. For months at a time after I left. I did the work most of the other agents couldn't."

Cormac leaned back with the hint of a smile curling at the right side of his mouth. Declan sensed *bravado*. His father was proud of his work.

He felt his mood darken another shade.

You'd do it all again if given the chance.

Declan stared at the floor a moment, quelling his urge to grab the man across from him and shake him. Scream at him. Hit him for what he'd done to the abandoned little boy he'd been. For what Cormac had done, abandoning his mother. Indirectly, he'd signed her death warrant.

"Mom disappeared. Did you know that?"

Cormac shook his head. "Not until about a year later."

Declan saw his father's expression soften. Pride had given way to...*regret?* Maybe. He looked sincere, but as an undercover officer, wouldn't he be adept at Oscar-winning performances?

Declan turned his attention to Seamus. "And you didn't know he was alive?"

Seamus shook his head. "No. I swear, Declan. Tonight I saw him for the first time since he left."

"I couldn't tell Seamus either," said Cormac. "He loved your mother. He couldn't have kept it from her."

Seamus shifted in his chair, clearly uncomfortable to find his brother had known he'd had feelings for Declan's mother.

Cormac patted Seamus' knee. "I always knew you'd take care of my family."

Seamus glared at his brother, and Cormac pulled his hand away.

"It wasn't fair of you to put me in the position you did. To make me take care of your grieving family when I couldn't do anything to make their pain go. Men came. Dressed like cops. Told us you died of a drug overdose."

Cormac nodded. "Yes. That way, I could send Erin money, and she would think it was my pension." He raised his hands to create air quotes around the word pension as he said it. "She could get on with her life."

Declan scoffed. "And more importantly, you could get on with yours."

Cormac nodded. "That's fair."

"Why are you back now?"

"I've been on Jamie Moriarty's trail for years. I'd been using Assistant D.A. Jason Walsh to trap Stephanie, so we could leverage her for information on her mother. Maybe draw Jamie out of hiding. But an asset I was using for the job killed the D.A. *Accidentally*, he said, but I have my doubts. He's got this weird thing for animals..."

"Miles Davis," said Charlotte.

Cormac turned to her. "You know his name?"

"He tried to kill me with a python and an alligator."

Cormac didn't react to Charlotte's odd confession. It was as if she'd said *gun and a knife.*

Declan leaned forward in his chair. "But you knew that, didn't you?"

Cormac nodded. "That might have been my fault. I'd asked him to stop you from helping Stephanie. He might have misunderstood what I meant by *stop.*"

Declan's cheeks flared with heat. "You asked a man obsessed with killing people with wild animals to hurt Charlotte?"

Cormac waved his hands before him as if trying to block the words his son spat at him.

"*No.* No, I *never* asked him to kill her. I mentioned to him I wanted you"—he nodded toward Charlotte—"out of the picture. He then took it upon himself to slide a snake through your window."

"But why would you work with a psycho like that?"

"He had a thing about Jamie. Hated her. Spent years hunting her. He claimed he had information..." Cormac drifted off and sighed, holding his son's steady gaze. "I didn't know about the animals. I made a call, and it was a bad one."

"But he'd already killed Jason," said Charlotte.

Cormac winced. "At that point, I thought Stephanie had killed Jason." He ran both hands over his head, pulling back his thick, dark hair from his forehead. "I'm afraid, in trying to catch a monster, I may have created one."

"Or at least enabled one," mumbled Charlotte. She looked at Declan. "Miles tried to kill Jamie before, you know."

"I know." Cormac's head cocked. "Wait. How do *you* know that?"

"Jamie told me."

Cormac cocked an eyebrow at Declan, who scowled.

"They're not partners. Jamie kidnapped her friends and threatened to kill everyone if she doesn't clear Stephanie."

Charlotte nodded. "And the good news is now we know Stephanie is innocent."

"*Innocent* might be a stretch," said Cormac. "In planning this whole thing, I did some digging on your ex-girlfriend. Did you know—"

Declan held up a hand. "We don't have to get into her past right now."

Cormac glanced at Charlotte. "Right. Of course." He pressed his lips together as if he'd fallen into deep thought.

Seamus stared at Cormac. His best scowl had been pointed at his brother since they sat.

"What're ya cookin' up, Mac?"

"Huh?" Cormac's mind appeared to return after a trip away. He looked at Seamus. "Don't call me Mac."

"I always called you *Mac* when we were kids."

"We're not kids."

"Nevertheless, I know that look. What do you have percolating in that head of yours?"

"Nothing. I'm just thinking, if Jamie is in contact with Charlotte, there has to be a way to use that to draw her out."

Charlotte laughed. "Sure. I can draw her out. I just do *nothing*. Stephanie goes to jail, and then Jamie shows up to kill everyone I know."

Cormac's eyes widened. "Maybe...?"

"No," said Declan and Charlotte together.

"We're not using my friends as bait. She'd kill half of them before you got to her...*if* you got to her at all," added Charlotte.

"You don't have much faith in me," muttered Cormac.

"You already admitted to chasing her unsuccessfully for years, getting a D.A. killed, and losing control of your animal freak," said Declan.

Not to mention being a lousy father and abandoning your family.

Cormac shook his head. "It doesn't matter. It wouldn't work anyway."

"Why?" asked Charlotte.

"I don't think she'd be the one doing the killing. It wouldn't be enough of a challenge. We know she has a little cadre of hired killers working for her. We suspect that's how she makes most of her money these days. Contract killings."

Declan's attention shot to his father. "Does she have a paragliding sniper?"

"What?"

"A paragliding sniper tried to kill me. Like the snake and alligator, we thought the paraglider might have been sent by Miles' boss—"

"But now we know that's *you*," said Charlotte.

Cormac shook his head. "It wasn't me. I don't even know what a paragliding sniper is, but I can tell you I didn't hire one." He rolled his attention to Charlotte. "The snake and the alligator, that was unintentionally me. Yes."

"So if it wasn't you..."

Declan frowned. "Then it *was* Jamie. Stephanie warned me I might be on her naughty list."

Charlotte's brow knit. "But why? You're helping to get Stephanie out of jail for her."

"She thinks I'm a bad influence on Stephanie."

Charlotte laughed. "That's rich. You told me Stephanie said you inspire her to be *good*."

"That's what Jamie considers a bad influence."

"So, Jamie thinks you're stealing her daughter from her?"

Declan considered this. "From her control, yes. Maybe."

If Jamie had a treasure trove of killers, why wouldn't she want her talented and trained daughter to be the jewel? Who could she trust more?

Seamus stood and walked to the refrigerator to grab a beer. "It would be nice if there were fewer out to kill you both. What about this lunatic with the snakes, Mac? Can you do something to keep him away from Charlotte?"

Cormac nodded. "I called him off. He's headed back to the swamp he crawled out of."

Charlotte sat bolt upright. "No!"

All eyes turned to her.

"Miles is the one who killed Jason. I *need* him. He needs to go to jail instead of Stephanie."

Seamus returned with two beers. He held one out to Cormac, who waved it off. He tried Declan and Charlotte, who both declined. He shrugged and put them both down in front of himself.

"Stephanie probably *should* be in jail," muttered Cormac.

"I don't disagree," said Charlotte, "But she didn't commit *this* crime, and Jamie's going to kill everyone I care about if I don't get her daughter out of there. The problem is, she doesn't remember much of what happened in the warehouse."

Cormac looked up and to the right as if he couldn't believe what he was about to say. "Because I hit her on the head."

"What?"

"I hit her on the head. He shot at her—I needed her down but couldn't let her see me. I couldn't let that idiot kill her. It didn't hit me 'til after he'd shot *at* her to trick her into shooting Walsh. Frame her for murder, which was never the plan. I was going to pin *kidnapping* him on her."

"But why would you think Jamie would try and help Stephanie if she were arrested?" asked Charlotte. "She's not exactly mother of the year."

"We had some evidence she'd been taking an interest in her daughter lately."

Something about Cormac's eyes told Declan his father wasn't sharing the full truth. "So let me get this straight. You were *there*? In the warehouse?"

"Yep. Hiding behind the rolls of moldy carpet."

"Why?"

"Like I was supposed to trust Swamp Thing to get it right?" He shook his head. "Though even I never dreamed he'd get things as wrong as he did."

"So you didn't know the A.D.A was already dead?"

"Not then. I didn't find out 'til afterward. The freak wasn't following my plan. That he had his own agenda. I'd only asked him to bring Walsh to the warehouse and tie him up. I didn't want to get one of my men involved."

Charlotte sniffed. "Because it isn't legal to frame people, even if you're doing it to lure a serial killer?"

Cormac glanced at her from the corner of his eye. "Something like that."

Declan held up a hand. "Hold on. So what happened after you knocked out Steph?"

"Miles ran, and I went after him. He got away, and by then, you'd showed up, so I couldn't go back in to check on Walsh."

Charlotte's head cocked like a side-eyed egret hunting fish. "If Miles thinks Cormac wants me dead, couldn't we use that to draw him out?"

"Use you as bait?" asked Cormac.

Declan shook his head. "Absolutely not."

Cormac pulled at his chin. "No, hold on, it's a good idea. Problem is he could be halfway into the Everglades by now."

Declan's shoulders unbunched a notch. "Good."

"How'd you find him in the first place?" asked Charlotte, and Declan knew she wasn't going to let it go. His back tightened again.

Cormac leaned over and cracked Seamus' spare beer to take a sip. "Serendipity. I'd followed a few leads and rumors about a man who'd tried to kill Jamie and lived to tell the tale. I staked his Daddy's land and caught him during one of his rare trips to civilization." Cormac hung his head and shook it back and forth. "The four days I spent on that farm were four of the most disturbing days I've ever spent in my life."

"So you can't reach him anymore?"

"I can call him."

"Call him."

Declan straightened. "Stop. *No.* We just got him away from

you."

Charlotte looked at him with the eyes of a child begging for a toy. "We *need* Miles. We need him to clear Stephanie."

Declan hooked a thumb toward his father. "What about him? He knows Stephanie didn't do it. He can testify for her."

Cormac laughed. "That's not going to happen."

"What do you mean?"

"You think I'm going to walk into court and testify that I was there? Every part of that makes me an accessory to the death of an A.D.A."

Declan glared at his father. "Yes. And it's the truth."

"Well, that *truth* isn't coming from my lips."

Charlotte leaned over and put a hand on Declan's knee.

"We'll draw Miles out and grab him. I won't be in danger. We'll make it so we can see him coming a mile away. And anyway, he's pretty bad at killing people." She looked at Cormac. "Could you call him now? Tell him you changed your mind, and you need me dead?"

Cormac tapped his fingernail on his teeth. "I think if I tell him you really *are* working for Jamie, he'd be mad enough to come running."

"Ah, but if you haul him in for killing the fella in the warehouse, will he flip on you?" asked Seamus.

Cormac shook his head. "He thinks my name is Jim. He's only caught a glimpse of me chasing after him. And while he didn't leave any fingerprints, I'm sure his DNA is all over the crime scene."

"And he has a long history of hating Moriartys, so the idea he wanted to frame Stephanie could easily be his own," added Charlotte.

Cormac looked at her as if he were impressed. "Exactly."

Declan rubbed his forehead. "I realize no one is listening to me, but I still don't like the idea of Charlotte being used as bait."

"We'll pick an ideal spot for the sting. Keep her safe."

"But what *is* the perfect spot? We don't know what animal he has left in his bag of tricks," said Charlotte.

"Let me see if I can get hold of him first." Cormac stood and pulled his phone from his pocket. He walked away from the group to stare through the back slider at the pool in Declan's backyard.

"You swim?" he asked.

He nodded, and Cormac mimicked him, nodding his approval. "I used to swim some."

Declan looked away.

Like that means we're tight now.

The volume was loud enough on his father's phone for Declan to hear it ringing until a voice answered.

"I thought we were done."

"Miles. I've changed my mind. New information. Charlotte Morgan *is* working with Simone. We need her dead, or she'll blow everything."

"Huh. Got me just in time. Was about to burn this phone and drop off the grid."

"Sure. Good. Can you make it look like an accident?"

Miles snorted. "That's my specialty. That's why you need me."

"Right. And I assume you'll be using an animal of some sort?"

"Yep. That's how I work. Don't look like an accident if there's a bullet in her." Miles laughed a low, throaty chuckle.

"Don't look like an *accident* when you throw an alligator at someone," muttered Declan.

Charlotte muffled a giggle with her hand. "*And* he cut my window. Are we supposed to believe the python cut the window with his teeth?"

Cormac turned away from them. "What, if you don't mind me asking, Miles, will your weapon of choice be this time?"

"Depends where she'll be. How much room I got to work with?"

"I'll get back to you with that information. Not long. Maybe an hour. Okay?"

"I'll be here."

Cormac hung up and turned back to the group, smiling.

"So, Charlotte, what animal would you like to be attacked by today?"

CHAPTER TWENTY-EIGHT

"What other animals would be in Miles' repertoire?"

Cormac sat back down and set his phone on the table. "That's a good question, Charlotte. I don't know that we can pigeonhole him into a particular creature, but maybe we *could* decide between small and large. Portable and less portable?"

"Speaking of pigeons, if she's *inside,* it probably won't be a bird or anything too big," suggested Seamus.

"You think he has trained birds?" asked Charlotte.

Seamus shrugged. "Who knows? I'm thinking anything is possible at this point."

She scrunched her nose in disgust. "If we try and make him go small, he might choose a *bug*. I think I'd rather face a lion."

"Depends on the bug," said Cormac, the side of his mouth curling into a smile. "Maybe he'll try and smother you with butterflies."

Declan rubbed his fingers against his temples. "This is the dumbest conversation I've ever had. 'If my girlfriend had to be attacked by a deadly animal, what animal would I want that to be?'"

Charlotte laughed and stood to pace. She needed to stop staring at Cormac. He looked a *lot* like she imagined Declan would look as an older man—a little more barrel-chested perhaps, but handsome, his dark hair flecked with gray. It was strange to see someone so similar and yet so different. She couldn't imagine how Declan must be feeling, faced with his aging doppelganger, meeting the father he'd long thought dead.

For now, they had too much to plan for Declan to confront his father, and he seemed grateful for the distraction. They *needed* to stay on topic. After all, they *were* picking the way she might die.

"What deadly animals are left?" she asked. "What are the possibilities?"

Cormac had also seemed rattled upon seeing his son, but the more they talked about the case, the more at ease he appeared. The strange reunion had become just another day at the office for him.

"When I was staking out the farm, he had cages for everything, big and small. He had this fifty-gallon bin of cockroaches—"

Charlotte slapped her hand over her mouth to keep from shrieking.

"He couldn't kill me with cockroaches, could he?"

Cormac shook his head. "I think they were for *feeding* something bigger."

"Why aren't we just staking out his place again? Why are we putting Charlotte's life in danger?" asked Declan.

"Way ahead of you. I already planned on putting men on his place, hoping that's where he'll go to get the animal for the job."

Declan looked away, visibly frustrated. "She shouldn't have to be involved. This is *your* problem."

"Here, here," mumbled Seamus as he finished his beer and retrieved the spare from where it had migrated toward Cormac.

"Blade—" Cormac stopped as all eyes turned to him.

"What about Blade?" Declan's expression darkened, and

Cormac's shoulders slumped.

Cormac huffed a sigh. "Blade's one of mine."

"*What?*" Declan stood. "You planted a spy in my *shop*?"

"That explains a lot," said Charlotte.

Cormac stood to face his son. "Not a spy. A protector. I knew these things with Jamie were coming to a head and knew you had a past with Stephanie—I needed to make sure you were safe."

"Since when did you give a damn about me?" Declan took half a step forward toward his father.

Seamus rose to his feet and pushed his way past Cormac to stand between father and son. He put a hand on Declan's arm.

"Easy, Dec. If anyone is going to beat the stuffing out of him, it's going to be *me*."

Declan jerked away from Seamus' touch and walked to his sliding glass door to stare into the backyard, his hands on his hips.

Cormac sighed. "Declan, I have so many things I want to tell you."

Declan shook his head.

"No water."

"What?"

"No water. I don't want Charlotte anywhere near water. Alligators, sharks, water moccasins, jellyfish...the water is too hard to control.

Charlotte perked, happy the conversation had returned to the capture of Miles, though it was clear Declan and his father needed to have a long talk.

Like *months* long.

But not *now*.

Even after a long talk, Declan might never forgive the man, and no one could really blame him. But she could see that Declan knew, for now, Cormac was a necessary evil. He had the resources and research to help them end Jamie's reign of terror for good. It had to be hard for Declan, being forced to work with his father before he had the time to *talk* to him. She wanted to go to the window and throw her arms around him.

The best thing she could do, for now, was to keep the topic on the situation at hand and away from father-son relationships until Declan could steal some quiet time to process his father's reappearance.

"I agree with the water thing," she said. "I don't want to be swimming with things I can't see."

Cormac, who stood staring at the back of his son, looked away and cleared his throat. "No, of course not."

"And not near people," added Charlotte. "We can't put other people's lives in danger."

"You have a car?" asked Cormac, his expression shifting from concerned to inspired.

"Yes."

"Then that's it. I'll tell him you'll be driving somewhere far away tomorrow. That's how he tried to kill Jamie. He put spiders in her car."

Charlotte shivered. "Bugs. I *knew* it."

"That *would* be a great way to keep things contained," agreed Seamus.

Cormac nodded. "Exactly. Spider bites are easy to cure when you're prepared for them. Anyhow, you'll never even get in the car. All we have to do is *watch* the car and catch him when he comes to fill it with whatever creepy-crawly he's chosen."

"So Charlotte will never be in danger?" said Declan, turning to face the group. His mood lifted.

Cormac shook his head. "No."

Charlotte sighed. "I'll just never be able to drive my new car again without thinking there's something crawling around my ankles." She looked at Cormac. "Can you try *really* hard to get him before he opens my door?"

"Of course." Cormac smiled and dipped to grab his phone from the table, dialing as he strolled toward the kitchen. "I'll give Miles a call back and set the trap."

Charlotte walked to Declan. He'd resumed staring out the window. She put a hand on the small of his back. "How are you doing?"

He jumped, clearly too deep in his thoughts to notice her approach. "Hm? Oh. I'm fine."

"I know it's late, but do you want Seamus and me to give you two some time to talk?"

"No," said Declan. "Absolutely not. I think I've had enough of him for one day. I need to..." His voice trailed off.

"Process?"

He nodded.

"Understood."

Cormac wandered back toward the sofa. "It's done. You need to pull the men off your house around eight tomorrow morning. Told him you'd moved base camp here, but your car is still there."

Charlotte nodded. "Good. But one question. If we catch him, how do we prove *he's* the one who killed Walsh? What if he didn't leave any DNA at the scene?"

"Stephanie saw his lightning tattoo. She can identify him." Declan glared at Cormac. "Since you made it clear you won't."

Cormac frowned. "No. I won't. But Stephanie's recollection is hardly useful. She has a motive to convict someone other than herself."

"That's a good point," said Charlotte.

"Ah, hold on..." Cormac tapped his phone screen. "Jason was killed by tetrodotoxin. From this." He held up his phone to show them the photo of a fish floating in what looked like midair. Beige, spiked, and spotted, it had large eyes and an almost smiling little mouth. Its face reminded Charlotte of E.T. from the movie of the same name.

"A pufferfish?" she asked.

Cormac nodded. "This is what Miles used to kill Jason. Like I said, the family farm was empty while we were waiting for him to show up, but I stopped by the place once after contact just to see if I could find his research on Jamie. That's when I saw the cockroach bin. I took this picture of the saltwater tank in the basement. I think because it was the least disgusting thing there. I hadn't thought of the fish as a weapon at the time."

"Maybe we can find the store where he bought the fish, too," offered Charlotte. She paused as an unsettling thought crossed her mind. "Did he put Jason in the tank?"

"Miles force-fed it to him if I had to guess. Jason's body would have become paralyzed, starting with a numbness in his lips and his fingertips. I remember thinking I smelled vomit as I ran past him after Miles, and that's consistent with ingesting poorly prepared fugu. At some point, his lungs seized, and he more than likely suffocated before his brain shut down."

"What an awful way to go," said Declan. "How do you know all this?"

"I've eaten fugu before. Prepared by a master, of course."

Charlotte stood with her mouth agape, imagining the horror of the A.D.A.'s death. She cleared her throat and tried to smile away her fear.

"On the upside, I'm feeling better about the spiders."

CHAPTER TWENTY-NINE

"This is all too weird for me. I'm going to bed," said Seamus, yawning. He poked a finger at his brother. "You and I will be having a long talk tomorrow."

Cormac grinned. "If by *talk* you mean another fistfight, I'm looking forward to it."

Seamus snarled his lip and stormed down the hallway to the guest room he'd been occupying for months.

Charlotte yawned as well. "I'll call Butch and Andy and tell them I need them to move tomorrow morning. Hopefully, I can convince them. I'll tell them it's Jamie's idea." She looked at Declan. "In the meantime, I think I'll try and get some sleep. Tomorrow could be a big day."

Declan moved toward Charlotte and hugged her to him for longer than he meant to. Embarrassed, he let her go.

She gave his hands a squeeze and then waved to his father. "Goodnight. Nice to meet you, Cormac. Even if you did accidentally try to kill me."

Cormac chuckled. "You too."

Charlotte shuffled toward the back of the house.

"She's a keeper," said Cormac, glancing at Declan.

Declan allowed himself a little smile. He felt tired. He didn't want to talk. He didn't even want to fight anymore.

"Do you need a place to stay?" he asked.

Cormac seemed shocked he would ask. He looked at his watch. "It's almost three now. I have a hotel at the beach, but I'd rather stick around here tonight if you don't mind."

"No. That's fine. I'll get you a blanket."

"Don't bother. I'll be awake. I need to make some calls and get the ambush ready. I can have some men move Andy and Butch by force if need be. Lot of moving parts to arrange in a couple of hours."

Declan nodded and headed toward his bedroom.

"Maybe sometime tomorrow you'll let me explain better," called Cormac after him.

Declan stopped and spoke without turning.

"There's nothing to explain. You abandoned us. Mom was alone. She ended up dead, and you still didn't come back."

"I didn't know she was dead."

Declan turned. "But you knew she was *missing.*"

"Eventually. Much later. I was undercover. I couldn't check in on you very often. I had to—"

Declan felt his anger flash. Turning on his heel, he took a step forward. "That's just it. You *didn't.* You didn't *have* to. You *chose* to."

Cormac sighed. "You're right. I didn't want to leave you, but your mother and I weren't getting along anymore. Best case scenario, my life with you was going to end up a string of weekend visitations anyway."

His jolt of adrenalin fading, Declan found himself exhausted again. He closed his eyes and held up a palm.

"What's done is done. Let's just get through this thing. I need you to concentrate on keeping Charlotte safe."

"Charlotte will never be in harm's way. But—" Cormac grimaced.

"But what?"

"I can't say the same for your other girlfriend."

"Who?"

"Stephanie."

Declan scowled. "Ex. Not *other. Ex.*"

"Right. That's what I meant. I have an idea for her."

"She can take care of herself."

"I suspect you're right. But maybe not against one person."

Declan's sleepy eyes widened. "Jamie?"

Cormac nodded. "When we arrest Miles and get Stephanie released, I want to make it look like she was released for cooperating."

"For turning on Jamie?"

"Exactly."

"Jamie will kill her. You know that."

"I do. That's the point. She'll want to do that personally."

Declan studied his father's face. He didn't look like a man who'd just come up with a good idea. No animation. No urgency. He looked like a man methodically working his way *through* a plan. One that had been in place a very long time.

"This was your strategy all along, wasn't it?"

His father nodded.

Declan frowned. "I don't know if Stephanie will agree to it. Her relationship with Jamie is complicated. She both hates her and longs for her approval."

"That's where you come in. She listens to you. I need you to talk her into helping us."

Declan stared at the ground and traced a line on the tile with his toes.

Now it makes sense.

He looked up at Cormac. "That's why you're here. So you could use me to manipulate Stephanie?"

Cormac shook his head. "What? No—"

"How did you get this case in the first place? Because they discovered your son had dated Jamie's daughter?"

"No, I mean, that's possible, but—"

"Did the undercover gig that kept you from me as a child just end last week?"

Cormac's brow knit. "No, it's been over for years—"

"So you've been free to visit me for *years*, but you still didn't come until you needed me to work on Stephanie?"

Cormac's posture deflated until he resembled a week-old balloon. "Look, I didn't know if you'd even *want* me to show up."

Declan pressed his lips into a tight line, staring at his father, before turning to head for bed.

"There was only one way to find out, coward."

CHAPTER THIRTY

I don't know how stupid they think I am.

Miles hung up the phone and looked at the cracked face of his watch.

Two forty-five a.m.

That didn't give him a lot of time to prepare. He'd told Jim he'd be ready to rig the girl's car at eight a.m., but he knew a trap when he saw it. All they had to do was watch the car. If he got within twenty feet of that car, they'd jump him.

FBI Man thinks he's so smart.

Miles chuckled.

So smart he told me about the new safe house.

Miles raised his binoculars as the bedroom light extinguished in the house he'd been watching. The girl, her stupid fluffy dog, the boyfriend, and two old guys, one he expected was Jim, were inside.

Jim never had any intention of taking down Jamie. *If he did, he never would have fired me.* Jim was scared.

She'd probably paid him off.

I knew it.

Miles didn't have time for traitors.

He put down the binoculars and turned the ignition key of the enormous truck he'd stolen.

"You're all going to die tonight."

CHAPTER THIRTY-ONE

Declan and Charlotte lay in Declan's bed on their sides, facing each other. The moonlight fingered through the window blinds enough for her to see his eyes.

"Are you okay?" she asked. Her eyelids felt dry and heavy, but she couldn't decide if she wanted to steal an hour of sleep or power through. Her mind raced with everything they'd talked about. How could she sleep with so much going on?

Declan smiled. "I'm fine."

Charlotte let a few more seconds of silence tick by.

"Because I'm here if you want to talk about anything."

"I know. I'm fine."

"I know." Charlotte took a deep breath. "You know what's funny?"

"What?"

"I'm nearly thirty, and I still can't help thinking what Mariska would think about the fact I'm sleeping in your bed."

Declan chuckled. "I think she'd be okay with this."

"Because she likes you?"

"No, because there's a Soft-coated Wheaten wedged between us with her butt in my face and her paws pressed against you."

Charlotte giggled. Abby lay upside down in the bed between them, her back paws pressed hard against her, one on her chest and the other firmly planted in the notch of her throat.

"She's like a furry chastity belt."

"And even without her, we've got my long lost father and my uncle in the next rooms, so Mariska has nothing to worry about."

"No, hanky-panky."

"Definitely not—"

The sound of glass breaking made all three of them jump. Abby burst into a barking jag as Charlotte grabbed the dog to keep her from leaping out of bed. She looked to the window in time to see what appeared to be a huge black tube thrusting through the broken glass of Declan's window. There was the roar of an engine, and Charlotte felt hot air strike her face. She squinted and turned away.

"What is it?" she screamed over the howl of the engine. It sounded as if a tractor-trailer had parked just outside Declan's window.

Before Declan could answer, a shower of black spat from the tube's gaping maw into the room.

At the open bedroom door, Seamus and Cormac appeared. Each running from a different direction, they nearly collided in the hall.

"Outside!" she heard Declan scream at them, and the two men bolted for the front door.

Abby leapt from Charlotte's arms toward the window, Charlotte flailing, too late to stop her.

"Abby!"

Charlotte swung her legs over the bed to reach for the Wheaten, but Declan's hand slithered around her waist and jerked her back into the bed.

"Don't get out!" he barked. He'd shifted into soldier mode.

Charlotte watched Abby land on the low dresser beneath the broken window, scrabbling to keep her balance. Quick as a ferret, she squirmed between the invading black tube and the jagged pane to disappear outside.

No!

Charlotte heard a man outside yell over the sound of roaring machinery. She turned to Declan.

"I have to get Abby!"

Declan's face stopped her from moving. His jaw was clenched, his eyes wide and wild as he pointed past her toward the tube.

Charlotte followed his arm and, for the first time, really *saw* the substance spewing from the flexible pipe in the window.

What she'd thought was some sort of chunky black dirt didn't act like dirt when it hit the ground.

It moved.

The floor pulsed with activity.

It wasn't dirt.

Insects.

Charlotte covered her mouth with her hand.

The floor writhed with spiders, cockroaches, ants, and larger bits she suspected might be scorpions. It was hard to make out the bodies in the dim light, and that only made everything more horrifying.

The cockroaches felt out of place. Certainly, cockroaches couldn't kill them. They'd joked about it earlier in the evening. Yet, somehow their creeping brown bodies arose in her the most panic. They certainly added to the vileness of the horde. They moved faster than the other bugs. Perhaps Miles had meant them to be herders, pushing his victims toward the slower but more deadly members of the battalion.

Or maybe he just had a lot of cockroaches he didn't know what to do with.

Either way, they were surrounded. She and Declan sat on a

mattress ark, adrift in a sea of multi-legged death.

A loud *boom!* echoed nearby, and Charlotte jumped.

"Was that a gunshot?" she asked.

Without answering, Declan reached over her to grab the bed sheets on her opposite side. Thanks to the Florida heat, even with air conditioning, they'd been lying on top of them, and she felt them tug beneath her as Declan pulled them over her and toward him.

"Make a sushi roll!" he screamed over the engine.

It took her a moment, but Charlotte came to understand his unusual request. They ate sushi together often. They always sat at the bar, where they watched the chefs roll their food into neat little rice tubes. In this case, the sheets and top cover would be the seaweed wrapper and rice, and *they* would be the tuna stuffed inside.

It was a brilliant plan, except for one thing.

They were on the bed.

They still had to drop to the floor.

This is going to hurt...

Together they rolled into the bed linens to create their human sushi roll, hoping the sheets would shield them from the insect army.

"Hold on," Declan said in her ear, his body pressed against hers. "You're on the edge of the bed. I'm going to roll us off so I land first. Try to keep your skull from knocking out my teeth..."

Charlotte whooped as she felt herself falling and stiffened her neck to keep her head from bouncing off Declan's. They hit the ground, with Declan taking the brunt of the fall. She heard the air escape his lungs.

"We have to roll out the door."

Rolling and scrunching like an inch worm, they worked their way through Declan's bedroom door. Charlotte strained her neck to catch a glimpse of the bugs through the top of their roll and had to take a deep breath to quell her panic. Her arms were pinned to her sides like the piece of tuna she'd been reduced to. If any of those bugs started down their little linen tube from the top or bottom...

Charlotte heard the sound of bodies crunching beneath them. Worse, she *felt* it.

"So *gross*," she muttered through gritted teeth as they folded their legs in to clear the doorway. They crumpled, rolled, and stretched their way down the hallway toward the living room until they felt they were a safe distance away.

"Unroll," said Declan.

Charlotte rolled with him until they were freed from the wrap. She leapt to her feet, jumping and shaking for fear something might be on her as Declan stood and did a similar dance. He half pushed her through the wide open front door, which hung at an angle, its doorknob missing.

Charlotte used Declan's friendly shove to gain momentum as she ran into the yard. She had to find Abby. In the clear, she stopped and surveyed the scene.

A large truck sat feet from Declan's bedroom window, where it had jumped the curb and left deep tire tracks in his front lawn. Printed on the side in bright coral and green colors, *Tropical Landscaping* shone beneath the glow of Declan's front entryway lights. Near the foot of the truck, Seamus and Cormac hovered over a man lying prone on the ground. She realized the engine roar had stopped. The flexible pipe they'd seen in the bedroom snaked from the back of the truck before threading through the broken window. Abby sat a few steps away from Cormac, Seamus, and the unmoving man, her tongue lolling from all the excitement.

Charlotte ran to her and began to inspect the dog for cuts. There were a few small streaks of blood on her front leg. She'd been lucky.

"Stay back from the window," said Cormac, a phone against his ear. "There are spiders and ants and—" He rolled his eyes so hard his head moved.

She glanced up at the window and hefted Abby into her arms to move the dog to the relative safety of the curb, far away from any bugs falling from the truck.

"Did Abby catch herself on that broken window?" asked Declan coming up beside her. He handed her his phone, and she used the flashlight to inspect the Wheaten. After poking through Abby's light tan fur, she was able to find the cut, but it wasn't deep. She hugged Abby to her.

"What were you doing? You can't go jumping through windows," she scolded.

Declan cradled Abby's snout and kissed her nose. "Are you okay, dummy?"

Abby gave his cheek a few slurps.

Charlotte rolled back to sit on the grass and then, thinking better of it, stood. "She seems okay. What just happened?"

Declan straightened and put his hands on his hips.

"It looks like Miles—"

"Do we know it's Miles?" she asked, interrupting.

Declan looked at her as if she'd just asked if the grass was green. "He just tried to kill us by pumping bugs into my house with a mulch shooter. I think it's safe to say that's Miles."

Charlotte turned to the truck. "Is that what that is? A truck that shoots mulch?"

"Yes. You never saw one before? The landscapers walk that tube around the plants, and it pumps mulch from the tank, so they don't have to haul and place it."

"That's pretty neat."

"Mm. I hate to break it to you, but the mulch shooter really isn't the big news here."

She shrugged. "It's still pretty neat. Great idea."

Declan put his finger under her chin and pointed her attention away from the mulch truck and toward the front door. "*Anyway*, to get back to us nearly being stung to death by insects, it looks like Miles tied a rope to the front door knob and secured it to that tree," he said, nodding at the large palm in his front yard. "He was trying to seal us in with the bugs."

"That was the gunshot we heard. Cormac must have shot the knob off to get outside."

They turned to watch Seamus and Cormac drag Miles' body from the back of the truck to the middle of the lawn. Charlotte guessed they were trying to keep him from being eaten by his own little monsters.

"They should open up that guy's skull for science," said Seamus as he approached, clapping his hands together as if Miles had been dusty.

Miles lay still, his hands now cuffed behind him. Cormac was barking orders to someone on the phone as he wandered out into the street to continue talking, undisturbed by bugs.

"What did you see when you came out?" asked Declan. "Did Cormac shoot him?"

Seamus hoisted up his pajama bottoms, his pale, bare chest glowing nearly as white as the gray hairs snow-capping his still-perky pecs. It was easy to see he'd been a bulldog scrapper as a younger man.

How much had changed, really?

"We found him like that, in a heap at the back of the truck. I think he fell and clipped his head on the bumper of the truck. He's got quite a gash."

Declan nodded, and Seamus waddled off toward Cormac on his thick, bowed legs, still trying to keep his thin pajamas from sliding off his nonexistent butt.

"Is he dead?" asked Charlotte, taking a step toward Miles. The large cut on his head glistened, matting his hair with blood.

Charlotte gasped. "There's Stephanie's coral." She pointed to the roadwork of red lines working their way around Miles' neck, peeking above the stretched crewneck collar of his t-shirt.

Declan squatted beside Miles and grabbed the blood-stained shirt with two hands. He ripped it down the back and tore a large piece away, revealing more of the lightning tattoo.

The two of them paused to study it.

"That's kind of amazing," said Charlotte.

Declan pressed the fabric against the man's head to slow the bleeding.

"He needs an ambulance. Make sure Cormac is talking to 911 and not just his own people."

Charlotte nodded and moved to Cormac. She overheard him talking, now in a more civilized tone. While he'd been on the phone for some time, she guessed he'd called *his* people first. Now she could hear he'd gotten around to calling 911.

She moved back to Declan. "He's calling them now." She glanced at Abby, who'd lowered herself into the grass by the curb. The excitement had worn off, and now she wanted to get back to sleep.

"You think Abby knocked him over?" she asked.

Declan nodded. "Or startled him. Either way, I'm sure she had something to do with him hitting his head."

Charlotte stared down at Miles and shook her head. "There had to be easier ways to kill us."

Declan snorted a laugh. "You'd think so."

Charlotte squatted down beside Abby and scratched behind her ears.

"You're our hero." The dog rolled to her side and stretched, ready for her belly rub. Charlotte leaned down to whisper in her ear. "But don't ever do that again."

CHAPTER THIRTY-TWO

Charlotte knocked on the window of the Cadillac parked outside her house. With a snort, Andy jumped in his seat and then rolled down his window, his eyes bleary as he peered out at her.

"Hey, I wasn't sleeping. I was just resting my eyes."

Charlotte glanced across him at Butch, who sat with his chin pressed against his chest, lightly snoring. The two of them took turns during the day and kept each other company at night, taking turns sleeping, theoretically.

Andy's hand shot out, and he smacked his friend in the stomach.

"I gotcha!" Butch screamed. He stared through the front window for a few seconds before his brain kicked in, and his head swiveled toward them. He offered Charlotte a sheepish smile.

"Oh, hey. I wasn't sleeping. I was just restin' my eyes."

Charlotte nodded. "I feel safer already."

"You're up early."

Charlotte yawned. "You have no idea." She spotted a bug on her shorts and flicked it away. It was only a fly, but she had a feeling she'd be a little more panicked around bugs in general for a while.

She spotted movement from the corner of her eye and turned to see Tilly slapping down the road in her purple, terry slippers and yellow housecoat, an ornate yet dainty floral teacup in each hand.

"Fortification for the troops," she said, handing one to Andy. He passed it to Butch and then kept the next for himself. Charlotte smelled coffee.

"You want one?" asked Tilly.

Charlotte shook her head. "No, but you're just the person I wanted to talk to."

"Me?"

Charlotte nodded and steered her a few feet away from the Cadillac.

"I think we need to have a heart-to-heart."

Tilly frowned. "Uh oh. Why does it sound like I'm in trouble?"

"I didn't make a big deal about it at the time, but I think you know more about the witness protection people under Jamie's thumb than you've let on."

"What makes you think that?"

"The way Butch and Andy looked at you when we started talking about the others. The way Andy elbowed Butch in the stomach when he mentioned inviting Pollock Johnny to a *meeting*."

Tilly pinched an invisible thing off the tip of her tongue. "I thought you might have noticed that."

"Uh huh. I'm also going to guess you might have some sort of support group going for these guys."

"Who? Butch and Andy?"

"All of them. The WITSEC people are stranded here, thanks to Jamie."

"You think that?"

"I do. You being an old victim of the witness protection program yourself, I think you feel bad for them."

Tilly snorted a laugh. "Feel bad for them? That doesn't sound like me."

Charlotte cocked her head. "Tilly…"

Tilly seemed to shrink beneath Charlotte's expectant glare. "Fine. Let's say, hypothetically, I might know something about something. Why do you care?"

"I'm wondering what kind of talent you have in that

group?"

"What kind you looking for?"

"I need someone who can trace a call and maybe use *that* trace to follow other activity on the opposite end of the line."

"Landlines or cell phones?"

"Cell on both sides, I think. Who uses a landline anymore?"

Tilly nodded. "I know a guy who can hack a phone."

"How about a pickpocket? Do you have one of those?"

"You're making me sound like the Walmart of criminals."

"If the shoe fits..."

Tilly offered a low, guttural giggle. "Pickpocket, you say? The old-school talent. A year ago, I might have had *two* for you on that front, but I think the one's lost a step. His hands are getting a little shaky."

"Can you arrange a meeting with these people?"

"I can take you to the pickpocket right now. She's just down the street."

"Really? In Pineapple Port?"

Tilly nodded.

"And she's definitely anti-Jamie?"

"Oh, they're all anti-Jamie. That goes without saying. It's the core tenet of the group."

"And Butch and Andy are members? Because between you and me, we caught the guy trying to kill me last night. I'd like to tell Butch and Andy, but I need them to pretend he's still at large, and I don't know what good actors they are."

"Why do you have to pretend?"

Charlotte looked over her shoulder. Butch and Andy stood chatting over their coffees, stretching their legs, clearly uninterested in what she might be sharing with Tilly. Still, she lowered her voice a notch softer.

"We're going to get Stephanie freed, but we want to make it look like she flipped on her mother to get out."

"Jamie will kill her."

"We know."

Tilly gasped. "You want to draw her out?"

"Yep. You think it could work?"

"I do. I don't think she'd hire out to kill her own daughter. Not even she could be that cold."

Charlotte rolled her eyes. "It's so tacky to hire out and not kill your own children."

"Exactly. The question is, how is she going to do it? She can get pretty creative..."

Tilly pulled what looked like a plastic magic marker from the big floppy pocket of her housecoat and took a drag off one end. A puff of white mist billowed from her dark red lips, and Charlotte caught the scent of vanilla custard.

"Is that a vape pen? Are you finally trying to stop smoking?" she asked.

Tilly nodded. "Doing pretty well, too, all things considering."

"Considering what?"

"Considering I don't want to quit."

"Ah, you'll be happy when you're done. Good for you."

"Thanks."

Charlotte stole another glance at her bodyguards. Butch had finished his coffee. The cup hung from the tip of his pinkie finger as he talked.

I could use some coffee.

She turned back to Tilly and tried to push away her craving for caffeine a little while longer. "So, do you think I can tell Andy and Butch what we're doing? They seem awfully afraid of her. I'm afraid they'll crack."

Tilly took a drag and stared at the Cadillac. Andy's sausage fingers pinched the delicate handle of his teacup as he sipped his coffee. He looked like a father playing tea party with his child.

Tilly shook her head. "Let's keep it close to the chest a bit longer. I'm not saying you can't trust them, but they're the ones Jamie has her eye on right now, so whoever her spotter is in the area might notice if they forget themselves."

"Spotter?"

Tilly waved a hand in the air as if she were backhanding the face of the entire neighborhood. "Oh, you know, she's got someone else around here checking in on them."

Charlotte looked around. If that was true, she'd have to be more careful sneaking in and out of her house. "Okay. They didn't notice I didn't sleep at the house last night."

Tilly nodded. "They've been out of the game a long time."

"Lucky for me. Can you take me to the pickpocket now? Is it too early?"

"Nah, she gets up early." Tilly shuffled past her to the Cadillac and thrust out her arm to retrieve her cups. The boys handed them over.

"We're going to go visit a sick neighbor if you guys want to take a break. I'll keep an eye on her."

Andy nodded. "I could use a bathroom break."

"Me too," said Butch.

"Go get yourselves some breakfast," said Tilly.

The boys got back into the car and drove off, Andy hanging his arm out the window to wave goodbye as they rolled away.

Charlotte started down the road in the opposite direction, Tilly slapping alongside of her. Tilly made a left and stopped in front of a house that looked very much like all the others in the neighborhood but for a statue of a female pirate in the front yard, nestled between two palm trees.

"Pandora the Pirate is your pickpocket?" asked Charlotte, recognizing the home.

"Think about it," said Tilly.

Charlotte gasped and put her hand over her mouth. "Oh my gosh. It's so *obvious* now."

Pandora had received her nickname, *Pandora the Pirate,* because it seemed every time someone in Pineapple Port lost something, *she'd* find it. Someone mentioned it was as if she were always discovering buried treasure, and the idea stuck.

Charlotte could barely remember a neighborhood get-together where someone didn't misplace their wallet or pillbox or purse and Pandora wasn't the one to find it, forgotten on a table here or there.

"She returns things these days."

Tilly grinned and knocked on Pandora's door. "She has to hone her skills. Use it or lose it."

The door opened, and Pandora appeared, wearing a floral-patterned tracksuit. She wore red reading glasses attached to a gold chain around her neck and held a paperback book in her hand.

She tilted her head as she eyed her visitors. "What are you two doing here?"

"We have a proposition for you," said Tilly.

Pandora's expression soured for a moment as she glanced down at the book in her hand.

"I was in the middle of a good chapter."

"It can wait."

She looked at her watch. Charlotte noticed it appeared both expensive and too large and guessed it was a man's watch.

"It's early."

"It's important," said Tilly.

Pandora huffed. "Fine. Come on in."

Charlotte and Tilly entered to find the familiar layout of that particular style of modular home. Pineapple Port only had a few different models, and Charlotte had seen them all.

Pandora put her book on the kitchen island. "Would you like a cup of coffee? I have the pods. I can make you one?"

"No, thank you," said Tilly.

Charlotte looked longingly at the coffee machine.

Shoot.

Pandora lifted a mug of coffee from her kitchen island to her lips. "So, how can I help? Do you need me to man a craft booth?"

Tilly shook her head. "I need your other talents."

Pandora trilled a laugh, her eyes darting in Charlotte's direction. "Shuffleboard?"

"We're taking down Jamie Moriarty," said Charlotte.

Pandora sputtered her coffee and lowered the mug, raising her other hand to cover a cough. When she'd cleared her airway, she looked up at them with teary eyes.

"Did I hear you right?"

"Yep. We have a plan to smoke her out."

"Don't say *smoke*," muttered Tilly reaching for her vape pen, but she smiled her most cat-like grin. Charlotte saw how excited she was by the prospect of bringing Jamie down.

"They're going to make it look like her daughter flipped on her. Draw her out of her hidey-hole."

"Really... That lawyer? That's her daughter? I saw the name on an office down the street. Nearly drove into a telephone pole staring at it."

"That's her."

Pandora scowled. "She's in on it? The daughter?"

"Yes." Tilly looked at Charlotte. "Yes?"

Charlotte nodded. "I have Declan talking to her now."

Pandora's pale, makeup-less lips wrapped into a tight circle. "Oooh. I like this. Makes me nervous, but I like it."

"So, will you help?"

Pandora smiled and raised her mug as if to cheer. "Oh, I'm *in*."

Charlotte smiled.

Jeeze, I need some coffee.

CHAPTER THIRTY-THREE

Declan tapped on the jail waiting room's plastic picnic table and glanced at his watch. His eyes felt tight from lack of sleep. Sleeping in his own bug-riddled house hadn't been an option, so after talking to the police, taping plastic over the broken window, setting off bug bombs, and sucking up the bodies with a Shop-Vac, he'd given up on the idea of sleeping altogether.

He had professionals there now, but it didn't matter if they tented the house and pumped it full of poison for a week. He suspected he'd never be able to sleep there again without feeling as if something was crawling over him. He was considering moving.

He rested his head in his hand.

I am definitely getting a new bed.

He heard a muffled scream and, through the glass, saw Stephanie being led to the door of the room where he was sitting. A thrashing girl was being pulled away by a guard. The prisoner only had eyes for Stephanie. Wild, *angry* eyes. She screamed again at her and spat on the ground as the guard on her arm was joined by another, and the two of them dragged the agitated woman away.

Stephanie never glanced at the woman straining to reach her. Her own guard opened the door, and she walked toward Declan with a smile as if she were coming to interview him for a job, and there *wasn't* a prisoner behind her suggesting ways she might die horribly.

"What was all that about?" he asked as she sat.

"What?"

"The girl screaming profanities at you in the hallway? Don't tell me you didn't notice."

Stephanie glanced over her shoulder. "Oh, was she talking to *me*?"

Declan chuckled. "Making friends wherever you go."

"If you must know, I took over the little cottage industry she had going on in here."

"You're making long-term plans?"

Stephanie shrugged. "Better safe than sorry."

Declan lightly slapped the table with both palms. "Well, you can give her back her business. You're being released."

Stephanie's eyes widened. It wasn't often Declan was able to surprise her, and he felt a flash of what almost felt like pride.

"I am?" Stephanie's expression darkened. "Wait. Why?"

"You're supposed to be happy."

"Not until I find out *why*. They found the guy with the coral tattoo?"

"Yes. We did. The hard way."

Stephanie's body relaxed as if she'd just been struck in the neck by a tranquilizer dart. "So it really is over? They can tie him to Jason's death?"

"Yes. And we're fast-tracking things for you."

"How so?"

"We—" Declan didn't want to tell Stephanie about his father's reappearance. Better to keep things uncomplicated. Best to not muddle her decision-making processes. Or give her ammunition. She was too cunning. Any weakness he showed her, she'd find a way to use it to her own advantage.

"We have someone from the FBI helping us."

Stephanie frowned. "Uh oh."

"Not *uh oh.* But we will need a favor from you."

Declan tried to look upbeat about the plan his father had shared with him. The plan *he* had to sell to Stephanie.

Stephanie's expression shifted from partly sunny to thunderstorm. "I assume there are conditions to my fast-track release?"

"Yes. We need to pretend we *don't* have Miles."

"But I'm still released—"

Declan saw the moment Stephanie put the pieces together.

"You want to use me as bait to draw out my mother? Make her think I flipped to get out?"

He nodded. "Yes."

"This is the FBI's idea?"

"Yes. But—"

"I'll do it."

Declan blinked.

Did I hear that right?

"You'll do it?"

Stephanie nodded. "I'll do it."

"Why? I mean, you're sure?"

"Yes. I've been working out my mommy issues in here with a friend. I think I need to stop Jamie. I need to be released from *her.*"

Declan wasn't sure what to say.

That was way too easy.

"Great. I guess. I mean, yes, that's great."

"What do you need from me?"

Declan's head tilted. He thought he'd still be arguing and hadn't loaded the next step details in his brain. "From you? Nothing really. We're getting a team together, and we have a plan..."

Which could end up with you shot, but we'll worry about those details later.

"When do you think I'll be out? Now?"

"No, not this second, but soon."

Stephanie seemed relieved. "Good."

"Good? You wouldn't rather get out now?"

She shook her head. "No. I want to say goodbye to someone." She stood. "Let me know when you know."

Declan nodded. "Will do."

CHAPTER THIRTY-FOUR

Tilly and Charlotte stepped onto Pandora's porch. Their plan had been shared, and Charlotte's stomach was growling by now. Now she needed coffee *and* bacon.

"I'll be in touch," said Tilly.

Pandora smiled and held out what Charlotte recognized as her own phone. She'd had it tucked safely in her pocket. She slapped her hand to her hip, searching for it.

Gone.

"I knew better," said Tilly, pulling her own phone out from her bra.

With a sheepish grin, Charlotte reclaimed her phone and followed Tilly to the sidewalk. Tilly had someone on her own phone, but she finished her conversation before they hit the curb.

"My hacker says we can come over. He'll be outside."

Tilly started down the road in the opposite direction of her house.

"Are we taking my car?" asked Charlotte.

"No. We don't need a car."

There were no homes within walking distance that weren't in Charlotte's own neighborhood. "The hacker is in Pineapple

Port, too?"

Tilly continued to shuffle forward. "Yep. He's over on Sea Oat Drive. Why? Did you think he'd have to be fifteen to be a hacker?"

"Now that you mention it, yes." Charlotte felt a flush of embarrassment. Here she was supposed to be a detective, and she'd never even noticed the interesting people living in her own neighborhood.

"He used to have a house over in Albacore, but he moved here recently."

Charlotte smiled. "They all move here eventually."

Charlotte spotted a man outside what she guessed was his home, wearing a white tank top and pajama bottoms checkered with cartoon robots. In his hand, he held a pink leash, but she couldn't see the dog at the other end. Only when they moved closer did she realize why.

There was no dog at the end of the leash.

It was a *cat*.

The man's gray kitty wore a matching pink harness. Its face was shaped like a sideways egg, the ears large and the coat thin and wavy. It picked its way through the bushes of his garden, stopping to sniff or dig through the mulch with a swipe of its paw. It didn't seem troubled by the leash at all.

Cat and owner did not appear dissimilar. The cat had great tufts of white hair sticking from its ears, as did the man at the opposite end of the leash. Both were overweight. Both had whiskers. Neither looked particularly happy to see Tilly.

The man nodded in her direction, and Tilly held out a hand as if she were asking Charlotte to admire a trophy. "Charlotte, this is Gryph."

Charlotte held out her hand, and the man grimaced. He bent his arm and lowered his elbow to touch her fingers.

"He doesn't like to touch people," muttered Tilly.

"You're looking at the leash," said Gryph, giving Charlotte a lazy once-over with his gaze.

"I am. Sorry. I didn't know you could walk a cat."

"I hate the smell of litter boxes. Reminds me of my ex-wife." Gryph wiped the back of his hand across his nose with a loud sniff, seeming suddenly agitated.

Charlotte nodded as if she understood.

I hope the smell of litter boxes never reminds anyone of me.

Gryph leaned over and picked up the cat, who hung limp in his arms and seemed to grow three notches more annoyed. "Come on in. We shouldn't talk out here."

Gryph glanced around as if every gutter, bush, and bird's nest in the vicinity had a tiny camera hidden inside. Charlotte thought him paranoid until she remembered *her* home *was* currently blanketed in cameras. Tilly had cameras stationed all over the neighborhood for her own obsessive surveillance.

Maybe Gryph wasn't so crazy to think he might be watched.

Charlotte motioned to the cat's wavy coat. "I've never seen hair on a cat like that."

"They all have hair. Except for the hairless ones," said Gryph opening the door.

"No, I mean the *wavy* hair."

"Chip is a Devon Rex. He doesn't shed very much, which is important for my work."

Charlotte walked inside and felt her jaw slipping slack. She'd expected to see the usual configuration of a modular home. A kitchen, a living room, a comfy chair, and some knick-knacks. The largest difference from home to home was usually whether it had hardwood, vinyl, or carpet or what the occupant's obsession happened to be. Some of the ladies loved roosters and some dolls. Some collected china plates.

Gryph was his own man. The home appeared as if someone had gutted the place and turned it into a Radio Shack. Checkered vinyl squares led to a living room area, sitting empty but for tables lining the perimeter, stacked with computers from various decades. Monitors, laptops, and other blinking devices she couldn't identify covered every inch of the tabletop. One table held a pile of cell phones.

It was a little like a low-rent Bat Cave.

"Hold it," said Gryph, pushing past them and setting the cat on the kitchen counter. "Stay in the blue box."

Charlotte looked down to find a blue-tape box had been laid out on the vinyl flooring, creating a small virtual prison.

Gryph sat his pudgy frame in a rolling office chair, the only available seating in the room.

"What do you need, Tilly?"

Tilly hooked a thumb toward Charlotte. "Not me, *her*."

"Tilly said you're good with phones?" said Charlotte, pulling hers from her pocket.

He snorted. "I *invented* them."

Charlotte paused. "You invented cell phones?"

"Basically." Gryph waved at the air. "All the important parts."

Charlotte couldn't help but scan the modest modular home.

Gryph pointed at her. "I see what you're doing. You're thinking, *Shouldn't this guy be rich if he invented cell phones*?"

"Thought crossed my mind," admitted Charlotte.

"They stole it from me. I had all the ideas, and the companies banned together and stole them from me. Bell Labs, Motorola...both of them."

"You worked for them?"

"No. I worked at home. But they must have found out what I was doing and sneaked into my house." Gryph's voice grew high and strained, the veins in his neck bulging. "They must have taken pictures of my circuit boards because there's no way—"

"Okay, easy, Gryph," said Tilly holding up a hand. She turned to Charlotte. "He gets a little worked up when you talk to him about cell phones. But it's not good for your blood pressure, is it, Gryph?"

He took a deep breath. "No." He grabbed the cat from where it sat on the floor beside him and pulled it into his arms to stroke it.

"It helps to pet Chip."

Tilly nodded. "Sure it does."

Charlotte looked at Tilly, and she motioned for her to begin.

Charlotte swallowed. "I have a phone number for someone we're trying to trace, but when I call it, I think there's another line that is then forwarded to her somehow, like a call service. I'm wondering if I get the first woman on the line, can you follow where she sends us? The third line?"

Gryph scowled. "You just want to know where the second phone on that side is?"

"I'd like to know everything about it if that's possible. Calls it makes etc. I'd like to track it—"

"You want me to clone it," said Gryph flatly.

"Yes, I guess."

"Do you have the sim card of the other phone?"

"No. That's the point. We're trying to *find* the other phone. We don't have it."

"Right. Well, one thing at a time."

Gryph thrust out a hand. "Give me your phone."

Charlotte hesitated. *Does every person Tilly knows want to take my phone?*

Gryph continued to hold out his hand. Charlotte moved to take a step forward.

"Uh uh," scolded Gryph, pointing to the blue line.

Charlotte grimaced and stretched to hand over the phone without crossing the tape.

Gryph took the phone and then pushed off to roll his chair toward the never-ending row of tables behind him. He plugged her phone into a laptop and began typing.

"Is this the number? Declan?"

"No, it's marked Jamie."

"Ah, got it."

Charlotte felt a nervous wave roll through her body. She didn't like the idea of handing her phone over to someone who could apparently do *anything* with it.

"Are you sure we can trust this guy?" she whispered to Tilly.

Tilly shrugged. "Probably."

"Probably?"

"Well, he *is* a criminal."

Charlotte rolled her eyes.

Gryph unplugged her phone and rolled it back to her. "Give Jamie a call for me. Try and keep whoever answers on the phone for a bit."

"Okay." Charlotte took a moment to work on a reason to call Jamie and dialed.

"Dirk's Auto Body," said the woman, answering. Apparently, the donut shop had closed.

"I need to talk to Jamie."

"We don't have a Jamie here."

"Yes, you do. And she'll want to talk to me. It's about her daughter."

The woman paused. "May I ask who's calling?"

"It's Charlotte. Do we have to go through this every time?"

"Hold please."

Charlotte glanced at Gryph to find him typing again. Strings of numbers rolled across the screen in front of him.

"What do you want?" said Jamie's voice.

"We have a development here I thought you should know about."

"What makes you think I don't know that already?"

"Then you know why I'm calling?"

Jamie paused. "No."

Charlotte couldn't help but smile, feeling she'd won some

small victory.

"Stephanie's being released."

"She is? You found the person who framed her?"

"No."

There was a pause before Jamie's voice returned lower and more measured than before. "You mean they're just letting Stephanie go for no apparent reason?"

"Yes. Lack of evidence, I guess. But she'll be free, so there's no reason for you to bother me anymore. That was the deal."

"They have another suspect?"

"I don't know."

Charlotte heard the anger flash in Jamie's voice. "Then you didn't do your job, *did you?*"

Charlotte heard a bang, and the line went dead. She looked at Tilly. "That didn't go well."

"I got it," said Gryph. He stood and handed her another phone.

"What's this?"

"It's Jamie's phone. Cloned. Any calls she makes or receives, you'll see."

"Can I answer them?"

"Go to this app to listen in." He pointed her to an app on the phone. The icon for it looked like an owl's eyes.

"Wow. Thank you. This should help a lot."

Gryph thrust his hands in his pockets and nodded. "Great. That'll be three thousand dollars."

Charlotte gaped. "What?" She looked at Tilly. "I didn't bring any money."

Tilly put a hand on her arm and began leading her toward the door. "You'll have it by the end of the week, Gryph."

He crossed his arms against his chest. "I'd better."

Charlotte was nearly through the door when she stopped and turned back to Gryph.

"Do you do tracker devices?"

"How do you mean?"

"Like a device I could slip into a person's pocket in order to track them."

Gryph pressed his lips tightly together as if in thought. "I could, easily enough. How soon do you need it?"

"Yesterday."

"I can do tomorrow. Six hundred."

"Deal."

Tilly pushed on Charlotte's back. "Let's get out of here before you're broke."

Charlotte chuckled. "Oh, I'm not paying for any of this."

CHAPTER THIRTY-FIVE

Charlotte had everyone meet her at the apartment above The Anne Bonny at one o'clock to plan their trap for Jamie. Cormac wore the same clothes he'd had on the night before, though he'd removed his jacket and had untucked his shirt. It was clear he'd never gone back to his hotel to change. She pictured him on the phone all day, barking orders to someone.

What is it about Declan's relatives? They show up, and they never leave.

Cormac and Seamus sat side-by-side on a striped, gold, and green sofa that should have been put out of its misery back in nineteen eighty-five. They were sharing an enormous tin of peanuts. Whatever animosity there had been between the two brothers had dissipated overnight, and they looked like any two boys lazing on a sofa in front of a television, waiting for their mother to come home. Both had their feet on a coffee table so worn and scratched it looked like someone had saved it from a wood chipper at the last second. Both wore shoes.

"Don't take your shoes off, love," called Seamus from his perch. "I haven't had this place cleaned since I bought it, and the floors make your feet black."

Charlotte looked down at the orange carpet beneath her

flip-flops. It had worn into a grease slick.

Charlotte shivered. "Not a problem."

I guess it's better than a house full of black widow spiders.

Maybe.

She padded over to a wooden chair across from Cormac and perched on the very edge of it, trying to touch as little as possible.

From her seat, she had a better view of the Bingham brothers' cuts and bruises from their scuffle the night before. Seamus had busted his brother's lip, but Cormac had caught him on the cheekbone. A deep purple bruise rimmed with yellow cupped Seamus' left eye, like a dark crescent moon lying on its back.

Charlotte turned her attention to Cormac. "Do you have an expense account with the agency you work with?"

Cormac tossed another peanut in his mouth. "Yes."

"Where do you think he gets all them fancy suits?" asked Seamus, winking at her.

Charlotte nodded. "Good. I need three thousand, six hundred dollars."

Cormac scowled. "Why?"

"For this." Charlotte held up the phone Gryph had given her.

"What is it?"

"A clone of Jamie's personal phone."

Cormac's jaw creaked open. "You're serious?"

Charlotte nodded.

Declan appeared from the back of the apartment, wiping his hands on a towel. He seemed to grow increasingly disgusted by the towel until he tossed it toward the tiny kitchen in the corner.

"Your bathroom is disgusting," he said to his uncle.

"I told you, it was like this when I bought the place. I haven't had time to clean up."

"You don't need to clean it up. You need to burn it down."

Declan grabbed the back of another wooden chair and placed it beside Charlotte's before sitting down.

"Your girlfriend made me a clone of Jamie's phone," said Cormac, holding up the device.

Declan nodded. "Great. You don't mind if Charlotte does something you haven't been able to do in—how many years is it you've been after Jamie?"

Cormac frowned. Apparently, Declan and his father hadn't spent the morning working out their issues.

"He's got you there, Mac." Seamus laughed and slapped his brother on the shoulder a little harder than he had to. Seamus wasn't ready to forgive Cormac quite yet, either. A few more passive-aggressive taps like that, and the two of them would be rolling on the ground again.

Declan looked tired. Charlotte couldn't remember seeing him ever look so *drained*. The fact they'd had no sleep the night before didn't help.

I probably look like forty miles of bad road myself.

"How are you holding up?" she asked, leaning toward him to lower her voice and still be heard.

He shrugged. "I'm good. I called in a company, and bugs are dying as we speak. But I honestly don't know if I'll ever be able to sleep in my room again."

"Don't think they can get them all?"

"I don't know. Hopefully. I stuffed a towel under my bedroom door, and not many made it out of there before I went in with a can of spray in each hand like a gunslinger."

Charlotte laughed. "How'd it go with Stephanie?"

Declan stretched his back, yawning as he reached for the sky. "She's on board."

"Oh, *good*. Nice job."

"Don't thank me. She's apparently had some sort of epiphany that has inspired her to throw her mother under the bus."

Charlotte chuckled. "With her, probably *literally*."

"How about you? The cloned phone is huge. Anything else?"

"Tilly hooked me up with *everything* we need."

Seamus had closed his eyes, his hands crossed over his belly. Cormac sat studying Gryph's phone like a child with a new toy. Feeling Charlotte's eyes on him, he glanced up.

"Has she used her phone? Do we know this works?"

Charlotte nodded. "She used it twice on my way over here. Her assistant called to let her know she has a flight booked for tomorrow morning at eight forty-five. I haven't had the chance to look up the gate, but that will be easy enough."

"You got a flight number? Did she say what airport she's leaving from?"

"She mentioned the flight number, and I matched it with the leaving and arrival times to find the airline. She's leaving Buenos Aires to come here."

Cormac grimaced. "It's tempting to have her picked up there, but *no*. We need to catch her in the act, and better to get her on American soil to avoid complications."

Charlotte perked. "Oh, that reminds me. We need eyes on her from the moment she steps off the plane, which means we need to buy tickets to get to her gate."

Cormac nodded. "Not like the good old days when you could roam wherever you wanted in an airport. I'll send some men."

Charlotte shook her head. "She'll spot FBI a mile away. We don't want her on her toes."

"You have a better idea?"

"Yup. I have two women *perfect* for the job. Jamie will spot them within seconds of getting off the plane."

Cormac's brow knit. "You just said I couldn't send in my men *because* they'd be spotted."

"Yes, but spotting agents and spotting two doddering old ladies inspire very different reactions. Jamie's not stupid. She knows this could be a trap. If she sees my ladies, she'll think *I'm* trying to trap her. She'll laugh to think I'd try. If she spots guys talking into earpieces...whole different ballgame."

Cormac sniffed. "Hm. I don't love the idea of using civilians. How will your spotters be spotted? You're going to have them wave at her?"

"Don't worry about that. I'll just tell them *not* to be spotted, and it'll happen naturally." Charlotte smirked. "Plus, Jamie might recognize one or both of them by sight. I don't know how much she's researched my friends while planning to slaughter them all. Either way, she'll know they aren't a real threat."

Cormac stood and thrust his hands in his pockets, staring at the ground as if in thought. "And we have someone to bug her?"

Declan groaned. "Don't say *bug*."

Charlotte chuckled, nodding. "Once the spotters see her, they'll notify Pandora, who'll drop the tracker on her."

"Who's Pandora?"

"My pickpocket. She'll tag her without her knowing."

"You have a personal pickpocket now?" asked Declan.

Charlotte grinned. "I think I do."

"Why not just have Pandora meet her at the gate? Tag her there?" asked Cormac.

"Even with a disguise, Jamie might recognize Pandora—she's one of her witness protection clients. Better to have Pandora do her thing at the pickup curb where it's busy, and she can move away quickly. Plus, by then, Jamie will have spotted the two women following her and think she's already one step ahead."

A rattling snore ripped from Seamus' gaping mouth, and Cormac kicked his foot. Seamus opened his eyes with a snort.

"Huh? What? Did I miss something?"

Cormac shook his head and returned his attention to Charlotte. "You said Jamie made two calls?"

"She made a call to someone asking for what sounded like a *Barrett*? He said he could get it for her on this side. I assume he meant this side of her flight."

Declan's chin lifted. "A Barrett?"

Charlotte nodded. "I think so. That call was a little hard to hear. You know what that means?"

Declan grimaced. "It's a sniper rifle."

"Did you catch a name? The number's on the phone?" asked Cormac, picking the cloned phone off the table again.

"The number should be on there."

"I'll run it through the system and see if it's a known arms dealer."

The phone in Cormac's hand rang, and everyone straightened except Seamus, who had fallen back to sleep, a thin line of drool slowly rolling from his mouth.

Charlotte jumped to her feet and showed Cormac where to tap on the listening app. Cormac hit the speaker, and a woman asked if the recipient of the call was willing to accept a call from prison. The woman on the other end of the line agreed.

"Hello?"

"*Stephanie*," lipped Declan. Charlotte nodded.

"So you're free?" asked a new voice. Charlotte recognized it as Jamie.

"No. I mean, soon. They, uh, caught someone else, I think," said Stephanie, stammering.

"Really? Well, that's good. I guess Charlotte did her job."

"I guess."

"I thought I'd come to see you."

"Why?"

"I'm your mother. I need a reason?"

"You're *my* mother. You *do* need a reason."

Jamie ignored the comment. "I have something for you."

"What?"

"Something that should help you going forward. In case they *don't* have someone else to pin this on."

"What?"

"You'll see when I get there."

Stephanie sighed. "Fine. It's not like I can stop you."

"You know that big fountain outside the Baptist church down the road from your office?"

"Yes."

"Let's meet there. I'll bring a little lunch for us. It will be a nice picnic spot."

Stephanie barked a flat laugh. "You want to have a picnic with me?"

"Sure, why not?"

"Fine. Tomorrow?"

"Tomorrow. I already have a flight scheduled."

"Okay."

Stephanie hung up, and the line went dead.

Declan chewed at his lip, looking as if his mind had packed up and taken a vacation.

"What are you thinking?" asked Charlotte.

His gaze snapped to hers. "There's an office park not far from that fountain Jamie mentioned. The one building is tall."

"Tall enough for Jamie to snipe from?" asked Cormac.

Declan nodded. "It would be perfect."

"So this is it. We know where Jamie's going to be at one o'clock tomorrow. She'll be on that roof."

Charlotte lowered herself back onto the edge of her seat. "And even if you have trouble pinning Jamie to her other crimes, you'll have her on the attempted murder of her daughter."

Cormac grinned. "Exactly."

CHAPTER THIRTY-SIX

"Wait. I need to get an Auntie Anne's Pretzel." Mariska veered away from Darla's side and headed for the airport kiosk.

"Now? You have to eat *now*?"

"My blood sugar is low."

Darla clucked her tongue. "You don't have blood sugar problems."

"Yes, I do. And who knows if her plane will come in on time. We could starve to death waiting for her. She's coming in from Mexico."

Darla's expression pinched. "I think Charlotte said her flight was coming from Buenos Aires."

Mariska nodded. "Right."

"But you said Mexico."

"Same thing."

"I think Buenos Aires is in South America somewhere. Our tickets are to Rio de Janeiro. I think this is the South American wing of the airport."

Mariska paid the woman and took her pretzel. "Right. Mexico."

"Give me some of that." Darla tore a hunk of the pretzel for herself as they continued to Jamie's gate.

"I should punch her in the nose," said Mariska.

"Who?"

"This Jamie person."

"We're supposed to be *sneaky* for Charlotte's plan. Punching the woman in the nose as she's stepping off the plane wouldn't be very sneaky."

Mariska took a bite of her pretzel. "I know. We *will* be sneaky. But after what she did to Bob and me—kidnapping us from our homes in the middle of the night..."

"You're right. You should punch her in the nose."

"I should."

"But we have to stick to the plan."

"I know."

"We—" Darla spotted another kiosk. "Hey, do you want some lemonade?"

"That's a good idea. We'll probably get thirsty from the salt on the pretzel."

"Does this have salt on it? Or just sugar?"

"Both, I think. We'll get thirsty either way."

The women veered toward the kiosk covered with images of dancing lemons and ordered their drinks.

"They have lots of good stuff in airports. We should come here more often," said Darla, poking a straw into her drink.

They headed toward Jamie's gate again, both sipping in silence.

"This is it," said Mariska as they grew close.

Darla surveyed the area, searching for an inconspicuous place to settle camp. "Let's sit over there across the hall. We can still see where they'll be deboarding, but we won't be too close."

Mariska followed where she pointed and nodded her approval. "Good idea."

They wandered to a large bank of empty chairs and sat down.

"I have to pee," said Mariska the moment her tush hit the seat.

Darla looked at her watch. "You better hurry. She's going to be here soon."

Mariska stood and tottered back down the hall. Darla looked over her shoulder at Jamie's gate, feeling nervous butterflies dancing in her tummy. Would they recognize her? Would she be wearing a disguise?

Darla slapped her leg and let out a groan.

A disguise. We should have worn a disguise.

How could she have missed a chance to wear a disguise? She'd been *looking* for a chance to wear the blonde wig she bought for Halloween three years ago. *Stupid.*

Darla spotted Mariska returning with another woman in tow.

"Is that your friend?" said the other woman, pointing at Darla as they neared.

What fresh hell is this? Weirdos seemed to gravitate to Mariska, and this lady didn't look like the brightest bulb on the tree. She wore one tall white and one short red sock beneath the bells of her flapping blue pants.

"Come sit with us," Darla heard Mariska say.

Darla groaned. "What's going on? Who's your friend?" she asked, with what she hoped was enough strain in her voice to make it clear to Mariska that she shouldn't involve random women in their spy operation.

Mariska didn't seem to notice. "This is Mindy. She's from Detroit. I met her in the bathroom. We think her grandmother and my grandmother might have known each other."

"No kidding. Hi, Mindy."

"Hello to you."

Mindy sat across from them and ruffled through her purse. Darla leaned as Mariska took a seat beside her.

"What are you doing?" she whispered through gritted teeth.

"If there are three of us, we won't look so much like *us*," whispered Mariska. She tapped her temple with a bright pink ceramic nail. "Pretty sneaky."

Darla rolled her eyes.

Mindy pulled her phone from her purse.

"I'll show you my crafts," Mindy announced as if they were in for a treat. She flipped through the photos on her phone, thrusting out the screen for Darla and Mariska to glimpse every third or fourth photo.

"I made this vase for my granddaughter. You can see the glitter on it. She likes flowers. I painted it purple because purple's her favorite color."

Darla nodded and glanced over her shoulder. Jamie's plane had arrived at the gate.

"These are placemats I made by weaving together recycled plastic," said Mindy so loudly that Darla's head jerked back in time to have a phone thrust toward her nose. Her eyes crossed, trying to see the photo on the screen. "I cut them from clothes-washing bottles mostly. Some soap and some softeners, but you can use anything, and it helps save the environment."

Darla glared at Mariska, but Mariska refused to make eye contact with her.

Even you know what you've done.

Mindy clearly had decided she didn't want her new friends to miss *any* of her photos. She held the screen toward them *as* she flipped through, her nails clicking on the glass as she tapped and slid photo after photo.

"That's outside my house where we were digging a new septic system. That's my daughter-in-law, that's me and my favorite horse, that's my Maltese when I painted her pink with food coloring for an Easter party, that's the duck pond when it froze over—"

Darla saw a flash of red slide by. "Was that *blood*?"

"Hm? Oh..." Mindy flipped back a few photos to what looked like a scene from a horror movie. "We slaughter our own pigs at the farm."

Mariska gasped and covered her mouth with her hand. "I

thought you lived in Detroit.

"Just outside the city. It's a working farm."

"For the love of—" Darla pulled her gaze away and noticed the woman at the counter in front of Jamie's gate was changing the city of departure behind her to Bogata.

"Something wrong. It says Bogata."

Mariska followed her gaze. "I think that's in Africa. I'll go check."

"Oh no, you don't," said Darla standing quickly. "You stay here with Mindy."

"Did I show you my Imperial Shitzu?" asked Mindy.

Darla strode across the hallway to the woman at the desk.

"Is the plane from Buenos Aires still coming in here?"

The woman shook her head. "No, I'm sorry, they're coming in at gate twelve now."

Darla checked the gate number on the wall behind the woman.

"But this is gate forty-eight."

"Yes. They moved the flight."

"But how far away is *twelve*?"

The woman smiled. "Oh. It's pretty far. Maybe an eight-minute walk?"

Darla gasped. "Which direction?"

The woman pointed back the way they had come. "That way."

"Is it still on time?"

"It came in about five minutes ago."

"Holy—" Darla heard a little scream escape from her lips and covered her mouth to stop it.

We're going to ruin Charlotte's whole plan.

She turned and saw Mariska still looking at Mindy's phone.

No. Not *us*. *Mindy* and her phone scrapbook from hell are ruining Charlotte's whole plan.

Darla walked as fast as she could back to Mariska. She could hear Mindy flipping through photos as she approached.

Tic tic tic.

"They changed the gate," she said, grabbing her purse.

"What?"

"They changed the gate. She's coming in at gate twelve, and the plane's already been there five minutes."

Mariska yipped and began rocking back and forth until she'd revved enough momentum to propel herself from the chair.

"We have to go, Mindy. I hope you have a nice trip."

Mindy frowned. "You have to go? That's a shame. I didn't get to show you our chicken coop."

"I don't want to see your damn slaughtered chickens," said Darla breaking into a jog.

"Slow down! I can't walk as fast as you," called Mariska.

Darla turned to see Mariska trailing behind her and motioned for her to hurry.

"You're going to have to walk faster. We're going to *miss* her."

"I can't!"

Frantic, Darla twirled like a whirling dervish, searching for a way to move Mariska *faster.* As if answering a prayer, a man appeared in the hallway before her, driving a small motorized cart. He parked beside her, nearly clipping her hip as she spun. Lumbering from the cart's torn plastic seat, he made his way on bowed legs toward a woman who appeared to be waiting for him at one of the gates.

The cart remained beside her.

Key in the ignition.

Unattended.

"Cart," she said, grabbing Mariska's arm as she came up beside her, panting.

Mariska huffed. "Oh, good. You got us a driver?"

Darla glanced at her. "Sure. Yep. Get in."

Mariska moved toward the passenger seat, Darla prodding

her in the back as she climbed. Once she was secured, Darla ran around the opposite side and hopped in the driver's seat.

"You're the driver?" asked Mariska.

"Yep."

"I don't understand. Did you rent it? Do you put quarters in it to make it—*whoop!*"

Darla stomped on the pedal, and Mariska flew back with a squeal.

Mariska steadied herself by leaning on Darla's shoulder. "You're stealing this," she hissed.

"Yes."

"You're going to get us *arrested*."

"Can't help it. We have to get to gate twelve. Charlotte will never forgive us if we mess this up."

Darla wove through commuters and vacationers on their way to their gates. The cart wouldn't go very fast, but it moved speedily enough that avoiding people unprepared for her approach became a challenge.

A man wearing a large sombrero wandered directly in front of her, and Darla swerved hard to the right, nearly taking out a suitcase rolling at the side of a woman wearing form-fitting running clothes.

"See? Mexico!" said Mariska, pointing at the sombrero as it flew from the man's head and rolled down the hall.

"Move it! Move aside!" barked Darla.

As they closed in on gate twelve, Darla spotted a woman matching Jamie's description ahead of them.

"Is that her?" she asked, taking her right hand off the steering wheel long enough to point.

Mariska's hand appeared from her purse, holding the image of Jamie that Charlotte had provided them for identification.

"I can't tell. Does she look like this?"

Darla glanced at the flapping photo, trying to compare it to the woman ahead of her. There was a scream as a woman dove out of her way, and Darla shifted her attention back to driving. In her attempt to avoid the cart, the screaming woman stumbled into a man whose backpack swung from his shoulder and fell to the ground in front of the vehicle.

Darla swerved, caroming into a silver trashcan. The resulting clatter sounded like an entire brass band had marched off the edge of a building and fallen to the sidewalk below.

Jamie's head swiveled, and Darla watched a smile spread across their quarry's face.

"She's seen us," she whispered to Mariska.

The cart stopped, the trashcan wedged beneath its front.

Jamie turned and continued walking.

Darla looked away, only to find all eyes on them.

"Let's go."

Mariska huffed. "I spilled half my pocketbook—"

"Let's *go*." Darla hopped out of the cart and followed Jamie. She glanced back to find Mariska grabbing Lifesavers and a mini-pack of tissues from the ground before following.

Darla watched Jamie gain ground on her as she wove through the crowd. The woman was too fast. Darla looked behind her to see Mariska wincing, her legs bothering her from the stress of rushing.

Darla grunted, trying to find a new gear and close the gap.

I'll never keep up.

She pulled her phone from her pocketbook and called Charlotte.

"We're following Jamie now. She's on her way out."

"Okay. Let us know when she gets to the luggage claim or an exit."

"I'll try. She's fast. And..."

"And what?"

Darla took a beat, bracing herself to deliver the bad news. "I think she saw us."

"That's okay. Keep an eye on her."

Charlotte seemed unfazed.

"Do you understand what I'm saying? I think Jamie knows we're following her."

"Don't worry. Just try and keep track of her."

"Okay..."

"Is there anything else?"

Darla glanced behind her.

"We might be arrested at any moment."

"What? Why?"

Darla saw Jamie stop at her luggage carousel.

I've done it. I've caught up with her.

Darla grinned.

"Long story. She's at luggage carousel four."

"Great. That's perfect. Call me back when you get to your car. Let me know you're safe."

Darla grimaced. "I will. Maybe. If we're not arrested. But even then, you'll be my first call. Bye."

CHAPTER THIRTY-SEVEN

Declan knocked on Blade's door.

I shouldn't be doing this. I don't have time.

He glanced at his watch. In a few hours, he'd be headed to the top of a building, hoping to stop Jamie from shooting her own daughter. Yet, here he was at Blade's house, his father standing behind him.

Why?

For some reason, he felt the need to confront the giant who'd been hiding in plain sight, pretending to be his employee, when all along, he'd been spying for his father.

He couldn't help himself.

I should just fire him and forget he ever existed.

Nope.

Can't.

My feelings are hurt, and, dammit, I want an explanation.

Though Blade had always been a bit standoffish with him, on some deeper level, he'd felt they'd become friends.

Was it all an act?

No sooner had Declan parked outside Blade's house than his father pulled up behind him. He didn't know whether Cormac had guessed where he'd been headed or if the old man didn't trust him.

Maybe Cormac thought he was on his way to warn Jamie. The idiot had already nearly *killed* Charlotte with his misplaced suspicions.

It didn't matter. He glanced at his father to be sure the old man knew he'd been spotted and then ignored him, choosing to head for Blade's door without further conversation. Cormac shadowed him and now stood behind him, silent, as they waited for a response.

Blade opened the door looking flustered, a towel wrapped around his waist. His grin collapsed like a faulty umbrella upon spotting his boss, standing behind his "boss."

Blade's eyes softened. He almost looked as if he might cry.

"I'm sorry, man."

"Can I come in?" asked Declan.

"Me too," added Cormac, waving like a wise guy.

Blade stepped back and let them both inside.

Cormac peeked behind the living room table. "That freaky cat of yours isn't here, is he?"

"He's with his *real* daddy," said Blade, sounding defeated. Declan couldn't be sure if Blade's disappointed tone had to do with himself or the neighbor's cat. Maybe both.

Blade sat on the sofa. The bottom edge of the furniture had been shredded into a wig of flower-print threads. Declan chose to sit on the edge of a worn reclining chair.

"I guess you're pretty mad," said Blade.

"That you were a spy in my own shop?" Declan spat the sentence before he could stop himself. He hadn't thought he was as angry as he was. He stared at his toes and took a deep breath.

Blade shifted in his chair, lifting one foot and then the other. Declan couldn't tell if he was uncomfortable with the topic or wanted to cross his legs and couldn't in the bath towel he wore without flashing the room.

"I want you to know I love working at your shop. I really

do. That wasn't fake. Dec, I have more fun—"

Declan's head snapped up. "Did you just call me *Dec*?"

Blade's enormous forehead scrunched into a rowed hillside fit for farming. "Yeah?"

"That's the most affection you've shown me since you started."

Blade frowned. "I apologize for that too, man. I was protecting myself. I like to keep people who might be killed at arm's length. It's too hard on me."

"You thought I might be *killed*?"

"Well, sure. I assumed that's why Cormac had me watching you."

Declan looked at his father.

Cormac shrugged. "If Jamie caught wind of how close I was to her."

Declan scoffed. "Were you, though? Without Charlotte's help?"

Cormac dismissed him with a wave. "Don't pretend to know about my investigation."

Declan rolled his eyes and turned to Blade. He felt his anger toward the big man dissipating. Blade looked so sad it was hard to stay angry. And Blade was only doing his job. His *father* was the jackass who'd put him in the shop.

"You were always sweet to Charlotte," Declan muttered.

Blade smiled wide enough to flash the gap where his first molar used to be. "Well, sure. Why would anyone ever kill Miss Charlotte?" He caught himself. "I mean, until recently."

Cormac raised his right hand, index finger pointed to the sky, and circled it. "Okay, if you guys could wrap up this bromance, we've got work to do."

Declan ignored his father, his mind drifting to thoughts of the pawn shop. Sales had *soared* since hiring Blade. Staying mad at the man would be a poor business decision.

"Does this mean you're going to leave me? I mean, leave the

Hock o'Bell?"

Cormac dropped his raised hand to his side with a thud. "Of course, it means he's going to leave—"

"I'm not leaving," said Blade.

Cormac's gaze snapped to Blade. "What?"

"I quit, Cormac."

Cormac's mouth hooked to the right, the tilt of his head following. "You're *kidding* me."

"No. I'm due for retirement, and I quit. I like it here in Charity. I like working with the people and selling in the shop." He looked at Declan. "I mean if you'll still have me."

Declan almost yelped with joy, but he caught himself and cleared his throat. "Sure. I mean, I'm not the sort who holds a grudge. And you *were* trying to protect me, anyway."

Cormac barked a laugh. "Come *on*. This is ridiculous. Blade, you've been threatening to quit for fifteen years."

"I mean it this time. I found my place."

"Selling old people's old stuff to other old people?"

"It isn't just old *stuff*. It's stuff people loved."

Declan silently echoed Blade's words, his lips moving as he repeated the phrase.

Stuff people loved... There's a new slogan in there somewhere...

Cormac expelled a loud puff of air. "I don't know what's going on around here. This place is crazy. Miles is killing people with animals, and my best guy is leaving me for a pawn shop full of—"

"Well, I'm happy you're staying," said Declan, cutting his father short before he felt the need to smack him. He stood and thrust a hand toward Blade.

Blade grinned and stood, nearly losing his towel in the process. He caught the cover with one hand and shook with the opposite hand. "Happy to be here."

Cormac flopped back in his seat with a defeated sigh. "Fine. You can go. I can't stop you. But can you do me a favor and operate the drone for this operation?"

Blade nodded. "Sure, boss. I wouldn't leave you hanging."

Declan released Blade's hand. "What drone?"

"The drone that's going to watch everything go down. It will keep an eye on Jamie, Stephanie, and us making the capture."

"So you can post it on the FBI's Instagram?"

"No, smartass. It's for safety."

"Us?" Blade's head cocked. "Is Declan going with you?"

"No—"

Declan shook his head. "That's where you're wrong. I *am* going."

"Absolutely not. It's too dangerous."

"Look—I've met Jamie. She knows me. I'll be an asset if we need to talk her down. And both Stephanie and Charlotte are involved. I'm *going*. End of discussion."

Cormac rubbed his head with his right hand as if it were a balloon he wanted to stick to the wall. "I don't know..."

"You know I'm trained," added Declan.

"That was years ago."

"I'm younger. I'm faster. And you've already proven yourself incompetent."

Cormac poked the air in front of Declan. "Hey, you better watch that mouth—" Cormac stopped and pressed his lips into a hard line. He looked away and stared at a lamp as if he were trying to move it with his mind.

"I can run the drone from the shop, so we won't have to close," suggested Blade.

Declan smiled. He'd been wondering who was going to watch the store while he was out capturing serial killers with his long-lost father. "That would be great."

"You're worried about the shop?" Cormac's eyes grew wide and mocking. "Afraid you'll miss *Betty* when she comes to look at the china?"

"Betty likes the china," said Blade, a touch of growl in his tone.

Cormac retracted his telescoping neck. "I was kidding. There's really a Betty?"

Declan nodded. "There are like *six* Bettys. But the one who likes china is Blade's favorite."

Cormac clapped his hands together. "Alright. This is nuts. I declare this touching scene *over*. We need to get rolling if we're going to catch Jamie on that building."

"So I'm going?" asked Declan.

Cormac nodded. "Yes. But let's go before I change my mind."

CHAPTER THIRTY-EIGHT

Declan and Cormac met Charlotte and Stephanie at the meeting spot beneath a wooden pavilion not far from the fountain where Stephanie would play *bait*. The two women were arguing, Charlotte shaking a bulletproof vest at Stephanie in an attempt to make her take it.

Charlotte spotted Declan and thrust the jacket at him. "I borrowed this from Frank. She won't put it on."

Declan scowled. "Didn't he want to know why you needed a bulletproof vest?"

Charlotte lowered the jacket. "Okay, maybe I *borrowed* it without asking. She still needs to wear it."

Stephanie's lip curled. "It's going to ruin the line of my suit."

"Put on the vest, Steph," said Declan.

"She won't shoot me."

"She *will*."

Declan saw Charlotte wince at the delivery of his bitter truth. Stephanie remained unmoved. For a moment longer, she stood defiant, eyes blazing. Then the fire fizzled, and her shoulders released. She held out her hand.

"Fine. Give it to me."

Charlotte hung the jacket on Stephanie's hand, and as she moved toward the nearby public restroom, Charlotte looked at Declan.

"Thank you. I've been trying to talk her into that for fifteen minutes."

"No problem."

She placed a hand on his chest, but he felt little beneath his own vest.

"You look sexy in your tactical gear," she said.

He felt himself blush. He was dressed like a badass soldier, yet Charlotte could make him feel like an embarrassed little boy with a single sentence. "Thank you. How are you doing?"

Charlotte shrugged. "I'm fine. Cormac's men are covering all the entrances. I'm just hoping Jamie won't spot them turning people away from the park. I'm a mess of nerves thinking things might not work. All I have to do is sit here and hope I don't see Stephanie's head blown off. She's got the hard part."

Declan raised a hand to shield his eyes from the sun and survey the area. Beneath the roof of the pavilion, Charlotte would be safe from any sniper.

"Just be sure you stay under here. And if we read this all wrong and you see Jamie approaching, do not approach *her*. Let me know, and then get out of here."

"Right, right. I got it, soldier boy."

The walkie-talkie his father had provided Declan crackled to life.

"I just saw her enter the building."

He pulled the radio from his hip and held it to his mouth. "Was she carrying a bag or anything?"

"Pretty large gym bag. Yes."

Declan grinned at Charlotte. "Got her."

"I need you to get back here," said Cormac.

"On the way. Out."

Declan kissed Charlotte and let his lips linger a moment longer than his typical PDA kiss. "You're all good?"

"All good."

The door to the restrooms opened, and Stephanie paused, staring at them.

"Oh, you two are just so *adorable*." Grimacing, she smoothed the lines of her jacket, where it puckered near the edges of the bulletproof vest. "I look like I've gained thirty pounds."

"You can't even see it." Declan shook a finger at her. "Don't give Charlotte any more trouble. She's here to keep you alive."

Stephanie rolled her eyes. "She's not going to shoot me."

"I know she isn't because you're not going to give her a shot. You're going to stick to that tree line, remember? Make her feel safe you're following the plan, but give her *no* shot."

Stephanie stared out to the tree line and nodded.

"Declan, I need you here now," crackled Cormac's voice.

Stephanie looked at his walkie-talkie. "Did she show up at the building?"

"She did."

Stephanie paled. "She's not going to shoot me," she mumbled.

Charlotte put a hand on Stephanie's arm. "Don't take it personally. She's insane."

Stephanie jerked away from Charlotte's touch. "Why would I take my mother trying to kill me *personally*?" She walked to the edge of the pavilion. "Let's do this."

Declan nodded to Charlotte, gave her one more quick kiss, and then jogged toward the office park.

He found his father waiting at the fire escape door where they'd arranged to meet.

"About time."

"Sorry, we were getting Stephanie ready to go."

"Ready to head up?"

Declan nodded. He was about to charge into the stairwell when his father grabbed his arm.

"Dec, before we do this. I want you to know I really am sorry. Sorry for leaving you, and sorry I was such a selfish prick. At the time, I thought I was doing the right thing."

Declan stared into his father's eyes. It felt as if something else was there now. He seemed...*sincere*. Declan looked down with a quick nod.

"Okay. We can talk later, Cormac."

"You can call me Dad."

"Yeah, I don't see that happening any time soon. Let's take this one step at a time."

"Fair enough." Cormac clapped him on the back and then tapped Declan on the head. "I hereby deputize you to help me bring down this homicidal maniac."

"Is that official?"

"No. I'm not an old-timey sheriff, but if you have to shoot her to save your life or the life of anyone else, do it. I'll figure out the paperwork afterward."

"That sounds comforting."

Declan and Cormac moved into the fire escape stairwell, their guns drawn.

"What if someone comes into the fire escape?" asked Declan as they started up the stairs.

"I've got men at every door to keep them from coming out or Jamie from getting in. She took the elevator right to the roof."

"People inside?"

"Yes. I couldn't close the office. She would have known."

"Aren't the workers going to be suspicious of the FBI guys guarding every fire escape and every elevator?"

"They're dressed as repairmen. If someone makes a stink about leaving, we'll deal with it—"

The crack of a rifle shot stopped both men in their tracks.

"She couldn't have—"

Declan bolted up the last flight and pushed open the door. A rifle mounted to a tripod sat at the opposite edge of the building, the side facing the park. A large black bag lay on the ground beside it. Jamie was nowhere to be seen.

"Where'd she go?" asked Cormac coming up behind him.

Declan ran around the stairwell and spotted a dark rope tied to an air-conditioning unit. The rope led over the side of the building.

"Over here!" he screamed, sprinting for the side of the building.

He reached the edge and looked down. Jamie was already on the ground, unhooking a rappelling harness.

"Freeze!" he screamed, pointing his gun at her.

She looked up and grinned before bolting for the trees.

Cormac shouted behind him.

"Shoot her!"

Declan fired. Bark burst from the side of a pine near where Jamie had disappeared into the tree line.

Declan's gaze traveled in the direction he'd seen Jamie headed, and he whirled to face his father.

"She's headed toward Charlotte."

CHAPTER THIRTY-NINE

"Stephanie!"

The gunshot still echoed in her ears as Charlotte sprinted toward the fallen form of Stephanie. The blonde wasn't moving. She ran just inside the tree line where Stephanie *should have been*. Charlotte slid to her knees as she moved close to the body, nearly tripping over Stephanie as she tried to stop her momentum.

Charlotte knew it was best not to move an injured person, but she couldn't tend to Stephanie if *she* were the next one to be shot. She jerked the body into the trees until she felt safe they had cover.

Hands scrambling to locate the wound, Charlotte tore open Stephanie's jacket. She spotted a hole through the chest pocket of her shirt, just above her heart.

It must have gone through the vest?

Charlotte slapped Stephanie's cheeks.

"Wake up. Wake up."

She ripped away Stephanie's shirt and struggled to remove the bulletproof vest, chanting Stephanie's name as she worked.

"Wake up, Stephanie, wake up, Stephanie—"

She stuck her finger into a hole in the vest that lined up with the hole in Stephanie's now torn shirt. She felt the bullet flattened there.

Is my finger in her chest?

She pulled out her finger.

No blood.

She pulled back the jacket expecting to see blood. There was none. Just a bruise near Stephanie's right breast, throbbing above the lace of her bra.

Charlotte's head cocked.

What a gorgeous bra. Where does she get underwear like that?

Charlotte shook her head, getting back to the crisis at hand. Stephanie wasn't bleeding, but she was also not moving.

Is she breathing? Was there a second shot she hadn't registered?

Charlotte put her hand in front of Stephanie's nose, but she couldn't feel anything. She couldn't tell if her chest was rising. She dipped her ear toward Stephanie's parted lips.

"Stephanie? Stephanie? *Oooph!*"

Stephanie gasped and sat up, slamming her face into the side of Charlotte's head. Both of them bounced in the opposite direction, Stephanie to the ground and Charlotte back on her butt.

Both raised their hands to their heads.

"What are you *doing*?" barked Stephanie, cradling her nose.

"I was trying to see if you were breathing."

"By kissing me?"

"Don't flatter yourself." Charlotte rocked back to her knees. "I was trying to see if I could hear you breathe."

"You're an idiot."

"*You're* an idiot. You walked right into a bullet. I saw you. You purposely left the tree line."

Stephanie sat up, grumbling, trying in vain to pull her shirt together. Finding the buttons had been torn away, she glared at Charlotte.

"You *ruined* my shirt."

"I was trying to save your life."

"I was *fine*."

"You walked into a bullet. On *purpose*."

Stephanie closed her eyes tight, her jaw bulging as she grit her teeth. "I needed to know if she'd shoot."

"She shot. Look at your chest." Charlotte saw the expression on Stephanie's face shift to what she could only describe as *pain*. By closing her eyes so tightly, she seemed to be sealing herself from the world, as if her eyes were doorways for bad things to enter. She raised her hands and covered her ears.

She wasn't in physical pain.

Her mother had shot her.

Charlotte couldn't imagine what it must feel like to discover your own mother wanted you dead. It had to be devastating.

"I'm sorry," she mumbled.

Stephanie released a breath. Her body relaxed, and she opened her eyes, lowering her hands from her ears. She seemed almost serene. As if some other person had assumed control of her body. Her gaze flicked to Charlotte.

"Yeah, well, keep your face out of my face."

Charlotte couldn't tell if Stephanie knew she was saying sorry for Jamie's betrayal, not for clunking heads. She let it go.

Stephanie gingerly touched the bruise on her chest, wincing.

"That really hurt."

"I bet."

"Did they get her?"

Charlotte realized she hadn't received a call. She'd been so worried about Stephanie that she'd forgotten about the other half of the operation. "I don't know."

"Charlotte!"

She heard Declan screaming somewhere to her left.

"That's Declan," said Stephanie, head swiveling.

Charlotte scowled. "I know."

"He's running." Stephanie's eyes grew wide. "Is she coming this way?"

Jamie's loose.

Charlotte stood and scanned the trees, trying to figure out the most direct path Jamie might have taken from the office building to their current location. She pulled her gun from her holster. For once, she'd remembered to bring it when it mattered.

"Give me your gun," said Stephanie.

"What? *No.*"

"I need to be the one to kill her. Give me your gun."

"No—"

Stephanie lunged toward her and then yelped in pain, grabbing her chest as Charlotte jerked away from her.

"You probably broke a rib. I wouldn't move. It could stab your heart or lung, and you'll be dead before an ambulance can get here."

Stephanie's eyes were filled with tears and fire, her lip trembling. "Give me your gun. Let me kill her."

"No. She wants you dead as it is. Don't give her an excuse to try again."

Stephanie laughed. "You think she'll hesitate to shoot *you*? She was willing to shoot her own *daughter*."

"Because she thought you were going to turn on her."

"Yes. With me, maybe she needed a reason, but she'll shoot you for existing. For standing between her and *me* when she wants me dead."

Charlotte felt her stomach grow woogy.

Stephanie had a point. Was there a place they could hide? It's not like there was a handy cave or a closet nearby. They'd have to stand their ground.

Charlotte did her best to force down her fear. "No. Be quiet—"

"Step away."

Charlotte whirled at the sound of the voice behind her.

Jamie stood behind her in a torn dress with a handgun pointed at them.

Charlotte's hand tightened on her own weapon.

"If you're wondering if you can lift that before I shoot you, the answer is no," said Jamie.

Charlotte took a step in front of Stephanie. "You can't kill your own daughter."

"It was you who cooked up this trap, wasn't it?" asked Jamie.

Charlotte didn't know what to say.

"Did you know that's the only reason you're not already dead? I liked the idea of keeping you alive. You're fun."

Stephanie groaned, glaring at Charlotte. "What is it about you? First, my boyfriend. Now my mother?"

Jamie's attention shifted to her daughter. "And *you*. Your DNA has become a liability."

Stephanie shifted and sucked in a breath, clearly in pain. "Why should I have any loyalty to you?"

"I made you who you are."

Hearing Declan call out again, Charlotte's attention moved beyond Jamie. He was getting closer. Jamie would have to make her move and run very soon.

But I know something you don't, Jamie.

There was more than just Declan somewhere behind Jamie.

There was also a large drone sweeping through the sky, dodging trees.

Ramming speed, Mr. Blade.

Charlotte tried not to wince as the drone approached at high speed, aiming for the back of Jamie's head. Charlotte looked at Jamie's gun, still pointing at Stephanie. If it went off when the drone struck her—

"Behind you!" Charlotte screamed at the last possible second.

Jamie turned, the movement of her body shifting the gun away from Stephanie just enough. It fired as the drone plowed into her forehead at full throttle.

Jamie flew backward as if someone had jerked her on a string. The gun spilled from her hand and landed, whirling not far from Stephanie, playing its own deadly game of spin the bottle. The drone crashed to the ground, buzzing and twisting like a wounded beetle. Charlotte jumped on Jamie as she fell. She straddled her foe, pinning her arms. Jamie didn't fight her. She seemed dazed. The blow had left her face cut and bleeding.

"I'll kill you," said Stephanie, reaching for the gun. She cried out with the effort as Declan arrived, panting, his gun drawn.

"Get the gun," said Charlotte nodding to the gun at Stephanie's fingertips.

Declan leapt over Jamie's feet to snatch the gun as Stephanie's clawing fingers strained to reach it.

"No!" moaned Stephanie, sounding more like a wounded animal than an angry woman. She looked up at Declan. "Shoot her. Shoot her for me."

Declan shook his head. "Lie still."

Stephanie closed her eyes and lay back down, her fists clenched.

Jamie's eyes fluttered open, and she stared up into Charlotte's face. Her eyes shifted to the left to stare down the barrel of Declan's gun, which he now held trained on her. She returned her gaze to Charlotte and grinned. One of her front teeth had been knocked free by the drone.

"This isn't over," she said.

Charlotte felt a rush of adrenaline and pushed harder on Jamie's trapped wrists.

"It is today."

Cormac arrived, sweating. He rested his hands just above his knees, panting. "Assessing the situation," he said between gasps for air. After a moment, he pulled a pair of handcuffs from the belt of his tactical uniform and slapped one end on Jamie's right wrist. He tapped the side of Charlotte's arm.

"You're going to have to release her if I'm going to finish this."

Grudgingly, Charlotte released her grip on the handcuffed hand. She'd enjoyed having Jamie pinned. This could have been the only time she'd ever have control over her. The one time she knew where she was.

Cormac finished cuffing Jamie and lifted her to her feet to pat her down for weapons.

Jamie glanced at Stephanie.

"When they call you into court, don't be stupid."

Stephanie's lids opened, her gaze as cold as if her eyes were chipped from ice. She smiled at her mother.

"Nice teeth."

Charlotte heard ambulance sirens wail in the distance.

CHAPTER FORTY

Charlotte, Blade, and Declan were standing behind the counter of Declan's pawn shop when Stephanie entered. It had been a week since their showdown with Jamie, who remained in custody, charges mounting against her as various law enforcement agencies built their cases against her.

"Well, if it isn't the hero who took a bullet to capture the most prolific serial killer of all time," said Declan. Stephanie had been hailed a hero in the national news. The press couldn't get enough of the serial killer's legal-eagle daughter, bringing down her evil mother singlehanded. Or at least that's how most of the stories read. Somehow, Charlotte's and Declan's parts in the capture had been largely overlooked. Cormac, of course, had never been there.

Stephanie tossed her hair over her shoulder with a flick of her head. "I'm *flooded* with calls from producers. They want to make a movie about the girl who captured her killer mother. But I'm sure you two are fielding offers as well."

"I didn't get any calls from producers," mumbled Charlotte.

Declan chuckled. "Why would we? We're chopped liver." He closed his register drawer. "So why did you squeeze this visit into your busy schedule?"

"Oh, I thought I'd swing by and thank you both for stopping me from killing my mother."

Charlotte smiled. "See? I told you you'd regret it if you did it."

Stephanie rolled her eyes. "I'm being *sarcastic*. You're both morons. You know she's going to get out."

Declan shook his head. "No. They have her dead to rights."

"How do you figure?"

"She tried to shoot you from the rooftop."

Stephanie's eyebrows raised. "Did she? Did *you* see her pull the trigger?"

"No, but she was the only one there. The only one rappelling down the building two seconds after we heard the shot—"

"Sure, logic dictates she pulled the trigger. But the law isn't about logic. Hell, I could get her off *that* charge with one WestLaw search and a low-cut blouse."

Charlotte frowned. "That's depressing to hear."

"It doesn't matter. They'll pin other murders on her," said Declan.

Stephanie poked at a stuffed bear propped on a bureau to her left and then recoiled as if the fur was made of spider webs. "You're so naive. Mom has friends. She hasn't avoided capture all these years without help. She'll be out in a month."

"We'll see," said Charlotte, her mind already racing for ways to prove Jamie was the killer they knew her to be.

Stephanie shrugged. "In the meantime, I'm thinking I might have to become a defense attorney. I hear there's an opening in the D.A. office."

Charlotte winced. "Come on..."

Stephanie grinned. "What, too soon?"

~~ THE END ~~

Want more? FREE PREVIEW!

If you liked this book, read on for a preview of the next Pineapple Port Mystery AND the Shee McQueen Mystery-Thriller Series (which shares characters with the Pineapple Port world!).

Thank you!

Thank you for reading! If you enjoyed this book, please swing back to Amazon and leave me a review — even short reviews help authors like me find new fans!

REVIEW ON amazon

ABOUT THE AUTHOR

USA Today and *Wall Street Journal* bestselling author Amy Vansant has written over 30 books, including the fun, thrilling Shee McQueen series, the rollicking, twisty Pineapple Port Mysteries, and the action-packed Kilty urban fantasies. She's also the founder of AuthorsXP.com - a site for authors (marketing help) and readers (free and deal books!).

Amy lives in Jupiter, Florida, with her muse/husband and a goony Bordoodle named Archer.

http://www.AmyVansant.com

FOLLOW AMY on AMAZON or BOOKBUB

Books by Amy Vansant

Pineapple Port Mysteries
Funny, clean & full of unforgettable characters
Shee McQueen Mystery-Thrillers
Action-packed, fun romantic mystery-thrillers
Kilty Urban Fantasy/Romantic Suspense
Action-packed romantic suspense/urban fantasy
Slightly Romantic Comedies
Classic romantic romps
The Magicatory
Middle-grade fantasy

FREE PREVIEW

PINEAPPLE PUPPIES

A Pineapple Port Mystery: Book Nine – By Amy Vansant

CHAPTER ONE

Mina gave the body on the ground one good kick with a sensible shoe.

It barely moved.

More importantly, it didn't make a sound. It didn't *complain*, which was unusual for that particular body.

She rested her knuckles against her lips and stared at the dead man, sorting her emotions. On one hand, Kimber's death meant she was out of a job. On the other hand…

Stop it. That's terrible.

Still…

Next door, the tiny Yorkie puppies had whipped themselves into a yipping frenzy. Mina rubbed her hands on her apron and waddled out of Kimber's room to the next door down the hallway toward the stairs. Opening it a crack, she made sure to use her foot as a wedge to block any chance of escape. Tiny noses and paws pushed at her shoe as she eased them back.

Struck by the irony that the same black working shoe that had just touched death was now swarmed by so much *life*, she allowed herself a little smile.

Mina slipped inside the whelping room and shut the door behind her. She wanted to lie on the floor and let them run all over her. The poor things had lost someone, too. The puppies' champion mother, Princess Buttercup, had suffered a complication during pregnancy and they'd lost her. She, Kimber, and presumably the puppies, had been devastated.

Since then, Mina had been the puppies' mother, keeping the little furballs alive and happy as best she could. Kimber had loved those dogs, but now he was dead...Mina supposed she'd have to sell them. She didn't have the time or the knowhow to raise them as show dogs.

She'd miss them. They were a tremendous pain in the neck but *so* cute. Even now one stared at her, dancing on his toes, readying himself to jump on her face the moment she lowered herself to the floor. He wanted to *pounce*. It was written all over his snout.

She was halfway to the floor when a stifled sob came from the closet. Mina fell back against the cabinet, startled.

"Who's in there?"

"It's me."

The slatted door of the closet slid open to reveal a woman sitting on the floor of the closet, half-tucked behind a laundry basket. As the light fell on her, her eyes flashed white.

"What are you doing in there?" asked Mina.

The woman shook her head. "He's dead."

"I know. Get out. Don't worry."

The stowaway crawled out of the closet, mascara smeared beneath each eye where she'd been crying. Standing, she smoothed her shorts and wrapped her arms around her chest.

"What am I going to do? He fell."

"You were there?"

"Yes. I mean, *no*. Not really. I heard a *thunk* while I was in here with the puppies and went to look. I think he tried to get out of bed and fell."

Mina frowned. "You shouldn't have been up here."

"I know. I wanted to see the puppies."

Mina shook her head and motioned to the door leading to

the hall. "Get out of here."

"What?"

"Get out."

"But—"

"I'll let them know it was an accident." Mina closed her eyes as the puppies tumbled over her toes, hoping she was doing the right thing. There was nothing she could do for Kimber, but she *could* still help the girl. She'd already been through so much and with her family history...

The young woman's hand reached out for the knob and then retracted. She turned back to Mina.

"What if they investigate?"

"What do you mean?"

"What if they think his death is suspicious? I touched things."

"What things?"

"Knobs. Maybe the bed posts?"

"Anything else?"

She looked down.

"The puppies. They were all over me. They must be covered in my hair, my DNA—" She looked at Mina, eyes telegraphing her rising panic. "What if they know no one but you is ever up here? What if the girls mention it and then they find *me* all over the puppy room?"

Mina watched a puppy steadily chew the end of her shoelace, the fabric tucked in the back of its maw, where its sharp little molars could grind away.

What am I going to do with you little rascals?

"Take them."

"What?"

Mina opened the closet and pulled out a small dog carrying case.

"Take them. No one will know they're missing. I won't mention them and I'll clean the room."

"They're *purebreds*. You want me to sell them?"

Mina cocked an eyebrow. "You mean so you can get *caught* and they *know* you killed him?"

"But I didn't—"

"You know what I mean. If you're caught selling his dogs—"

"Right. I understand."

"Just *take* them. I'll clean up before I call the police. You take the dogs."

"But what should I do with them?"

Mina began shoveling puppies into the crate. "Find them good homes. Loving homes."

"But where?"

"Figure it out. I can't do everything." Puppies packed, Mina closed the carrying case and pointed to the handle on top.

"Take it. Go."

The woman took the case as if dazed. Mina opened the door for her. She walked into the hall, the case rocking as the puppies inside rolled around, still playing. She paused and turned back to Mina.

"Thank you."

One puppy began to whine and the others joined in until Mina couldn't hear herself think.

"*Go*."

The young woman turned and jogged down the stairs as best she could with a box full of howling puppies hanging from one hand.

Mina stepped into the hall where she could look into the puppy room and Kimber's room at the same time.

No more puppies. No more Kimber.

What am I going to do with all my free time?

She was about to fetch her cleaning gloves when she heard it.

A *groan*.

She spun on her rubber heel and saw Kimber's hand move.

She gasped.

He's alive.

Chapter Two

Charlotte elbowed her way through the Pineapple Port post-holiday "Swap and Sell" crowd to find Mariska standing at her jelly and relishes table, making change for a customer. Mariska's normally perfectly poofed hair had wilted, flopping across her glistening forehead like a forgotten August flower.

Someone had had the clever idea of running a post-holiday bazaar to help the residents unload the things they'd received that they didn't want. It hadn't hit anyone until it was too late that presents gifted *between* the residents would end up on the tables, too. Now half the group sat steaming, glaring at the other half and the Christmas tree mugs and snowman tea cozies they'd gifted them.

None of the themed gifts bore any resemblance to the holidays Charlotte had known in Florida. It was December twenty-ninth and she wore a spaghetti-strap tank top sprinkled with palm leaves, not snowflakes. Outside, it was eighty degrees.

"I can't believe you're still here. You're usually sold out by noon," said Charlotte.

Mariska motioned to a last loaf of bread on her table, its powdered sugar top visible through a festive green wrapping. "My jellies have been gone for an hour. I've been trying to sell

Alice's fruit stollens. They're less popular *after* Christmas."

"She wasn't feeling up to selling?"

"No. That poor woman is in so much pain. Much worse than last year. I don't know how she does it."

Charlotte made a tsking noise. Severe arthritis and complications from lupus made each holiday tougher than the last for Alice. Whenever she baked one of her famous stollens, she chose one resident to serve as her 'bread elf,' a person to help her bake the breads, following her exacting instructions. But until this event, she'd always mustered the strength to sit behind a sales table.

Mariska poked the last loaf toward the edge of the table, nudging it half an inch closer to the potential buyers. "Without her here, the bread doesn't move."

"And stollen has an acquired taste."

Mariska smiled, her shoulders waggling as she lifted her chin. "Not like my jellies. Everyone *loves* my jellies."

Charlotte spotted 'Mac' MacBrady, Pineapple Port's retired Boston firefighter approaching. Mac was a tan, muscular man in his late fifties who'd had the local ladies swooning since his arrival, much to the amusement of his wife, Kelly. Kelly was selling only Irish soda bread at her own table—not unwanted gifts. Poison stares in her direction had less to do with rejected presents and more to do with jealousy over her handsome hubby.

"I'm going to buy your last loaf," said Mac, arriving tableside. "I need something different. If I have to eat another slice of soda bread I'm going to hang myself."

"Is fruit stollen a thing in Boston?" asked Charlotte.

Mac shrugged. "Sure. In the German neighborhoods. I love it. I like it with butter, but right now I'm so hungry I think I'll eat it here. Kelly tricked me into helping with setup and breakdown, so I'm stuck here for a while."

Charlotte chuckled. "Well, we all feel safer having you here.

You never know when a jar of Jalapeno jelly might burst into flames."

"My jelly would never do that," muttered Mariska.

Mac presented his money as Mariska passed him the last loaf. "I heard sirens a little bit ago. Was that a fire?"

Mac shook his head as he unwrapped the bread. "Ambulance."

"In Pineapple Port?"

He shrugged and spoke between bites, sugar powdering his lips. "Your guess is as good as mine. Kelly bet me twenty bucks I couldn't go a week without listening to the emergency scanners and I'm gonna win."

"Old habits die hard," said Charlotte, but her mind was already occupied worrying about the sirens. The average twenty-seven-year-old rarely had to worry about ambulance sirens, but Charlotte had been orphaned as a child and sent to live with her grandmother in Pineapple Port. When her grandmother died soon after, Mariska and the rest of the retirement community had unofficially adopted her, allowing her to remain in her grandmother's home and out of the orphanage. She knew from years of experience that sirens were never a good thing in a retirement community.

"Did you hear?" Mariska's best friend, Darla, appeared, craning her neck to peek around Mac.

"Where'd you come from? Why do you look so flustered?" asked Charlotte.

Darla nudged Mac aside with her hip to get a spot at the table. "I ran from my car. It's Alice."

Mariska perked and waved a few dollar bills in front of Darla's nose. "Let her know I just sold her last fruit stollen."

"That's the least of her worries."

Mariska frowned. "Why? It took me—"

Darla put her hand on Mariska's. "Sweetheart, Alice just *died*. They found her at home slumped over one of her own stollens."

Mariska gasped. "You're kidding."

Darla shook her head. "I'm not."

"Did she choke? How did she die? How did you hear about it?" asked Charlotte.

"Frank told me," said Darla, invoking the name of her Sheriff husband. "They don't know how she died yet. He said she doesn't look right, though. Little green around the gills or something."

"What does that mean?"

Darla shrugged. "They don't think she choked."

"Heart attack?" asked Mariska, clearly preparing to run through the usual list of culprits.

"Or poison," said Darla in a stage whisper.

"Poison?"

The three ladies turned to stare at Mac, who froze, mid-chew, staring back at them from above the stollen positioned at his lips.

"Poison?" he mumbled, his mouth full. He glanced at the chunk of bread remaining in his hand. "Excuse me a minute."

As he strode back into the crowd, Charlotte watched him spit the bread he'd been chewing into his hand.

Mariska slapped Darla's arm to get her attention. "I sold every last one of those stollens. Are you trying to tell me I might have poisoned everyone?"

Darla huffed. "Why do you think I ran here? I wanted to stop you from selling them just in case."

Charlotte frowned. Alice had been ill for a long time. Chances were good she'd died of natural causes. "Did Frank actually *say* anything about poison?"

"Only that she looked like her face was bloated or something. Or green. I forget the exact words he used. I just remember thinking, *that sounds like poison."*

"Why would anyone poison Alice?" asked Mariska.

Darla squinted. "You tell us. You were her elf. *You made the stollen.*"

Mariska's eyes popped wide. "I didn't *poison* her."

"I wasn't saying that. I was just kidding."

"It's not funny." Mariska shook her head so hard her dangling Christmas bell earrings chimed.

"What do you think we should do?" Darla tapped her front teeth with her fingernail while she waited for an answer.

Charlotte glanced up at the recreation center's stage, where a microphone used for the morning's announcements still stood. "I'll jump up there and ask everyone with a fruit cake to return them. Just in case."

Mariska rested her head in her palm. "This is *so* embarrassing."

Charlotte tried to leave, but Darla grasped her wrist and held her in place. "Charlotte, wait. Make sure you say fruit *stollen.* Tara sells fruit *cake.* If you tell people the fruit *cake* is poisoned, she'll have a conniption."

Charlotte sighed. Living in Pineapple Port was a little like being trapped in high school forever.

"Good point. Okay."

She again tried to make her way to the stage, only to have Darla jerk her back once more.

"Come to think of it, if you tell anyone *anything* is poisoned, there'll be panic. Maybe we shouldn't."

Charlotte frowned. "What am I supposed to do? Stand up there and tell them we accidentally put gluten in them?"

Mariska sniffed. "Gluten isn't a real thing."

"It's like global warming," agreed Darla.

Charlotte glowered at her. "Darla, I swear. I thought we had come to an agreement. Global warming is a *thing.*"

Darla waved her away. "I know, I know. We don't have time to talk about stranded polar bears now. There are people walking around here with poisoned fruit cakes."

"*Stollens,*" stressed Mariska. "But I didn't do it. Make sure you say that, too."

Charlotte rubbed her temples with one hand. She had to retrieve the stollens *and* avoid mass hysteria. Once, someone had confessed to accidently leaving one of the bingo balls out of the cage on bingo night and the residents nearly *rioted.* Implying poisoned stollens would have people apoplectic with hypochondria.

Slipping from Darla's grasp, Charlotte jogged up the stairs to the microphone, flipped the switch and heard the speakers crackle as she tapped the mike's wire mesh. The crowd's gazes swiveled in her direction.

"Attention...um...attention. If you bought a fruit stollen today from Mariska—"

"Why'd she have to say my name?" moaned Mariska, somewhere below her.

Charlotte continued. "Um, we need you to return them. The stollens. We used salt instead of sugar."

"I would *never* do such a thing," hissed Mariska.

"Will we get a refund?" asked a voice from the crowd.

"Yes. Full refund," said Charlotte.

Mariska moaned again.

Get *Pineapple Puppies* on Amazon!

ANOTHER FREE PREVIEW!

THE GIRL WHO WANTS

A Shee McQueen Mystery-Thriller by Amy Vansant

Chapter One

Three Weeks Ago, Nashua, New Hampshire.

Shee realized her mistake the moment her feet left the grass.

He's enormous.

She'd watched him drop from the side window of the house. He landed four feet from where she stood, and still her brain refused to register the warning signs. The nose, big and lumpy as breadfruit, the forehead some beach town could use as a jetty if they buried him to his neck...

His knees bent to absorb his weight, and *her* brain thought, *got you.*

Her brain couldn't be bothered with simple math: *Giant, plus Shee, equals Pain.*

Instead, she jumped to tackle him, dangling airborne as his knees straightened and the *pet the rabbit* bastard stood to his full height.

Crap.

The math added up pretty quickly after that.

Hovering like Superman mid-flight, there wasn't much she could do to change her disastrous trajectory. She'd *felt* like a superhero when she left the ground. Now, she felt more like a Canada goose staring into the propellers of Captain Sully's Airbus A320.

She might take down the plane, but it was going to *hurt.*

Frankenjerk turned toward her at the same moment she

plowed into him. She clamped her arms around his waist like a little girl hugging a redwood. Lurch returned the embrace, twisting her to the ground. Her back hit the dirt, and air burst from her lungs like a double shotgun blast.

Ow.

Wheezing, she punched upward, striking Beardless Hagrid in the throat.

That didn't go over well.

Grabbing her shoulder with one hand, Dickasaurus flipped her on her stomach like a sausage link, slipped his hand under her chin, and pressed his forearm against her windpipe.

The only air she'd gulped before he cut her supply stank of damp armpit. He'd tucked her cranium in his arm crotch, much like the famous noggin-less horseman once held his severed head. Fireworks exploded in the dark behind her eyes.

That's when a thought occurred to her.

I haven't been home in fifteen years.

What if she died in Gigantor's armpit? Would her father even know?

Has it really been that long?

Flopping like a landed fish, she forced her assailant to adjust his hold and sucked a breath as she flipped on her back. Spittle glistened on his lips, his brow furrowed as if she'd asked him to read a paragraph of big-boy words.

His nostrils flared like the Holland Tunnel.

There's an idea.

Making a V with her fingers, Shee thrust upward, stabbing into his nose, straining to reach his tiny brain.

Goliath roared. Jerking back, he grabbed her arm to unplug her fingers from his nose socket. She whipped away her limb before he had a good grip, fearing he'd snap her bones with his Godzilla paws.

Kneeling before her, he clamped both hands over his face, cursing as blood seeped from behind his fingers.

Shee's gaze didn't linger on that mess. Her focus fell to his crotch, hovering a foot above her feet, protected by nothing but a thin pair of oversized sweatpants.

Scrambled eggs, sir?

She kicked.

He howled.

Shee scuttled back like a crab, found her feet, and snatched her gun from her side. The gun she should have pulled *before* trying to tackle the Empire State Building.

"Move a muscle, and I'll aerate you," she said. She always liked that line.

The golem growled but remained on the ground like a good dog, cradling his family jewels.

Shee's partner in this manhunt, a local cop easier on the eyes than he was useful, rounded the corner and drew his own weapon.

She smiled and holstered the gun he'd lent her. Unknowingly.

"Glad you could make it."

Her portion of the operation accomplished, she headed toward the car as more officers swarmed the scene.

"Shee, where are you going?" called the cop.

She stopped and turned.

"Home, I think."

His gaze dropped to her hip.

"Is that my gun?"